That Cooking Girl

By Michelle L. Rusk

CHELLEHEAD WORKS

For John Peters,

My UK Dad, my Wise Mzee (uncle).

And the person who created Megan's character because she had to have a Welsh name.

How I miss you!

CHAPTER 1

"Gummy bears remind me of Christmas morning," Megan Marshall said nonchalantly as she picked up several from the brown-striped earthenware bowl that Stephanie Crowder held out to her.

"That's an odd combination," Stephanie said, taking the bowl back and grabbing a few for herself before she rolled her chair back behind the reception desk.

"Christmas morning?" Julie Martin asked. "They remind me of upscale candy stores. Remember when you could only get them at a candy store, not in a bag in the checkout line at the office supply store?"

The three women sat in the reception area of Thomas Public Relations in Albuquerque where they all worked, taking a mid-morning break. Thirty-six-year-old Megan loved her job writing copy, campaigns, or whatever Barry Thomas needed as the top PR firm in New Mexico. She knew Barry had worked hard to keep the local businesses working with him and not reaching outside the state for help. Julie also wrote copy, but she hadn't been there as long as Megan. And Stephanie was the heart of the company, directing calls wherever they needed to go. Sometimes she forgot to take off her headset when she left work in the afternoon, laughing at herself each time she did it.

"I think I really do love my job," she would say with a chuckle.

The three women often gathered together a few minutes each day to catch up and keep each other entertained, especially when there was a big deadline and they were struggling with words.

"My mom used to get us each a bag for Christmas– in our stockings," Megan added.

"Wow, we didn't have stockings," Julie realized, sitting back on the couch.

"I got chocolate. Lots and lots of chocolate," Stephanie added, her black curls bouncing around as she spoke.

"And they remind me of Duran Duran," Megan added, pulling her long blonde hair into a ponytail and tying it up with a hair band from her wrist, where she sometimes kept them, blending in with whatever bracelet she chose for that day. Megan leaned back in the chair and stretched her legs in front of her, revealing low black heels on her bare legs, coordinating with her turquoise shift dress.

"That's even weirder," Stephanie said, eating a few more, ignoring the fact that she was bursting out of her tight black skirt already.

Megan shrugged her shoulders. "I got the *Arena* album that year. And a poster. Oh, Simon. How badly I wanted to go to London. I thought life with the lead singer of my favorite band would be perfect."

"You were a Simon Le Bon girl?" Julie asked, raising her brown eyebrows. "You must be one of those lead singer girls? I much preferred the shadowy Nick Rhodes, the keyboardist."

"I liked men whose song lyrics didn't make sense," Megan said, laughing at the ridiculousness of it. And then she thought for a moment before she spoke. "I was never into actors. I think it's because they remind me of the theater people from high school. They were always so…"

"Dramatic?" Julie asked, laughing.

"Exactly. I thought it would be weird to be with someone who constantly thinks they are someone else."

"Not me, I don't care," Julie said. And then she added, "And then I marry an electrical engineer. Go figure."

"I think London is the most romantic city ever," Stephanie looking up dreamily at the Thomas Public Relations sign, as if it were a photo of the London skyline with The Eye and Parliament the focus of the shot.

"You've never been there," Julie asked her, looking at the bowl as if it wasn't worth it to leave any gummy bears behind and eating them one by one.

"I know, but I always thought it would be romantic."

Megan ignored her colleagues, setting off into her own world, remembering how she once dreamed that she would marry a rock star and they would divide their time between Los Angeles and England. And how listening to "Rock over London" on the radio every week inspired her.

Now she looked out the window at the Sandia Mountains and realized nothing in that dream had come true. Simon married a model and the last photo she saw of him, in a too small bathing suit, made her glad the "other" woman– what was her name anyway?– found a life with Simon. Megan sat forward, tracing her finger along the cover of the copy of *People* magazine on the coffee table, mostly across the name banner in blue across the top.

"Nate Matthews is the handsomest man ever," Julie said, looking over and letting out a sigh.

Megan looked down to see Nate– with his black hair and dark eyes– smiling back on the cover at her.

"I wonder if he'll ever marry," Julie said out loud. "He got me through grad school, that's for sure." She nodded her head and sighed again. "Every Wednesday night I watched that hospital show he was in. And if I missed it, I used to tape it. Imagine that, taping something! It sounds so old fashioned."

"Life before the DVR," Stephanie said to no one in particular as she sorted through the mail now that the candy bowl was empty. "I heard Nate Matthews has a new television show they're going to film here. They start pretty soon, too."

"How do you know these things?" Megan asked. "How old is he now anyway?"

"They deliver a newspaper here every morning, remember?" Stephanie reminded her. "I read it before all of you get it. Besides, I know you never read it anyway. I don't even think Barry reads it. If something happens, it seems like someone calls to tell him about it."

"I believe he's in his forties," Julie said pulling out her phone to Google it. "I'm sure Wikipedia has the right answer," she said sarcastically.

Megan heard her, but responded to Stephanie. "I don't read that section," she laughed about the entertainment news in the newspaper.

"They filmed the pilot in California, didn't they?" Julie asked. Stephanie and Megan started to feel left out of something. "And it got picked up so they're going to film it here. Something about a motel and Route 66."

"Megan! Megan! Are you out here?" Barry Thomas came flying around the corner, his tie flipped over to his back as he ran across the small reception area floor. Barry always looked rumpled in the office, but on television, in meetings, in photos, and out with the public, everyone saw a side of him that those who worked with him in his office knew was tough for him to keep up.

Disheveled was the word Megan always thought of.

And now– his tie taking up more space on his back than the front of his shirt– he looked like he was running from the enemy. He ran his hand over his balding head and took a deep breath.

"I'm right here," Megan said, standing up and straightening her dress, figuring he had gotten a phone call and needed her to write a press release. After five years of working with him, and helping him to build his public relations company, she knew if he got excited, it meant there was something they needed to do. And she would get it done without joining his drama.

"Barry, what has you all excited?" Stephanie asked, the three women looking puzzled at him.

He took a deep breath as if he had run across the city. "My producer friend down at the TV station lost a segment for the noon show. I need you to run over there and make those carob cookies."

"Cookies?" she asked, looking slightly confused. "You want me to go make cookies on television? Since when is that part of my job?"

"They lost their cooking segment. It was that chef at the Clean Plate. Apparently he had a nervous breakdown."

"One's nervous breakdown is your opportunity," Julie said. "You go girl."

"But my cookies?"

"I love when you bring those cookies." He held out his hand and she took it, Barry guiding her back toward his office. "We need to get a batch made for you to take. We've got time and they have an oven for you to use, but we need to hurry." He motioned for her to grab her purse from her office and follow him.

"What about the Scott campaign I was working on?" Barry stopped in the doorway of the office, his body halfway out, and looked at Megan. "We'll take care of it. Right now I really need you to do this. We have time before the election, but we don't have much time before the noon news."

Megan bit her lip as they drove to the grocery store closest to the office– which meant leaving downtown Albuquerque heading toward the University of New Mexico area. "We'll stop at your house and pick up whatever else you need," Barry said, parking his car and looking at his watch. "You have about eight minutes to shop and be back here. I'll follow you and carry everything."

Later Megan would tell Stephanie and Julie that she felt as though she were in a reality cooking show with a timeline she had to meet. But with Barry breathing down her back, there was no time to think.

At her house, conveniently close to the television station, while she pulled out packages of carob and her favorite stainless steel cooking bowl, Barry searched her cabinets. "I know you have some colorful dishes in here somewhere," he said, opening every cabinet but the right one. "Do you really have a waffle maker? I thought only married women had those."

Megan glared at him and then answered, "To the left of the sink." She put everything into a red and orange reusable shopping bag someone had given her as a gift. "Remember, I was married at one time so I still have some married girl things."

Sam, her "New Mexico special" dog as they called him, watched, keeping a close eye as the two of them went back and forth not just talking, but grabbing items from the cabinets. Sam was, at minimum, part pit bull, having been rescued by Megan as a puppy, curled up in the neighbor's carport, whimpering on a monsoon afternoon three summers ago. Megan guessed he had been dumped in her neighborhood, not unusual for people to do with the small park across the street.

Barry took two dishes– one blue and one bright green– and looked at Megan. "Do you have an apron?"

"It's kind of silly looking," she said, pointing to the pantry door. "It's a retro thing with a ruffle at the bottom."

Barry took a look at the pink and green print, laughed, and grabbed it. "It'll work."

Once at the studio, he ushered her through several doors, waving at security people. "Does everyone know you?" Megan asked, trying to keep up with him in her high heels and carrying two of the three bags of items she would need for the segment.

He stopped in front of an office. "We made it," he said to the person inside, Megan standing behind him but not able to see in.

A woman with long brown kinky hair walked out, looking around. Once she saw Megan, she smiled and held out her hand. "You must be Megan? Thank you for rescuing us. I'm Janet Smith. I produce the noon show here." She began to walk and waved Megan to follow. "Let's get your final batch made and measure out your ingredients."

Megan stopped. "Measure?" she asked.

Barry and Janet stopped to look at her. "Yes, measure," Janet said.

"I don't measure," Megan told them honestly.

Barry shook his head. "Megan, make it up. I'm begging you, make it up. You can do this in your sleep. I know you."

Megan sighed and kept following them into the studio where a fake kitchen was set up in the corner. "Ron Edwards cooked for us for years," Janet explained. "But he's been fired from Clean Slate for a social media mess over the weekend that he says was because of a nervous breakdown." She rolled her eyes before she spoke again. "I'm sure you heard about it. Anyway, we can't worry about the past. We need you to bake cookies."

There was no time to think or wonder more about it. Megan pulled her ingredients from the bag and Barry and Janet asked her what she needed. Without missing a beat, Megan started to bark orders. She had no idea what she was going to do or say on television, but she did know she could bake cookies.

Think about everyone who loves your cookies, she repeated to herself as she mixed the ingredients while measuring out the next batch that she would actually put together live on Albuquerque television. Did anyone even watch the noon news? she wondered.

After she slid the first batch out of the oven, she placed them on the cobalt stoneware plate, making sure they looked presentable. "This isn't a party where everyone will grab them without looking closely," she mumbled while the others were huddled in a corner discussing something else.

With everything ready for the segment, Barry guided her off to the side of the set and showed her a mirror and handed her the apron.

"The show goes on in ten minutes. You go on in twenty. I'll be right here," he said, giving her shoulder a squeeze.

That's when Megan began to get nervous, realizing what she was about to do. And what she had failed to tell anyone because of the timing. Her parents lived in Denver anyway. Maybe because it was local Albuquerque television, no one would see it.

"We forgot to get the recipe," Janet said, walking over with a rushed whisper. She handed a clipboard and a pen to Megan, motioning her to write it down. "We always post them on the web site."

The studio was cold and Megan shivered in her sleeveless dress. She couldn't decide, did her hair look better in front of her shoulders or behind? Or should she leave it in the messy ponytail from earlier? She wasn't having the best of hair days and here she was going on television.

Don't think, she repeated to herself. Just bake.

"You look great," Barry said, leaving the set. "Break a leg."

"I've never been on television," she whispered as he walked away.

He didn't hear her.

The host, Sally Baca, with her long black hair– as straight as Janet's was kinky– walked over to Megan, a stack of index cards in her hands. "These look great," she said, eyeing the cookies. "I can't wait to try one."

"You mean after we 'bake' them," Megan said, using her fingers for quote marks.

Sally laughed and someone called out, "We're on in five, four, three, two, go!"

The cameras went blindingly bright as they turned the lights to Megan and Sally standing behind the counter of the fake kitchen. As Sally talked, Megan wondered when they last updated it. There were no granite counters, just a simple Formica top.

"Thank you for joining us," Sally said, turning to Megan, with no mention of Ron or what happened. Megan knew Barry had suggested they not say anything. "I understand your cookies are well known in your circle."

Megan laughed and smiled, thinking she was just having a conversation with Sally. "It's true," she said. "I get requests for them all the time."

"And it's carob, not chocolate," Sally said, pointing a long red-painted fingernail at the bowl of carob chips on the counter.

"Yes," Megan said. "Not the ingredient only health food nuts in the seventies ate. Carob has come into its own."

As she mixed ingredients, she and Sally talked about food and a little about life.

"Why do you cook?" Sally asked, still eyeing the plate of cookies. Megan wondered if Sally had had breakfast.

"Cooking for me is a way of gathering people around my table and also sharing with them. It's a form of creativity. My mom taught me when I was young and it was one of the ways we spent time together."

Before she knew it, a director waved that they had thirty seconds remaining and Megan slid the plate of cookies over to Sally who looked as if she was going to devour them, despite her petite frame.

"Oh my goodness," Sally said, swallowing before she spoke. "I can't believe these have all sorts of healthy ingredients like flax and wheat flour."

She turned to the camera. "The recipe is on our web site and I recommend you make a batch today. I think I'm going to go home to make several batches."

Suddenly the director yelled, "We're out!" and Megan slumped her shoulders back, able to breathe. She ran her hands down her legs, across the apron, letting her body loose.

I did it, she thought.

"These are awesome!" Sally called, running off for the next segment after the commercial break.

Barry and Janet helped Megan grab her things and Barry whispered, "You were great!" He beamed like a proud dad on graduation day.

Once in the hall, Janet eating a cookie and passing the plate around to anyone who wanted one, said, "You were brilliant! Are you sure you've never done television before?"

Megan laughed. "Just pretend with my best friend growing up," she admitted.

She had forgotten how she and Kelly Connor would play not kitchen but television kitchen, taking their cues from Julia Child, a show they never watched themselves, but saw their parents hungrily devour.

"You're right Barry, she is great." Janet turned back to Megan. "Could you come back next week and cook again?"

Megan felt her breath slip out of her. She looked at Barry. "Of course she will," he said, realizing she wasn't going to answer.

"Great! Great! I have to go!" She took the last cookie and handed the empty dish to Megan. "See you then!"

CHAPTER 2

Around noon on Friday several weeks later, Megan looked out the window of her office and took a long look at the sky out west. Life hadn't changed a bit since her television experience over the past few weeks. She'd done three of them and it was as if she had one more weekly challenge, something new to do. No different than a new campaign to work on.

Not that she had expected to like to change. On the way back to the office after the most recent segment, Barry had said KRQE had the highest rated noon show in the city, but it was mostly housewives, either young with children, or senior citizen women.

"I'm neither of those," Megan had said, as he maneuvered his car back to the Simms Building where the office was. "I'm a divorced woman with no kids. And a waffle maker."

"I'm wondering," Barry said, pulling into his designated spot in the parking garage adjacent to the midcentury steel and glass building. "Was the waffle maker a wedding gift?"

"It was," Megan said.

"Why haven't you ever had a waffle party?"

Megan shrugged her shoulders as they walked back into the building and past the winding stairwell, the very one that Megan took to the second floor (as far as it went) and then caught the elevator to the sixth floor just so she could walk. "Maybe one day."

The waffle maker. She laughed thinking about how it was her mother's idea to put it on the wedding registry.

"Everyone has to have a waffle maker," Donna Marshall said as she and Megan made out a list of items they both thought she and Guy would need as they started their life together. When Guy left, he only took his favorite coffee mug, from New York City. Megan was left with the rest of the kitchen items. She either donated or upgraded many of them.

Except the waffle maker. Each time she moved it with her or opened the cabinet to where it sat behind the blender– a kitchen appliance she used often– she never took out the waffle maker. But she never tossed it away either.

"One day," she muttered every time, "I know I'll need it."

That day hadn't come, but still something kept it in the cabinet to the far left of her kitchen sink.

"That looks ominous," she mumbled, now looking at the storm out her office window, thinking it more resembled the monsoon clouds of July than a storm coming in January.

She went back to work, but within the hour she realized it was getting dark in her office. She turned on the small light she kept on her desk, as decoration mostly, and kept working.

"It's snowing!" she heard Stephanie yell down the hall.

"It is?" Kevin Poole– the social media guy– called back.

Megan turned her head to see the flakes starting to fall, a long way still to go from their sixth floor office. She pulled up the page for the weather report and it drew her eyes instantly to the red winter storm warning banner.

"We're getting a snow storm," Stephanie called out again.

The office was quiet, not unusual for a Friday, but while everyone was there working, the phones were silent, as if the falling snow kept the phones quiet, too. Slowly, the snow began to blanket the city.

"Everyone go home," Barry called from his office. "Get home before everyone else gets on the road. We know that no one here can drive in snow."

They never used texting or intercoms, always calling out to each other across the halls, making Megan feel like she were back in a college dorm at times.

"Here, here," called Kevin, a Minnesota native. He was out of his office in thirty seconds with his coat on and laptop in a bag. "I was just waiting for the boss's signal," he said to Megan as he strolled by her office on his way out. "People here have no idea how to drive in the snow."

Kevin lived on the far end of the city and Megan knew his commute would be treacherous if he didn't get out soon.

"You need to go home," Barry said, wearing his long overcoat, as Megan still sat at her desk fifteen minutes later.

"But I only live a few minutes from here," she protested. "All of you live in the new-fangled areas of town."

"We know you live in the classic part of the city. But go home. They said this could be a doozy. Spend the weekend working up recipes. You have a lot of work ahead of you."

While the snow fell, on and off through Saturday afternoon, Megan did just that at home. She pored over her cookbooks and her memory, thinking about her favorites, the recipes that taught her how to cook, and the dinner parties she had held over the years.

And the possibility of a waffle party. Nothing resonated with the waffles though and she turned her focus elsewhere.

Around 2 pm on Saturday, with everything looking white outside the window, Megan looked up from the notebook she was writing in and across the kitchen to Sam who was laying in the middle of the kitchen floor, two toys by his mouth, snoring away.

"Hey," she said, getting up, knowing he would sense her movement before he heard her and jump up. "You need to go out. You haven't been out since breakfast."

She opened the back door, barely able to move it because the snow had drifted up to it, and Sam walked to it, look outside, then looked at Megan, and went back to his spot on the light brown tile kitchen floor.

"You need to go," Megan said. "I know you. You need to go."

Sam ignored her and went back to sleep. As Megan walked back to her spot at the kitchen table, a two-person white ice cream table she'd bought at a yard sale, she remembered a similar day just about a year ago.

"Who would be out in a snow storm?" she had wondered on that day when the doorbell had rung, figuring it was a package the mail person didn't want to leave in the snow.

With Sam following her, Megan looked through the living room curtains to see a familiar face standing there. With a familiar smile.

Ryan Wilson.

Megan looked at Sam who looked at her. She moved quickly to the door and opened it.

"Aren't you glad to see me?!" he asked, his blonde hair dusted with snowflakes. "I drove through a snow storm to see you!" He held his arms open wide and Megan didn't move into them at first.

And when she did so, she took tentative steps. Wishing he hadn't come by.

"When did you get back?" she asked, stepping back so he could walk into the small foyer and shake the snow off himself.

"I barely made it in last night. I would have come to see you, but I was lucky to make it home with this snow. Some homecoming!" He pulled his boots off, making himself at home. Megan took his coat and hung it on a dining room chair.

"Now you can give me a proper hello," he said, revealing a ski sweater and jeans underneath the heavy, royal blue ski coat.

Megan walked into his arms and stood there, feeling somewhat like a limp flower, the kind that has outlived its time in the vase and should be thrown out. She wanted to tell him he should have called first, but she knew why he came without calling: she never would have opened the door otherwise.

"Convenient it was snowing," she would tell Julie on Monday. "Can you really shut the door on someone's face when it's snowing?"

"Yes," Julie blurted out, then covered her mouth. They had both laughed.

For twenty minutes he talked about his hike across the Appalachian Trail, what he'd been doing for the past five months. And then finally he looked at Megan.

"How are you? I missed you."

"That's nice," she said, keeping her arms folded in front of her chest. "I didn't miss you."

And it was true. How could she miss someone who didn't want to take the time for her? Who up and announced one day he was leaving for five months.

He looked as if he was pouting. His face was more chiseled than before. He needed to put some weight back on, that she could tell. She wasn't about to offer him any waffles though.

"I never told you I'd be here if you came back."

"But you are," he said. "Are you dating anyone?" Ryan looked around as if looking for signs a man had been in the house. A man outside of Barry.

"No. But it doesn't matter. I don't want to see you."

"You let me in," he said, holding out his hands with his palms up, as if to tell her she had made the right move.

"There's a snow storm," Megan reminded him.

"Let's go down the hall," Ryan suggested, reaching out to touch her leg.

"I think you need to go," Megan said, tilting her head toward the front door.

Don't let him in, she kept telling herself. Don't let him in.

"Fine," he said. "I can't believe this. I thought you'd be happy to see me."

When he was out the door, Megan leaned against it, proud of herself for turning him down.

Time doesn't always make the heart grow fonder, she thought. Sometimes it makes the heart wake up.

As she watched Sam sleep, she wondered if it had been worth it, a year later and she was still alone.

"Focus on the newspaper," she mumbled, pulling out another section to read, and lifting her mug of tea to her mouth.

*****

By Sunday night the snow had stopped and the streets were beginning to dry. Megan curled up under a blanket for The Golden Globes Award show, Sam hogging the other end of the couch and keeping her from straightening her legs.

"Yesssss!" Stephanie texted both her and Julie.

"Nate Matthews is up for best actor!" Julie wrote back.

"LOL," was Megan's short response.

He was handsome, she thought as he walked the red carpet before the awards with his girlfriend du jour. He did have that salt and pepper hair that she found attractive.

"I must be getting old if I like men who have graying hair," she had told Stephanie and Julie not long ago.

"Nah, you're just mature enough to know that typically an older man hopefully has his life together," Stephanie said, then looked at the photo of her bald husband on her desk. "But I still love my light bulb-headed Max."

"So who was the girl with him last night?" Julie asked on Monday morning. "I haven't seen her before."

"Well," Stephanie said, "we can Google it or we can wait for the latest issue of *People* to arrive and tell us all about her."

"I'm not that patient," Julie said, pointing at Stephanie's laptop. "Google it."

Megan watched the scene play out as Stephanie Googled Nate's date and they waited for the information.

"She apparently was a barista where he gets his coffee in Beverly Hills."

"So does that mean she's writing a script like the rest of the baristas or she quit work and is hanging out with him all the time?"

"What would you do all day if you didn't work?" Megan asked, confused by the concept.

"I bet I could find a few things to do," Julie laughed. "At least my house would be clean."

"You would have someone else clean your house," Stephanie reminded her. "You would follow him around between Hollywood and Mexico."

"Does he have a place in Mexico?" Megan asked.

"Sometimes I wonder what planet you live on that you don't know these things," Stephanie wondered. "He built some place on the ocean in Cabo San Lucas like the rest of the celebs."

"Imagine what that's like," Julie dreamed. "All the opportunity you have."

"And you would have the same ones if you would work," Barry said jokingly, sneaking around the corner without their noticing.

Julie straightened up where she was lounging on the reception area couch.

"Come with me," he ushered Megan, a piece of paper in his hand.

At the end of the hall, she sat down in the chair on the back side of his desk and waited as he got comfortable, adjusting the big chair he sat in.

"Janet called me this morning and said their numbers spiked with your segment. You're catching on." Megan nodded. "And do you know what people love about you?"

Megan shook her head, a little afraid of what he might say.

"Besides recipes they can use, they love the apron."

"Oh my God." Megan clasped her hand over her mouth. "You're not serious?"

"I am." He burst out laughing.

"But I look like some fifties housewife. I think my mom gave that to me as a joke a long time ago."

"Some fifties housewife who happens to be really smart," Barry said. He pushed his chair back and placed his feet on his desk as if that would help him think. "You need to get more of them. Ask your mom where she got them and go buy some more. And you need to get more dresses. Those straight dresses– don't they have a name?"

"Shift dresses."

"Yes, those. You look great in those. Not too young, not too old. Just right."

"The dresses I wear to work every day."

"Exactly. Just be careful on the color. You don't want to have that much pattern against the apron."

"And how am I supposed to pay for these?" Megan asked, squinting her eyes at Barry.

He sat up and laughed, reaching into his desk drawer and pulled out a pen, then looked for a sticky note. "Just bring me the receipts. I'll take care of it."

"Really? This is new territory we're venturing into, you know."

"I know." He looked up from jotting a note. "But it's one that will be worth it. What are you making next week by the way?"

"Paper bag pizza."

"Seriously?" Barry looked as if he didn't believe Megan and she laughed. "Doesn't it start a fire in the oven?"

"How do you think I made all those pizzas you ate at my house? Didn't you notice the paper bags on the counter?" It was a conversation every time.

"I guess not," Barry said, scratching his chin. "I guess I was a little preoccupied."

"With your dying marriage?"

He nodded and his face turned dark. Megan gulped, feeling bad that she had brought it up. "I'm sorry."

"No." he waved his left hand, one with the pen in it, at her. "Don't be. Sometimes we all need to move forward and let go in our lives. Even when we don't want to. It just wasn't meant to be. However, paper bag pizza is definitely meant to be. I'll look forward to tasting the samples of that after the show."

Megan rolled her eyes and walked out, cornering Stephanie and Julie for an online shopping trip.

Their eyes grew big and Stephanie turned back to her computer. "Trina Turk, here we come!" she said.

"Keep it under $200," Megan said, her hands on her hips. "I need more than one."

"When you reach national television she'll be calling you to wear her new dresses," Julie said.

"I don't want to be Trina," Megan said. "I'm Megan." She paused and turned to walk back to her office. "I have some work I need to do."

"Yeah, you have to shop."

Megan laughed and walked back to her office thinking about copy, not dresses.

CHAPTER 3

"That was baked on a paper bag?" Janet asked, her eyes narrowing while she watched Megan unpack the grocery store bags in the studio for the show.

"It's unbelievable," Barry said. "She's been doing it this way for years."

Megan laughed to herself, wanting to call Barry on what he hadn't realized but she bit her lip and kept unpacking, mentally preparing herself with the list of prompts she had written down; the most important points she wanted to share.

"I can't wait to try it," Janet said, not looking convinced, staring at the unbaked pizza. "Aren't you afraid this might catch fire?" she asked, looking up at Megan who laughed. "No. I've been doing it since I was in college."

"What if people worry about the chemicals from the ink? I know how weird people are."

"I've been eating her pizzas as long as I've known her," Barry said, waving it off. "They're apparently safe."

"I'll just use the Whole Foods bag," Megan said, holding it up. "I'm sure their ink is safe."

"We hope."

The frowning microphone man came around the corner to mic Megan. He walked around her, looking, then stopped. "I think you had a skirt on last week?"

Megan shook her head and looked at him, her hands on her hips on the sleeveless shift dress she wore, her apron laying on the counter next to the ingredients for the segment. She remembered that the last week she'd already had the apron on and they had clipped the microphone to the back of it.

He shoved the microphone pack toward her. "I'll need you to slip this up the back of your dress."

"I'd think that was a little risqué if I didn't know the industry," Barry joked. Janet looked as if she might lose it.

After the mic guy had walked away, Janet whispered. "He is the most unhappy person who works here. We only tolerate him because he does such a great job with sound."

"I'm sure your outfits annoy him even more," Barry suggested, pointing his head at Megan who was tying her apron in the back, around the dress.

"I love the color combo," Janet said, looking at the pale pink and green in the apron against the dark pink dress.

"So you don't think it's too early, still too much winter to wear this?" Megan asked, smoothing the apron across her dress.

"Ah, it's New Mexico." Janet shrugged. "It's so sunny here that I think people forget it's winter. Besides, I'm ready for spring."

"You're forgetting about that snow storm we had last weekend," Barry laughed.

"Those happen in the spring."

"Three minutes," the cameraman said.

"We'll talk more after," Janet said. She started to walk away.

"Break a leg," Barry smiled.

When the cameras turned their wheels and pointed toward Megan, she said a prayer, although she had never considered herself religious, that she wouldn't forget anything.

Before she knew it the segment was over and Sally the host was grabbing several more pieces of pizza. "I'm going to have to work out twice the days that you're here," she said.

A man Megan didn't recognize came around the corner with a stack of papers in his hand. "I don't know what you're doing," he said to her, pushing his oversized glasses up his nose with his finger.

"What do you mean?" Janet asked.

"You should see all the comments on the web site." He pushed the papers toward the trio.

"Are they complaining about chemicals in the paper bags?"

Barry snickered.

The man looked confused. "They're talking about how cool Megan is that she cooks pizza on a paper bag. And that she uses carob for cookies."

Megan was shocked. Barry let out a whoop before remembering they were still in the studio.

"Let's get out of here," Janet suggested.

In the hall, the man– Jason Brown, the social media techie guy for the TV station– showed them the ten comments already posted on the page about how excited they were about Megan's cooking.

"I think we're onto something," Janet said, letting out her own whoop, followed by a laugh.

"You can thank me later," Barry said.

Megan looked at the comments, unable to believe how quickly she was having an effect on people.

"Just what I planned," Barry told her, putting his hand on her back. "So how will you top this next week?"

For the first time, Megan panicked.

*****

They returned to the office and Megan headed down the hall when Barry stopped her. "I think you should have a dinner party."

Megan stopped and turned to look at him, the rest of the pizza on a stoneware dish in her hand. Two pieces she had kept for herself for lunch, hardly able to shoo the others away. "This is a ploy to eat more of my food, I know," she protested.

"Well, it *is* a ploy to get you to give me the rest of that pizza," he told her, nodding his head at the plate.

"No," Megan said, walking into her office, calling out, "It's my lunch. I made it, I should get to eat it."

She knew Barry wouldn't let up; he followed her in and sat down in one of the extra chairs. "The web is picking up. We could do an occasional series about dinner at your house." Megan's office faced the view of the north end of the city, in the direction toward Santa Fe sixty-some miles away.

"Besides," Barry added, "you need to learn to walk in higher heels."

"What?" She spun her chair around and stared at him.

Barry leaned forward, his hands cupped in front of him. "It would add to the image."

"But this is New Mexico. Who wears heels? I like my low heels."

"And I'm thinking more than New Mexico." Barry stood up. "Dinner party Saturday night. You can pick the guests as long as I'm invited. And I will have someone here this afternoon to help you with the heels."

After he walked out, Megan flopped back in her chair and sighed. It was a lot of work. Part of her felt as if she were making Barry's dream come true.

Two hours later, having eaten her two pieces of pizza and working on a marketing campaign for the visitor's bureau, Megan was interrupted by Barry with a Hispanic woman with long black hair trailing behind him. Wearing high heels, a big floppy hat in one of her hands.

"This is Maria," he said, bringing her into Megan's office.

Megan instantly felt like a little girl: much shorter and not as sophisticated as Maria, who oozed sexiness just by entering the room.

"Hello," Maria said, extending her arm, several silver and gold bracelets clinking.

"Hi," Megan said, jealous of the energy coming from Maria.

"Maria is an old friend of mine," Barry said. Maria laughed and Barry looked at her. "Well, it's true."

"College friends," she said. "But don't tell anyone how long ago that was."

Barry ignored her and turned back to Megan. "Maria's been working in Los Angeles as a celebrity stylist, but she moved back to Albuquerque a few months ago to do local movie and TV work so I've asked her to help us."

"We're going shopping," Maria giggled, not a girly giggle, but the kind that made Megan feel like she wanted to be with Maria. Even if she felt like she were in fifth grade again.

"You two head out to the mall and get started."

"Oh please, an Albuquerque mall for clothes?" Maria looked at him and laughed. She turned to Megan. "If we can't go to LA for clothes, we'll bring LA to us. Let me get my laptop."

Only Maria came back to Megan's office and they settled in at the big table in the conference room. "However, we'll go to the mall and pick out some heels, but I've got such great contacts in LA. There's no reason for us not to buy your clothes there. Do you have favorite designers?"

Megan realized her mistake since she hadn't actually bought any dresses the previous week when Barry told her to. Now someone else was going to buy them and she wasn't sure if what Maria liked was going to look right on her.

I'm not so sexy, she thought, watching Maria begin typing up a series of sites on the laptop.

Maria sized up the pink dress that Megan wore. Megan loved the dress before she met Maria, but now she was thinking otherwise. Was it too much bubble gum? "That's a great color on you. Hmmm." Megan felt better.

Maria started to type in another web address, talking to Megan at the same time. "What kind of image do you want to portray?" Before Megan could answer, she said, "I know Barry is in love with the fifties housewife thing, but that's silly. We want to make you elegant, a modern woman, but let's take some of the vintage details to make you unique. So like a sixties modern woman in the 2000s."

"Make me myself, I hope."

"Yes, of course. We can't lose you."

"My Barbies had some fun dresses," Megan said quietly, a little afraid.

Maria sat back and laughed. Megan felt stupid. And then Maria spoke. "Did you grow up in the seventies?"

Megan shrugged. "Late seventies, early eighties."

"Do you still have those Barbie dresses?"

Megan thought for a moment and then remembered her mom handing her a box when she went to visit once. "Please take these home. They want to be with you, not me." In it were her Barbies and their clothes.

"I do," she told Maria. "In a box."

Maria shut the laptop. "Then let's get them from your house."

When they arrived there, Megan pulled the box out of the guestroom closet and met Maria in her dining room. Maria could barely take her eyes off Megan's decorating, though. "You already have a sense of style that's your own," Maria said with a smile and a laugh, poking around at the paintings Megan had done herself when she didn't find anything she liked.

Maria walked into the kitchen, the white cabinets accented by orange tile. "I'm not an orange fan but this works." She stood in the middle of the kitchen and put her arms out. "I don't know what Barry thinks you need. I'm just going to help you find yourself to bring out your style in your clothes. You clearly already have it in your house."

Megan stood in the doorway, happy that Maria liked what she saw.

"Your closet is next, but I want to see the Barbies first," Maria said, breezing by Megan back into the dining room.

Megan opened the box while they stood around the table. Inside, the dolls looked like they were ready for a day at the beach or for a big outing. They were all dressed and smiling, their blue eyes open wide.

"Yours were never naked, were they?"

Megan laughed and shook her head. "But my guess is that my mom dressed them all before she put them in the box." Megan held up one in a red sundress. "Mom made this dress and it was her favorite."

Maria poked through the box, taking everything out and looking at the clothes. "I want to know what your other favorites are."

"That's easy." Megan laughed and dug through the clothes, shoes, plastic hangers, and accessories to find several dresses. The first one was pink with spaghetti straps, a long satin dress.

"Very simple, but elegant," Maria cooed, taking it from Megan's hands.

The second dress Megan picked was a flowing mix of oranges, pinks, and a small amount of purple and brown. "I'm not sure I'm into the off-the-shoulder look on one side, but I love the colors and pattern."

"Very Palm Springs," Maria said this time.

She continued to sift through the box and Megan could see she was thinking. Megan watched her, all the dresses bringing back memories of her own life and what she had learned from the dolls.

While Megan didn't say anything to Maria, what struck her was how much her Barbies had taught her to dream. She ran her fingers gingerly across a few dresses. The Barbies could have any life they wanted. And that life was the one that Megan had worked to build around her. But when she saw Ken, it reminded her that she wasn't quite there.

Her mom had taught her to dream big, not forbidding any Barbies in the house like her friend Kim's mother.

"That's silly," Donna Marshall had said the evening at home when Megan had announced to her that Kim's mom wouldn't let her have Barbies. "Your Barbies can be whatever you want them to be."

Megan wondered in that moment what became of Kim, but she was interrupted by Maria talking to her.

"The closet," Maria said. "Now I want to see the closet."

"It's not that big," Megan warned. "This isn't a big house."

"But this house has character," Maria reminded her. "I feel like I'm in Los Angeles. I never knew Albuquerque to have an LA feel. That's why I left."

"Well, it does at my house," Megan laughed, opening the door of her walk-in closet.

"You don't need my help," Maria laughed, taking a step back, folding her arms across her chest, and smiling. "I can help you to walk in heels and tie it together, but you definitely already have a sense of style. I'm just going to help you beef it up."

"You think so?" Megan asked.

"Why are you surprised?" Maria asked, running her left hand lightly across the dresses on the left side of the closet.

"Because Barry seemed to think I couldn't do this on my own. He just told me to buy dresses the other day and now he has you helping me. I'm confused to say the least."

Maria turned, looked at Megan, and then burst out laughing. "Oh, don't worry about him." She waved her hand as if to wave Barry off. "What I will say is that he believes in you and wants you to succeed. Maybe he thought I could make you better, but I know you're well on your way without me. Now let's go to the mall and get you some shoes."

"Do you work with a lot of celebrities?" Megan finally asked when they were back in Maria's white BMW convertible, heading to the mall via the freeway.

She watched Maria's hair blow in the wind, her large black sunglasses taking up most of her face, the big hat underneath her handbag where it wouldn't blow away. But she looked every bit the California girl transplanted back home in New Mexico.

"I did. I'm not sure if I'll go back or not." She turned to Megan while they sat at the stoplight to make a left into the Winrock Center parking lot, looking for the Dillard's department store. "I have an opportunity to head up the wardrobe for a new television show they're going to film here. It takes place in the fifties and into the sixties. I can't wait to get started." She let go of the steering wheel for a moment, motioning her hands as if she were grabbing something other than air. "Besides, love gets in the way," she said mischievously.

"Oh," Megan said. "You found love here?"

"I did. He hasn't figured it out yet."

With Barry? She wanted to ask, but didn't.

"But I love my work. And the industry is good here now so I can enjoy some time at home and let everything play out."

"Who is in this new show? Can you tell me?" Megan asked as they walked into the mall together, Maria taking long confident strides, Megan wishing she could look as effortless as Maria did.

Maria giggled. "It wasn't whom I work with so much as whom I lived next door to." She leaned over as she opened the glass door, "Nate Matthews was my neighbor when he was starting his career. He still lives there although now he seems to live all over the world. And he's not only starring in this show, but he's producing it as well. He's the reason I got the job. My mom's house needed to be sold– she moved to a retirement community in Santa Fe– so I'm living there until someone buys it."

Megan's eyes grew big, not hearing what Maria said about selling her mother's house.

Maria began to pick up shoes and inspecting them. "They do have a good selection here. This is where I came when I was in high school to get my shoes. I'm glad some things haven't changed."

Just then, Maria looked at Megan. "You're on your way. Nate Matthews isn't someone for you to just ogle over because I could totally see you two together. You just don't know it yet. But I've been around a lot of people and I see it in you."

"What do you mean?" Megan asked.

"Barry asked me to go to the dinner party at your house, but I don't need any proof." She took her hand and waved it from the top of Megan's head to her feet. "You are a beautiful, smart woman who can speak on television. And you can cook! You're going to go a long way."

A man with black hair and a moustache walked over. "May I help you two ladies?" He rubbed his hands together as if he were the Wicked Witch of the West and had found his prey.

"Yes," Maria said, smiling and ignoring his sleaziness. She pointed at several pairs of shoes. "We'll need all of those. Size?" She looked at Megan, her finger still pointing at the last pair.

"Eight," Megan said.

"Eight," she repeated to the man as if he didn't hear.

He moved quickly with the samples to the back room and when he emerged, carrying boxes as if they were pancakes, Maria started with her lesson.

"You need to wear them every day to get used to them. You'll never really get used to them, but you'll do it because you'll see how sexy you feel. We don't want you to ooze sexiness so much as we want it to be…," Maria thought for a moment, "just under the surface as if everyone knows it's there but they can't see it. Yes, that's it. You're giving off just a hint to keep them coming back."

She strutted across the empty area of the floor in her own heels, making it look effortless. "I used to practice with my mom's shoes and they were too big. Once I started to wear shoes my size, it was easy."

Megan buckled the first pair, her favorite, silver with straps dotted with rhinestones. She got up, wobbled a bit, and then took off walking. She wanted to look like Maria but when she turned around to walk back to Maria she saw the disappointment in Maria's face.

"You'll get it," she said. "I won't give up on you. Practice every day and we'll meet up in a week and see how far you've come." She gathered up the boxes for the salesman. "In the meantime, I need to get you back to the office so you can get home and prepare for dinner tomorrow night."

Oh yeah, Megan thought, having forgotten that she was due to cook the next night.

She quickly made out a menu and snuck out before anyone could ask her for anything, wanting to get to the grocery store before the workday ended and it got crowded.

While she stood in the produce section, deciding if she wanted to go with a Mexican or Italian theme, parsley in one hand and cilantro in the other, a woman around her age stopped her.

"Excuse me?" She asked, her cart half-filled with food items.

Megan looked up and smiled, having no idea who she was, the bunches of herbs still in her hands.

"Aren't you that cooking girl on TV?" the woman asked.

Megan felt her smile go wide as the woman asked. "I am," she said, confidently, finding herself straighten up as she stood there.

"You've renewed my interest in cooking," the woman said, her short curly brown hair bouncing as she talked.

"Thank you," Megan told her. "I have no idea who's watching since we are in the studio and I can't see the audience."

"Please keep doing it. I tried the cookies and the pizza. I'm looking forward to what's next."

"You'll see on Wednesday," Megan told her.

"Any preview?"

Megan laughed.

"I can wait," the woman realized. "I don't need to know now. It's kind of fun to tune in and not know what you're cooking until that morning anyway."

"And it's not fun for me to not know what I'm cooking," Megan muttered after the woman had left with her cart.

She sighed and took the cilantro, choosing a Mexican theme, making a mental note to use a calendar to map out her next few weeks of cooking demos for the show.

CHAPTER 4

It wasn't going to take much for her to make the chorizo, black bean, rice, and cilantro dish for dinner Saturday night so much as she felt like there was an extra expectation: Barry planned to bring a photographer friend.

"We might want to think about doing a film crew one time for one of these," he had said, leaning against the wall in the hallway of the office, his fingers massaging his chin.

"A film crew?" Megan asked. "For what?!"

"Eventually you're going to have your own show," he said as if it wasn't news.

"My own show?"

"You can't do cooking segments on the noon show forever. You need more time to delve into the cooking process and such."

"But shouldn't you have consulted me on this?"

Barry just laughed. "We're going all the way to the top."

Megan didn't tell him, but she was most worried about making sure she had enough ideas for the weekly segment. The idea of filling five minutes, even as fast as it went, freaked her out, but doing a full twenty-two minutes for a 30-minute show? She worried that would keep her up at night.

Now she stood looking over her dining room table on Saturday afternoon, fooling with the tulips she had placed at either end, cutting them down so they didn't infringe on the conversations of her seven guests.

Megan ran her hand over the top of one of the Danish mid-century dining room chairs, remembering all the family meals shared around it when she was growing up in Denver. Her parents had brought her the table and all eight chairs, plus the two leaves, when they moved out of the family home and into smaller one-story house where her dad said they would carry him out in a body bag.

"Please don't say that." Her mother would get upset and an argument would ensue.

Megan kept her thoughts on the holiday meals shared with her older brothers and their grandparents as they grew up.

"I hope you'll have the same memories I do," her mom had said, running her hand across the top of the table after they had set it up in Megan's dining room.

Megan didn't say anything, knowing full well her mother worried she would never marry again and have a family. But now it didn't matter. When her dad called her last it was to tell her that her mom didn't know him anymore and that because she kept escaping– his word– he was going to have to put her into some sort of facility where she would be safe.

Megan glanced at the clock in the kitchen and took one last look at the table before she had to get dressed and start dinner.

Barry and Maria were the first to arrive, Maria breezing in, Barry trying to look as elegant as she, but instead appearing as if he were stumbling behind. "I told him it was rude if you didn't know the photographer and he got here first," she said, rolling her eyes. She quickly forgot about Barry to gush at Megan's outfit.

She had chosen an orange shift dress she forgot she had. Even though it was March and not very warm, the kitchen felt like a June evening.

"And you have the heels on!" Maria exclaimed, clasping her hands together.

Barry took a look and smiled. "I knew you looked a little taller."

He handed Megan a bottle of wine and the three of them walked to the kitchen, Megan's heels clicking on the tile floor in her hall.

"This looks wonderful," Maria exclaimed, craning her head in the doorway to the dining room at the set table. "Who else is coming?"

"Um," Megan said, thinking, as she whisked a green chile and oil salad dressing, "My neighbors Jim and Josie…Sharon…" Before she could finish, the doorbell rang.

A man will long black hair pulled into a ponytail and a camera in his hand walked into the kitchen with Barry who had answered the door.

"Meet Zeke," Barry said, introducing the man. "The best photographer in town."

Zeke laughed and stuck his hand out to shake Megan's. "This is a great place you have," he said looking around at her kitchen.

"Isn't it great?" Maria asked, throwing her long black hair around. "It's not too funky, but has just enough that it's simple but cool."

"Thank you," Megan said, wondering if simple, but cool was a good way to describe herself.

It had taken her a long time to put the house together in a way she liked it. She could still remember the disaster it was when she moved in. It was just like the end of a relationship, one that she thought would last forever. She saw now that she and Guy were not meant to be, but it took them both several years into their marriage to realize it enough to actually say it to each other. By then they were housemates.

She still cringed to think about how much time she wasted, but she tried to push it aside. And then there was Ryan. She'd been single since then, the thought of even attempting a date making her tired. She tried to forget he had come by that Saturday a year ago during the snow storm, instead wishing he'd go hike the Appalachian Trail again.

Megan knew she had been lucky with the house. An elderly woman had died and her family was eager to unload it, even though it was in the historic Country Club area of town. The house was a little cut up, mostly because it was built in the 1930s, but Megan made it work and over time she was able to remodel rooms, one by one, and get where she was now: something she could truly call her own.

But in that process she had given up opportunities to travel. The money only went so far and she had spent it on making the place she lived something she loved.

"How long have you lived here?" Maria asked, her head still looking around as if it were her first time in the house, this time at the cookbooks that lined the wall behind the kitchen table, the white metal ice cream table with a glass top and chairs for two. Megan had recovered the chairs in a bright green and had she had spent hours sanding and painting the table gingerly from black to white.

"Ten years," she gulped. She stopped chopping the cilantro, the one item she had not cut yet and looked up, the knife still in her hand on the cutting board. "That makes me sound old. The only other time I lived somewhere that long was growing up with my parents."

"Time gets away from all of us," Zeke said. "I'm not sure I'm going to have time to explore everything here. We might need to do another shoot."

"And that means more dinner," Barry said, rubbing his slightly extended stomach. "I'm up for that."

The doorbell rang again, but before anyone could walk down the hall, Jim and Josie, the couple who lived on the park, walked in.

"The party can start!" Josie called, flipping her short brown hair back off her face as she walked into the kitchen. "J squared is here!"

They each hugged Megan and Jim placed a bottle of wine on the counter. "I brought the usual," he said, his hand pointing at the label of the Ponderosa Vineyard in Jemez. "The only one for Mexican food."

"Mexican-type food," his wife reminded him. "This isn't tacos."

"Yeah, yeah," Jim said, opening the drawer next to where Megan stood. "Did you move the wine opener?"

"It's there from the last time you opened a bottle of wine," she reminded him.

Sharon was the last to arrive. "It's a long walk across the park," she jokingly said, referring to Forest Park, the one that the houses all surrounded, Megan's just barely a block off the park. "I was afraid I might get lost."

Her long silver hair looked perfectly brushed as always.

"But you made it because you didn't want to miss a meal here," Barry teased her.

"Exactly," Jim, Josie, and Sharon all said in unison and everyone burst out laughing as Jim passed the wine.

Zeke began to take photos, giving himself a time out for a glass of wine and everyone gathered around the small kitchen counter with the two stools for chips and guacamole.

"I didn't grow up here," Josie told everyone, dipping a chip into the bowl of green. "I never ate an avocado until I was twenty-five when I came for graduate school."

"Oh you poor thing," Maria said, looking as if it were the worst thing in the world.

Megan had already cooked the rice and drained the beans. She browned the onion with the chorizo, giving the dish a red chile flavor, and added the black beans, rice, and cilantro. Around her the conversations kept moving along, Megan only half listening as she cooked, Zeke taking photos wherever he could.

When she ushered everyone into the dining room with a pot holder in her hand, it was as if she weren't there. They didn't need her for their conversations and that was okay. While she poured the mixture into a low wide serving bowl, heating up a pile of flour tortillas cut into fourths, she tapped her fingers on the tile counter and thought about how lucky she was.

This is what it's about, she said to herself, shutting her eyes and listening, not to anything in particular but the noise of the voices and the clinking of wine glasses that happens when people are drinking and having fun with the meal and their conversations.

Zeke was there to photograph the grand entrance, apron, dress, food, and heels.

"She's perfect," she heard Maria say in a dreamy way.

"I told you," Barry whispered to her.

After everyone had finished, their plates emptied, Jim asking jokingly if he could lick his until Josie elbowed him in the ribs, Megan questioned everyone. "Did you like it? Good enough for television?"

"Don't our plates give an indication?" Sharon asked, looking at her own.

"Well, maybe you didn't really like it and felt an obligation to eat it," Megan said.

She began to gather the plates and with the silverware piled on top, she told everyone, "There's dessert" and disappeared into the kitchen to load the plates into the dishwasher.

"That was incredible," Barry said, walking in behind her, looking for the other bottle of wine.

"Thank you," Megan said, opening the dishwasher.

"One day we're going to find you the perfect man," he said, stealing the last tortilla chip out of the wooden bowl. "Thank God you got rid of Ryan. If hiking the Appalachian Trail couldn't change him, nothing will. I wish he'd gotten lost on it or fallen off the side of the mountain."

Megan swallowed hard and tried not to let the comment sting. She knew Barry was right, but the wound was still there.

He disappeared back into the dining room to the group of voices that permeated the house, making it warm and happy.

Megan followed him a few minutes later with her upside down lemon meringue pie.

"Oh my," Sharon said. "I've been waiting for this since the last time."

"You've had it before?" Maria asked, her eyes growing wide across the table.

"We're lucky if we get it once a year," Josie laughed.

"Once a year? You've had it that many times?" Maria looked envious.

"I have people over about once a month," Megan told Maria. "I figured Barry would have let you in on that fact."

"As long as I'm included in the future," Maria said.

"Where are Julie and Stephanie?" Barry asked, taking a bite of the lemon part that sat in a meringue shell and then sitting back. "I probably shouldn't be eating this."

"But you are," said Maria, who sat to his left.

"They had family stuff," Megan said. "It's hard for Julie to get here because of the kids unless they can find a babysitter. And Stephanie and James had a wedding."

"I'm glad to be here," Sharon said.

"Me, too," Zeke said. "I get to photograph all future meals, right? Just so I can be invited. I won't eat all day next time."

Megan laughed and sat down to enjoy the pie herself.

After everyone had left, she pulled the tablecloth, with all the napkins on top of it, off the table and bundled it, setting it on the floor next to the washing machine to take care of in the morning with the rest of her laundry. Sam followed her, happy to have had lots of attention, but ready for Megan to stay in one place so he could sleep.

As she lay in the darkness, she thought about what Barry said. And the time before when he had joked with everyone, "I think Ryan is an enigma."

The group had laughed, and so did Megan. But inside she didn't understand why it had to be so difficult. She didn't expect the relationship to be perfect. but why couldn't she have what people like Julie and Stephanie have? Men who loved them and wanted to be part of their lives. And watching Barry and Maria– even if they hadn't quite figured it out yet– still there was an energy between them. Something drew them together and they made it look easy, effortless.

When Megan woke up Sunday morning, she looked out the window behind her bed to see it was still dark; clouds had rolled in overnight. She checked her phone to see that it was supposed to rain and snow all day.

She went for a walk with Sam and when she came back, it was beginning to snow.

"It always snows in March," Jim called to her from the driveway next door where he was picking up his newspaper, wearing his navy blue bathrobe and forgetting about their recent big snow. "It never fails."

Megan waved back and inside took a shower and settled in for day of working on future segment ideas.

After her shower, as she passed through her dining room, she saw on the table in the corner under the window the box with her Barbies and their clothes. She had forgotten to put it away before the party.

Megan walked down the hall and as she went to place the box in the closet where she found it, she saw the beer box underneath. A Coors box her dad had probably brought beer home in and her mom took one look at it and thought it would be good for something. She had a stash of boxes in the basement and when it was time to move, she said they made it easy for her to start packing up the house.

Inside this box were Megan's junior high and high school mementos including her yearbooks. And a stack of magazine clippings about Duran Duran. Megan smiled when she saw them and walked back into her living room where she had turned the television on softly, not paying any attention to what she put on.

As Megan leafed through the items, memories flooded back. She had forgotten how much she thought, no, she *believed*, that one day she and Simon Le Bon would marry. It seemed silly now, but at the time she saw it clearly in her mind.

When her mom let her and her two friends, Jackie and Cecilia, go to the Duran Duran concert the summer before their freshman year of high school, Megan could still remember clutching the program at the concert, the very one she had on her lap now, and watching Simon sing. While she knew that all around her she was surrounded by girls who also had a crush on Simon, but Megan thought she had something more than that.

Somehow she believed that she wasn't just another teen girl in the crowd; she was the one with whom he would spend his life.

When the dream died she didn't know. Probably when she got her first boyfriend. No, she thought, even with him, Martin, she didn't see a future. It was with Simon she saw her future as if she were bound for bigger things and by settling with some guy from high school, well, that's what it was, settling.

Megan looked up and turned up the television. It was a Nate Matthews movie on and she texted Julie.

"Nate is on TV," she wrote. "Wouldn't want you to miss it."

Julie texted back quickly, "I need some Calgon to take me away. The kids are screaming and the hubby is out playing basketball with his friends. And since I don't have any, I'll take Nate instead. What channel is he on?"

Megan settled into her couch, a little tired from the big dinner the night before and shopping with Maria the day before that. Across the room she saw the silver heels staring at her, waiting to be worn again. She'd slipped them off after everyone left in the living room and had forgotten to take them back to her room.

But for now she could watch the end of the movie, the part where Nate's character John goes to the home of the woman he's been meeting in various parts of the country and having some sort of a relationship, the part where he realizes he wants something more with her. He shows up at her house.

And there she is with her husband and kids.

As Megan watched, she wondered how someone could do that to someone else. Watching the pain on John's face as he realized she didn't really love him, he was just a good time.

While John, or Nate, or whoever he was, walked away from the house in the rain, the credits began to roll and Megan felt a cloud of sadness envelope her. She just didn't understand.

It's just a story, she told herself. They're telling a story. Hopefully the story ended happily.

CHAPTER 5

"We need to up the ante," Barry said, tossing a soft purple ball in the air as Megan sat down in the chair on the opposite side of his desk. Julie joined them, along with Kevin.

"What does that mean?" Megan asked, feeling a little nervous, sipping her to-go coffee from the new coffee shop two blocks away, Humble Coffee.

"It's time for social media," Kevin said, twiddling his fingers in the air.

"Yeah, he's been anxious to get you up on social media since the first day you were on the morning show," Julie said, rolling her eyes.

"I need a photo," Kevin, said picking up his pencil and starting to make a list. "You and I should talk after the meeting."

"We need a tagline," Barry added, looking out the window at the mountains while the others stared at her.

"You know what?" Megan said, not thinking much about what they had been discussing. "Every time someone stops me in a store, or at the gas station, they always say, 'You're that cooking girl.' Why doesn't anyone remember my name?"

"And you're blonde," Kevin lamented. "You'd think this would be the place everyone would remember your name since you're in the minority."

"That Cooking Girl! That's it!" Barry cried out, turning his chair around, dropping the ball on his desk, and letting it roll off the desk in front of Megan.

"What?" they all asked in varying degrees of wonderment.

"What are you talking about?" Julie asked.

"Oh!" Kevin explained, getting it. "That Cooking Girl!" He jumped up from the couch. "That's the tagline!"

"Like 'That Girl!'" Barry said, throwing up his arms.

"What's 'That Girl?'" Megan asked, wondering who she was being compared to.

The others stared at Barry.

"The TV show?" Barry got quiet. "That's what made Marlo Thomas famous. In the late sixties."

"Um, I wasn't born yet," Megan reminded him.

"Yeah, I was born in '69," Kevin said.

"Seventy-five," Julie chimed in.

"Okay, so I'm dating myself," Barry said.

"It's a great idea," Kevin said. He turned to Megan. "Let's go to my office. We have a bunch of copy to write. And I'll need photos."

He turned back to Barry. "We need a kitchen that suits Megan's look. Do you know anyone?"

Barry thought for a moment. "We have Megan's kitchen and I have some friends whose kitchen is larger, but just as much fun as yours." He looked at Megan. "We need something with an island. But we can use Zeke's photos at your house, too. We'll do dinner parties at your house and other filming and photos we can do at Julianne and Mark's place."

"Don't I get a say in any of this?" Megan asked, pretending to protest.

"You do," Kevin said, grabbing her hand. "Let's go."

*****

When Megan saw the Brennans' kitchen that afternoon in the North Valley, she knew why Barry had thought of it instantly.

The housekeeper had let them in, clearly not speaking much English, a toilet brush in one hand.

"Where are your friends?" Megan whispered as Marta took her toilet brush and disappeared through the door into the living room.

"She's probably at yoga," Barry whispered back, leaning toward Megan. "What do you think?" He threw his arms out for her to see.

Megan walked around and checked out the deep blue and green tiles. "It's definitely southwestern."

"And That Cooking Girl! We'll get you dishes that we can at least use for the photos. We still need the studio for the live pieces, though."

Megan took a step back. "Your friends don't mind if you we use their kitchen?" She looked around. It was a dream: filled with all the top of the line appliances and cooking utensils.

"Who wouldn't be excited if someone asked to use their kitchen for That Cooking Girl's social media and web site?" Barry questioned.

"But it's not mine," Megan said.

"One day you'll have your own," Barry reminded her.

Megan didn't say anything and Barry sat down on one of the stools. "Don't you ever dream?"

She thought for a moment, looked at the terracotta tiles on the floor, and then up at him. "No."

"Did you ever dream?" He looked surprised. "I can't imagine going through life without dreams. What motivates you? Keeps you going?"

She shrugged her shoulders, her hands stuffed in the pockets of her coat. "I did but they didn't come true." She thought of Simon. "So I guess I stopped."

Barry leaned forward against the tile, his tie crammed against the countertop. "Well, think about it because this is just the beginning."

Just then, a woman burst through the door. Julianne, Megan guessed.

"Hi!" she said, going straight to Barry and giving him a hug. Her graying black hair was tied back in a ponytail and she wore top of the line yoga gear on her skinny body, looking as if she worked out all day and never ate. "Does my kitchen work?" She looked across the counter and walked around it to Megan. "You're That Cooking Girl! My friends had been talking about you, but I hadn't looked you up and then Barry told me all about you."

Megan glanced at Barry who simply smiled.

"Thank you," Megan said, looking around. "Your kitchen is wonderful. Are you sure that you're okay with this?"

"Of course!" she said, grabbing a bottle of water out of the oversized stainless steel-faced refrigerator. She waved a hand as if to dismiss it. "We spent so much money in here. I think I ended up doubling what we had planned. Mark was sooo not happy with me that I went so far over the budget. But now! You using my kitchen! He's pretty excited to see some return. At least everyone can enjoy the kitchen." She leaned toward Megan. "Especially because I hardly cook. I usually pick up dinner from Whole Foods."

"Thank you," Megan said, feeling like there wasn't much to say because Julianne said it all.

When they were back in the car, Megan asked Barry, "What does Mark do anyway?"

"I think he launders money, but don't ever say that to anyone." He turned the car around on the gravel driveway to drive out to Rio Grande Boulevard.

Megan sat down at her desk in her office, opened her email, and spent a few minutes looking at it. She turned to the view outside her window, one that faced north toward Santa Fe and the Jemez Mountains.

Then she opened her desk drawer, looking for a tea bag for her hot water. That's when she saw a bag of gummy bears, the ones that Stephanie had given her for a joke the week before.

"I was worried you weren't eating enough," she had said. "Being that you are the cooking guru and I see how everyone steals whatever you make. By the time you get down the hall to your office, the plate you brought from the station is empty."

But really, Megan thought, Stephanie did it because her nephew needed to raise $150 for his middle school band where he played the trumpet.

"I'll pay you back for the bag," Megan offered.

"No way, this is my treat to you," Stephanie said. "I'm so excited to watch you rise into fame."

Megan opened the bag and started to eat them, one by one. They melted in her mouth.

Fresh, she thought.

And once again she was transplanted back to Christmas with the new Duran Duran tape. And poster. Megan thought about how clearly in her mind she envisioned a future with Simon LeBon, how they would live between England and Los Angeles. She had no idea what either place looked or felt like at the time, it all came from what she saw on television. Or envisioned in her mind.

When did that dream die? She wondered. And what replaced it?

Megan thought for a few moments, thinking back on her marriage to Guy. She thought it had been good, she thought they were happy. And then one day they looked at each other and knew it was over.

Dreams, she thought, I need to start dreaming again.

Megan pulled a blank piece of paper out from her printer and wrote, "Dreams" at the top.

But what did she dream about? What did she want? Did she still want to marry Simon Le Bon? Megan Googled Simon, who had long married that model girl Megan was so jealous of in junior high school.

He wasn't the cute guy she remembered. But maybe she had changed. When she and Guy got together, he was her dream. She thought they would live happily ever after together. Well, maybe it wouldn't be perfect, but they would stay together.

And ten years past their divorce she was still alone. What did she have to show for her life?

Public relations campaigns, of course.

CHAPTER 6

The social media took off after her next segment that Wednesday. Kevin had everything in place and once they announced it on the air, people jumped on following her.

"I'm going to have to teach you how to use it," he said. "You should be posting every day."

"Posting what?" Megan asked, from the conference room where they sat together using Kevin's laptop.

Kevin thought for a minute. "Post things you buy at the grocery store and an idea of how to use them. Post what you're making."

He went to lifestyle guru Martha Stewart's web site and showed her examples. "I'm not a photographer, but I know what people are following."

"I'll get Zeke to help you," Barry said, poking his head in the door.

"Are you always lurking behind the corner wherever I'm at?" Megan asked, rubbing her face when she saw him.

"I am." He pinched her shoulder lightly. "You'll never get rid of me now."

"Lucky you," Kevin mumbled.

"Yeah, lucky me."

When he left and they returned to her new Instagram page, Kevin lowered his voice and asked, "Are he and Maria dating?"

Megan started to laugh and realized she had to keep it down. She clasped her hand over her mouth before she spoke. "I think she's in love with him, but I'm not so sure he realizes it."

"For a man as successful as he is, he can be really dense," Kevin said, his voice serious which made Megan want to laugh even harder.

"When she and I went to the mall last week, she told me how much she likes him, but I was afraid to ask anything. He's still our boss."

"Yeah, but you could ask him. He's got this whole plan for your career, you know."

"I know," Megan said quietly.

"You're lucky. We're all going to make this happen," Kevin said, turning to her and patting her hand. "You deserve it."

Megan smiled and watched while he downloaded the Instagram app to her phone. Although she had no idea what she would do with it.

*****

"So I think you're right," Julie said nonchalantly to Stephanie as the three women took a break from work. "Nate Matthews is in town shooting a TV show."

"Maria said he is," Megan said, barely noticing, as she flipped through the latest copy of *Vogue* magazine, glad to be thinking about something other than food for a little while.

"My friend Lizzie saw him at her church on Saturday evening."

Megan looked up and watched Julie point her finger out the window. "That big Catholic church there."

"That's a beautiful church," Stephanie said. Then laughing. "And I'm not even Catholic."

"Did she talk to him?" Megan asked, putting the open magazine in her lap. "Does he go to church?" Then she wondered why she was asking.

"She said she waved at him during the sign of peace."

"Is that when you shake each other's hands?" Stephanie asked, looking proud of herself that she knew something about Catholicism.

Julie nodded. "But they were too far away for that so she just nonchalantly waved, she said." Then she looked at Megan. "Wait," Julie said. "What did you say that Maria said?"

"That's why Maria is here," Megan said, having forgotten all about it. "She's working on that TV show."

"Why doesn't anyone ever tell us anything?" Julie asked.

"It takes place…," Megan said, not really knowing anything.

"In the sixties. He owns a motel on Route 66. Seems sort of Fantasy Island-ish," Stephanie said.

"What do you mean?" Julie asked.

"Each episode is about the people who come through town, to his swinging place."

"That sounds more like 'Love Boat,'" Megan said. "I didn't think there was anything magical about the motel."

"There is something magical about Nate Matthews and that's enough to make the motel magical," Julie said with a shrug.

CHAPTER 7

Zeke was due at her house in twenty minutes to give her some pointers on how to take good food photographs. After that, Barry was looking for a food stylist to help.

"But we need to get you posting photos first," he had said after he called Zeke and asked for his help.

That Saturday afternoon Zeke arrived, ponytail intact, camera in hand, at Megan's doorstep.

"I don't have a digital camera," she admitted.

He shrugged his shoulders as he took off his leather jacket and placed it around the back of a chair of her kitchen table. "I'm sure you have a phone that has a camera." She picked up her smartphone from the counter. "That's all you need. We're just talking digital here. Anything you need that's for print, I'll take care of."

"You and Barry already discussed this?" she asked, not really surprised.

Zeke laughed. "It sounds like you're always the last to know."

Right behind Zeke, Maria arrived.

"Hello!" she called, walking in the front door. When she swept into the kitchen, her black hair pulled back into a bun on top of her head, she pulled off her sunglasses, and said, "I hope it's okay I walked right in."

Megan waved her off. "I'm not really sure my life is my own anyway."

"You have a very authentic life," Maria said, then turning to Zeke. "So what are we going to do?"

"I don't know how any photos I take are going to have anything I'm wearing in them when they're about the food," Megan pointed out, wondering why Maria was there.

Zeke and Maria laughed. "That's okay," Maria said. "You do your lesson with Zeke and I'll work on your wardrobe. I was thinking we should start doing a little more planning ahead of what you're going to wear. And then we can see how you're progressing in the high heels."

Megan still didn't get how her wardrobe had anything to do with the food, but she let it go.

Megan had made a red velvet cake with beets with an ombre red frosting that blended from red to orange.

"Seriously?" Zeke asking, turning the cake all around on its white pedestal stand. "That has beets in it?"

"It does?" Maria asked, walking back into the kitchen from the dining room. "And look at that color. Is there anything you can't do?"

"It does," Megan said proudly. "Do you need to take a photo of the cake as a whole or can I go ahead and cut it?" She turned to Maria. "I've never made a baked Alaska."

"Then maybe you should start. It looks like you can create anything you want."

"I want your photos to be edgy," he said.

Megan raised her eyebrows. "How does that go with my apron and shift dress theme?"

"That's the point," Maria interjected. "You're not what you seem on the outside." She laughed.

"Like don't judge a book by its cover?" Megan asked.

"Who does that?" Maria asked, looking so secure in herself. "I certainly don't."

"She does," Zeke whispered. "And I just met her at your party and I know that."

"She lived in LA," Megan whispered back.

"No one exists under their skin there."

"You two are too silly," Maria said, waving her hand and disappearing down the hall. "I'll be the judge of that. Let me know when the cake is cut so I can share a piece."

"No need to take a photo of the entire cake," he said, pulling out his tablet and opening a few web sites to show her what recent food photos on the most popular web sites looked like. "You can have a slice and even a slice that has a bite out of it."

Megan studied the photo and Zeke swiped his finger to another photo.

"And you can even have a smoothie that someone has had a drink from," he showed her.

Megan gasped. "That seems like sacrilege. It's not perfect."

"And that's just it," Zeke said. "It's about great looking food, but it's not about perfection. People want to know they can make it and won't have to live up to Martha Stewart."

Megan wondered about her own image as she cut the cake. Zeke took photos as she sliced it and then showed her what he had done and how important the light was.

As she handed him a slice of cake, then cutting another one for Maria, and finally one for herself, Zeke sat down at the kitchen table.

"I'm a little shocked you aren't married," he said, his eyes growing big after he tasted a piece. "This is incredible. You know the way to a man's heart is through his stomach."

"And no red food coloring No. 2 or whatever it is," she said sitting down, ignoring him. "Isn't that the one that people thought caused cancer in M&Ms, but really didn't?"

"If you don't have a boyfriend, you need one," he said. "Some man is missing out on having you cook for him."

"She's going to have a boyfriend soon," Maria sang, coming back down the hall, and laughed.

Zeke picked up the last of the frosting with his fork. "That's a good thing. Remember the boy who used to chase you around the playground at school?" Zeke asked, moving dishes around.

"Um, sure," Megan, said, looking at Maria, but really unsure what he was getting at.

Zeke placed his camera on the table and looked at Megan. "He's the one who really liked you."

"That would have been Ronnie Gallegos," Maria said, covering her mouth after she started to giggle.

Megan had to think for a moment. "Curt Stevenson." And then she started to laugh. "But I think it was only because we both wore glasses."

They looked at Zeke. "Whom did you chase around?" Megan asked. "We know it was someone."

"Tricia Vogel. She had this smile that could light up a room."

"What happened to her?"

"She moved away." He shrugged his shoulders. "I once thought about looking her up on the internet, but I decided to let the memory rest as it is. Sometimes it's better not to find out what happened to someone."

"By the time we were in high school, Ronnie turned into a fat slob." Maria rolled her eyes. "It grossed me out even more than when I wasn't interested in boys in third grade."

"I don't know what happened to Curt." Megan shook her head. "We moved away when I was in sixth grade."

"There's always a good man out there," Zeke said, picking the camera up again. "I think the biggest turn off in a woman is one who chooses men who don't treat her well."

"Why?" Megan asked.

"It shows she doesn't respect herself enough to have someone who really loves and cares about her."

Megan nodded and didn't say anything.

"You have gummy bears," Maria said suddenly, seeing the open package on the counter.

Megan laughed sheepishly. "Yeah, they've kind of become my motivation."

"Do tell," Maria said, sitting down at the table, neither woman paying much attention to the photographs Zeke was taking around them.

Megan felt a little embarrassed relaying her gummy bear story and Duran Duran.

"Does Barry know this?" Maria asked, looking like she was going to jump out of her seat and look for her phone to text him.

"Of course not," Megan laughed. "Why would he?"

"This is a great piece for them to use in your bio."

"That's good for today," Zeke said, starting his own conversation. "I'll email you these later."

"For today?" Megan asked, a little confused.

"We'll do it again," he said with an assuring smile.

"We have some other ideas," Maria added.

"You two are in this together?" Megan asked, pointing her finger each of them.

"We are," Maria said, picking out the green gummy bears. "We need to get photos of you prepping food and I'm thinking we might do some lifestyle stuff as well."

"For the web site?"

"For social media, for your web site," Zeke said. And Maria adding, "And your cookbook."

"Cookbook?"

"Yeah. Didn't Barry talk to you about that?" She was so nonchalant about it that Megan couldn't believe it was her own life they were speaking about.

"Uh. No."

"Well, that's going to be a huge part of this," Maria said. "We need to start gathering content so you should be thinking about that. Barry has a better idea of how many recipes you'll need."

After they left, Megan looked through her own cookbooks and finally sat back in her kitchen chair and sighed. It all felt overwhelming. She put on her workout clothes and walked outside into the bright sunshine of the mid-afternoon.

Mrs. Rosales, her neighbor around the corner, was outside with her little dog, Martino, who yapped away, acting like a security guard.

"Hi," Mrs. Rosales said, her long salt and pepper hair pulled back in a bun. "How are you today?"

"I'm well," Megan said, letting Martino run circles around her, Megan always slightly afraid Martino would bite her ankles.

"I need to make tortillas, but I thought I would come outside and enjoy a few minutes of warm sunshine today," she said, waving her hand all around.

"Me, too," Megan said. "Well, except that I don't need to make tortillas."

"Do you want some? I'll make you some," she said.

Megan thought for a moment and then asked, "Even better, would you show me how to make them?"

"Of course!" Mrs. Rosales's brown eyes grew big. Her eyes took over her face and skin, brown spotted from the sun. She motioned with her arm for Megan to follow her. "Martino, you come, too! I don't want you to get run over by a car."

Mr. Rosales had died five years before and Megan still remembered how all the neighbors had gathered at the church for the funeral to say goodbye to the man who tended to his roses as his retirement job. He was always working on the yard and after he died, Mrs. Rosales had all the grass torn out and rock put in. "I'm not going to mow it," she said adamantly. "And I certainly can't rely on my children to do the job he loved so much."

"I think he used to get down on his knees and made sure every blade was standing up," Josie once joked at the dinner table at Megan's house.

The house hadn't changed much since they moved in during the 1960s. They had raised three children in the three-bedroom house and making sure each one was ready for life was more important than any remodeling.

"I don't think they could afford it, but they wanted their kids to live in this neighborhood on the park," Josie had lamented. "I can't fault them for that."

Meagan looked around at all the statues of Our Lady of Guadalupe, including one in the front yard and one in the backyard, and the photos of Mr. Rosales and all their grandchildren. It was obviously a comforting place for Mrs. Rosales.

By then Martino had calmed down and was curled up in his little dog bed next to the refrigerator in the kitchen.

"I always wanted to teach my daughter how to make tortillas, but she's much too busy at the bank where she works. Instead, she just wants me to make them for her."

Mrs. Rosales pulled out a big stainless bowl and filled it with flour and water. "Have you ever made a pie crust?" she asked Megan, who nodded her head. "It's a lot like that. It takes practice to get the consistency right."

She set the bowl on the kitchen table in the middle of the kitchen and looked like she was playing with the dough. "You want it to be thick, but not so thick that you have to pound out the tortillas."

She pulled what looked like a flat cast iron pan out of a cabinet and placed it on the stove. "My mother gave this to me when I got married. She said if there was one thing I needed to have, it was a *comal*, a tortilla pan. I'm guessing your mother didn't buy you one?"

"My mom doesn't know how to make tortillas," Megan laughed, thinking back on how her mom loved to cook, but when it came to anything bread related, she left that to the local bakery. "I'm not sure you could even buy a dozen tortillas in the grocery store where I lived. But my mom thought I needed a waffle maker. Did you get one of those?"

Mrs. Rosales laughed. "No, I just made pancakes," Mrs. Rosales acknowledged with a smile. "But maybe I can teach you since my daughter won't learn and your mother doesn't know."

"I'm good with that," Megan said, trying to take mental notes. She knew the crew at work would be eating a lot of tortillas in the upcoming weeks.

As she got ready to leave Mrs. Rosales's house, she spotted a sewing machine in the laundry room off the kitchen. Hanging next to it were what looked like a bunch of aprons. But these weren't just any aprons, they looked like the very ones that Megan had been wearing on television with one simple ruffle at the bottom. It was as if the ruffle was the way to show the difference between a male and female apron.

"Do you make these?" Megan asked, stopping in the doorway of the yellow laundry room and pointing.

"Oh yes," Mrs. Rosales said, leading the way into the laundry room and taking one off a stand. "I like to display them so I can enjoy them," she said, her smile getting bigger as she showed off her work.

This one was pink with a brown ruffle.

"I was in love at first sight," Megan would tell Maria later.

"Do you think you could make me one of these?" Megan was feeling excited in a way she didn't expect. "I would pay you."

"Of course," Mrs. Rosales said. "You don't need to pay me though." She opened a closet door and behind it was more fabric than Megan thought the local fabric store had in its inventory.

"Holy moly," Megan said, walking up to the shelves, each stack by color and shade, touching them lightly. "How did this happen?"

Mrs. Rosales laughed. "I bought it on sale and one day I realized I had more than I knew what to do with. Roberto always teased me that he should have bought stock in the company so he could have recouped some of what I bought."

"When did you start making the aprons?" Megan asked, running her fingers along the incredible stitching.

"When I realized I could never use up all the fabric before I die. I'll make you as many as you want."

"But please let me pay you."

Mrs. Rosales shook her head and was adamant. "No. I will be happy to do that for you."

Megan set the bag of tortillas she had given her on the washing machine. "But I'm going to wear them on television."

"Oh!" Mrs. Rosales threw her head back and laughed again. "You're that cooking girl on the noon news! Wait until Jean hears about this. She loves to watch you. And all along you've lived several houses away from me. I'll make you the aprons. Jean will be jealous."

She had a sparkle in her eye which made Megan smile. "Okay," Megan said, knowing they could work it out later. "We have a deal."

On Monday she stopped by Barry's office to tell him.

"You what? Really?" He looked excited. "People love the apron you've been wearing. This will be great. Now you can have one to coordinate with every outfit. Did you tell Maria?"

Megan nodded her head securely. "I'm surprised she didn't tell you," she said.

Barry's face turned and he sat back down at his desk. "I kind of made her mad," he admitted as if he was putting his tail between his legs.

"Um, what happened?" Megan asked, almost afraid to find out what he had done.

Barry covered his face in his hands and then uncovered them. "I made her mad. It was so stupid and I feel so stupid that I can't even tell you what it was."

"Then tell her your sorry," Megan suggested, shrugging her shoulders. "I'm sure she'll get over it."

"It's not that easy," he said.

"But admitting you made a mistake is a big deal. That's a huge step in gaining someone's forgiveness."

"Really?" Barry asked, looking a little relieved.

"Yes," Megan said, thinking about how Ryan was never wrong. But she wasn't going to bring that up with Barry. "Just call her. I'm sure that's all she wants is for you to admit you were wrong." Megan leaned forward in her chair. "And I know men: you like to say stupid things."

Barry laughed and shooed her out of his office. "Okay, let me take care of this."

That afternoon as Megan was getting out of her car in the driveway thinking about how she needed to do yard work because spring was coming, she heard a voice calling her name.

Mrs. Rosales was walking toward her with something bundled in her hands– Martino running behind her as fast as his little legs could take him.

"Hello!" she said. "I've been waiting for you to get home from work," she said and she shoved the bundle into Megan's hands. "Here."

It was two aprons: one brown and pink, almost like the one she saw hanging in the laundry room, and the other one turquoise and orange.

"I know you liked the pink and brown one and I thought the orange and turquoise would be good with your blonde hair."

Megan wasn't even sure how react. She thought about crying, but all she could was smile and say thank you. "This is incredible," she said. "I love these. I can't wait to wear them on the air!"

Martino barked at Mrs. Rosales's feet, running in circles around her.

"And I can't wait to tell Jean you're going to wear my aprons!"

Before Megan could say anything else, Mrs. Rosales turned to walk back home with Martino following at her heels. Megan watched her and smiled. While it was obvious that this was important to Mrs. Rosales to show up her friend, it was more than that. She looked so happy.

"Oh!" Mrs. Rosales called. "When do you want to come over to have lesson two for tortilla making? I'll have more aprons for you by the weekend."

Megan laughed and couldn't believe what she was hearing. "Sunday will be great."

"After church, of course. Come over at noon and I'll have lunch for you."

Megan laughed again and ran her hand over the aprons in her hand. She couldn't believe what Mrs. Rosales had done for her. It seemed like at every turn someone was trying to help her. She said a silent thank you and grabbed her handbag and the bag of groceries she had and walked inside her house.

"Look at the apron!" Janet laughed when they arrived at the studio for the next segment and Megan had put it on. "Where did you get that?" Janet couldn't resist from touching it.

"My neighbor made it for me to wear on the air," Megan admitted. "It was a surprise. Isn't it great?"

"We're going to have a bunch of women who will want these," Janet said, looking surprised.

And Sally was more excited than Janet when she and Megan started the segment. "I can't stop looking at your apron," Sally said. "That is the coolest thing ever. Guys? You should get one for your sweetie," she said looking into the camera.

Megan thanked Mrs. Rosales on the air for making it and launched into her segment about black bean brownies. "You know spring is just around the corner," she said, looking at Sally while she poured the ingredients into a big bowl to mix them. "So for this Valentine's Day I'm suggesting black bean brownies with carob."

"Carob again!" Sally laughed. "But black beans?" she scrunched her nose. "That sounds weird."

"That's what you'll think until you try it," Megan laughed, sliding the dish into the oven and pulling out the brownies she had made and cut earlier.

Sally took a bite and was obviously wowed. "Those are black beans?"

"Yes," Megan laughed. "And if you want a mint flavor," she held up a bottle of mint extract, "just add a few drops of this."

After the segment ended, the staff gathered around the brownies and Megan took the ones out of the oven that weren't really baking.

"I can bake them at home," she told Janet. "There's no egg in them."

"It's another hit," Kevin said, meeting them in the hall and taking a brownie off the plate that Megan offered him. He held up his laptop. "People are going nuts over the apron."

"That's why we bring you along," Barry said, patting Kevin on the back. "We get validation before we even get back to the office."

CHAPTER 8

Sunday morning Megan walked over to Mrs. Rosales's house right at noon. She was a little nervous, but more excited to see what Mrs. Rosales would teach her.

When she rang the doorbell, Martino began his yappy bark and Megan smiled as she heard Mrs. Rosales talking to her dog. "I hear you, Martino. Yes, I hear you."

When the door opened, there stood Mrs. Rosales wearing what Megan guessed was her church outfit: navy blue pants and a red and blue top.

"Hello!" Mrs. Rosales said, her face lighting up when she saw Megan.

It's nice someone is so happy to see me, Megan thought, following her into the house.

"I don't have any new aprons for you this week," she said, leading Megan to the kitchen where the smell of something (Megan wasn't sure what) filled the air. "I got busy watching my *telenovela*. And I changed my mind. I want to show you how to make something else."

"Oh, it's okay," Megan said. "I just appreciate you making them for me. And teaching me."

They stopped and stood near the round kitchen table– the dark brown frame sticking out in the white tiled room. Mrs. Rosales sighed. "I wish Roberto were here to see my aprons on TV. He would be so proud." She paused as if she were saying a prayer. "God bless his soul."

And then she quickly lightened up. "But I bet he's glad I'm using some of that fabric I bought." She chuckled and walked to her stove where she stirred what looked like green chile. And maybe mixed with red chile. Megan stood behind her and watched.

"For many years, on Sunday mornings, I always made us eggs and chile after church." Megan listened as Mrs. Rosales moved around her small kitchen, a fluorescent light making everything look stark. "We went to church– walking in the nice weather. To San Felipe de Neri in Old Town, of course." She pointed as if the church were there and Megan could see it.

But she knew– the one on the plaza in Old Town.

"And sometimes some of the family would stop over and eat with us." She sighed. "Those days are long gone, but it's nice to be able to share it with you."

Megan watched her– and listened– as she explained the chile recipe, why she used corn tortillas instead of flour for this dish, and how her son would always eat the extra cheese when she wasn't looking.

She made up a plate of food and set it at one of the two place settings at the round table. "Go ahead," Mrs. Rosales said, pointing at the steaming plate. "Huevos rancheros, Rosales style. Just for you."

Megan sat down at the table and took a bit of the spicy, but tasty food. She sat back in her chair. "This is wonderful. You've been making this for how many years?"

"Since Roberto and I married," Mrs. Rosales chuckled, sitting next to Megan, but close to the stove where she could keep an eye on things. "We were so young. I was seventeen!"

"Oh gosh," Megan exclaimed.

"I wasn't even out of high school."

"I can't imagine."

"It was the way we did things. My children got married much later. But it worked for Roberto and me." She took a bite and chewed thoughtfully. "But it wasn't so easy. We were so poor. Chile we could get. Beans and rice, too. My meals were always simple because it started that way when we didn't have anything. And after three kids we still didn't have anything because they ate it all!"

Megan enjoyed the meal as she listened, glad for the new story, of someone who wanted to share with her. As she sat there, she was reminded of how Ryan didn't spend time with her. He didn't want to sit and listen to stories like these. He was too busy talking about what he was going to buy at REI for his hike on the Appalachian Trail. And she was reminded how much she missed these same stories from her mom about her life.

"Do you have a boyfriend?" Mrs. Rosales asked. "I'm guessing you aren't married."

"I was," Megan admitted. "I bought my house after the divorce."

"That's too bad. I'm sure there is a better man out there for you than one who doesn't care enough to keep a marriage. Roberto wasn't perfect, but he was faithful. I would never say otherwise, but we knew many couples where one cheated. And it wasn't always the husband! I comforted many friends whose husbands were sleeping with other women, but Roberto had to be there for several of his friends whose wives found a man on the side."

"You're lucky you had someone who loved you so much."

"Right until the end," Mrs. Rosales said. "He had just told me he loved me when he went to sit down and watch a football game. I thought he was sleeping, but he died right there in that chair." She pointed to the recliner in the family room that opened from the other side of the kitchen. "I suppose it's better that way than to linger with cancer."

They were quiet for a moment. Megan felt as if she were absorbing so much.

"Where is your family?" Mrs. Rosales asked.

"Denver."

"You live here alone?"

"Yes."

She looked at Megan and Megan began to feel like her current life was devoid of meaning next to the one that Mrs. Rosales had. Maybe her children weren't around, but it obviously had been filled with life and love. Lots of love. And food, of course.

"Do your parents visit? Or do you visit them? My son moved to Denver two years ago for his job. Took his family and the grandkids with him. I should go visit, but I'm so afraid to fly."

"They used to visit," Megan said, adding, "my mother has Alzheimer's."

Mrs. Rosales gasped and held her hand to her chest. "*Dios mio.* I'm so sorry. You're so young. How old is your mother?"

"She just turned seventy." Megan sort of snorted. "Not that she was aware of it."

"Why so young?"

Megan shook her head. "They don't know. She must have hit her head at some point." It was one of the few times she had talked about her mother.

"And your father?"

"He takes care of her, but he says the time to put her in a facility is coming. She's starting to try to wander out of the house. He has help so he can do other things, like golf. And stay sane."

"I wish I knew a nice boy to set you up with." She crumbled her napkin in her right hand and stood up from the table, taking her plate with her. "But not my sons! They're married, but I wouldn't set you up with them. Maybe I'll ask Father at church if he knows of any single men. You're Catholic, right?"

Megan laughed. "I am. I don't go much, though," she admitted. Or not at all, she silently mumbled, afraid to admit that to someone like Mrs. Rosales or she might not be invited back for lunch.

"Some time you can come with me. We'll scout out the church for single men!"

She laughed as she loaded the dishwasher and Megan got up to help. "No no no," Mrs. Rosales said. "You go home and rest up for your cooking thing on television. I'm sure you have plenty to do. Martino will help me with the dishes. Right, Martino?"

The little dog wagged his tail from his dog bed in the corner of the kitchen.

As Megan walked home she realized it was the first time in a long time where she felt connected to someone. Not like she was connected to everyone at work– the people who had made up her life for some time– but on another level. With her mother's illness, she felt disconnected from her family, and with her brothers living on the east coast with their families.

It feels good, she thought, as she turned the corner and crossed the street to her house.

*****

"Maria had a great idea at dinner last night," Barry exclaimed, flying into Megan's office like he always did. And when he stopped, his tie had flipped over his shoulder, making Megan chuckle.

"Stop it," he said, knowing she was laughing at him.

"I'm laughing with you," she said.

Barry sat down in one of the chairs and leaned toward Megan, looking around as if he had a secret. "You know, there are a lot of movies filming here right now."

"So I hear," Megan said.

"And television, too. But mostly movies."

Megan shrugged her shoulders. "Maria is working on one. But what does that have to do with me?"

"Maria suggested we have a fundraiser while we have these people in town."

"I still don't get how I'm involved."

"You would do the cooking."

"I'm not a caterer," Megan reminded him.

Barry held out his hand and shook his head. "No, not all of it. Just some of it. The cookies, of course. And maybe some appetizers."

"And how is this supposed to help me?"

"We're going to put you in front of a bunch of celebrities which will grow your audience. If just one person instagrams how great you are, your following will gather momentum outside of Albuquerque."

"But we don't have anything to sell yet."

Barry shook his head again. "You're worrying about something you don't need to. Once you have them as followers, when the cookbook comes out, they'll be first in line to buy it."

"For their personal chefs to make the food for them?"

"Exactly," Barry said, not catching Megan's sarcasm.

She stopped, then spoke again. "Wait... what cookbook?" While Maria and Zeke had mentioned it, Barry still hadn't said anything to her about it.

But Barry was gone before she could get the question out of her mouth.

Maria came in for lunch with Barry and stopped by Megan's office, taking off her wide-brimmed straw hat.

"It's only April," Megan said, watching Maria place the hat on a chair.

"It might be April, but the sun is already toasting me. I forgot how strong it is at altitude." She flopped down in the other chair and looked at Megan.

"Aren't you here to see Barry?" Megan asked, raising her eyebrows.

"I am. Did he talk to you about the fundraiser?"

Megan nodded her head and realized she wasn't going to get to finish reading her email.

"It's a great idea, isn't it? These people have enough money to make a difference for the poor kids in this state. And it gives you a chance to be in front of a different audience."

Megan nodded, she agreed. She just didn't know all the details. "Where will this take place?"

"At Barry's house, of course," Maria said as if there were never a question. "He has that huge house in High Desert overlooking the city. Imagine how it will look as the sun is going down."

"When everyone is outside freezing by the swimming pool. It is only April, remember?"

"We'll get heat lamps. Are you in?"

Megan nodded. "Yes, I'm in. I'm not sure I had a choice before."

"Great," Maria said, picking her hat back up and standing up at the same time. "You and I will talk more. Let me get with Barry. We need to do this quickly. I just have to find out who's here right now."

"Sounds like most of Hollywood," Megan laughed. "Sounds like there is plenty of work for you here."

"We'll see," Maria said with a sparkle in her dark brown eyes.

*****

Maria moved quickly planning the fundraiser, securing several actors and actresses she knew would come if she asked them.

"And I've got a few other Hollywood people coming as well," she told Megan when they sat down to work on the menu. "Producers, directors, and such."

"How many people are we talking about?" Megan asked, worrying the numbers would keep growing, and knowing full well her recipes weren't designed for this kind of party.

"Don't worry," Maria reassured her. "We'll have most of it catered. Let's just use this as a chance to showcase some of your best food. And you, of course. We need to pick out a cute dress and make sure you have the apron to match."

"Will I be cooking there or ahead of time?"

"I want you to make the cookies while we're there. We'll set you up at the island in Barry's kitchen and then they can eat the cookies as they come out of the oven."

Maria thought for a moment. "What else could you make?"

"How about those peanut butter dark chocolate cookies I made?"

"Ah, the ones where you dip the peanut butter cookies into melted dark chocolate? Those send me right to heaven." Maria put her hand on her heart as if she were going to faint.

"But I don't just make cookies," Megan reminded her.

"I know, I know," Maria said, looking at the notepad on her lap and her tablet in the chair next to her, the chair usually reserved for her hat. "But this is good for this."

Megan looked out the window and realized it was cloudy. No hat for Maria today.

"Is it all planned out yet?" Barry asked stopping by with a paper in his hand.

"Of course it is, darling," Maria said, waving him off. "We just need your house. We're good for the rest of it."

"See how she uses me?" Barry joked, looking at Megan.

CHAPTER 9

The day of the party, just a week later, the entire office staff arrived at Barry's house early in case there was help needed.

"Do you know who's coming?" Stephanie whispered into Megan's ear as Megan mixed up the first batch of carob cookies, wearing a dark pink spaghetti strap dress, her new heels, and the pink and brown apron Mrs. Rosales had made.

"Maria won't tell me," Megan said with a laugh and the shake of her head.

"Oooh, I'm not surprised. She wants to surprise all of us."

Megan slid the first batch into the oven and took a look over the kitchen sink at the city below them. Barry's house sat in the foothills of High Desert. He called it his "divorce house" because he'd had to move when he and his ex-wife split up.

"That's okay," he had said. "I like this one better anyway."

It wasn't as big, nor was it in an exclusive gated community, but it was still considered an exclusive part of town, where people lived in the desert, their houses planted with the desert still growing around them. No lush green lawns. And while most of the houses had the curved edges like something from Santa Fe, Barry's house had deliberate corners that made it look strong, not contemporary and modern. Megan could see Maria's small touches around the house: the once empty white walls now were filled with paintings and there were flowers everywhere. Color, Megan, thought, there is color in here.

"I should just live there," Maria had joked several days before to Megan while they were working on the fundraiser.

"Why don't you?" Megan asked.

Maria craned her neck toward the hallway of the conference room where they were working and then leaned forward to Megan, whispering. "He's not quite there yet. But he will be. My mom's house is on the market and has an offer on it so he'll have to make up his mind sooner than he thinks."

Here they all gathered at Barry's house in the foothills, transformed for a big fundraiser filled with celebrities and lights. Lots of lights. Candles floated in the swimming pool and slowly the lights of Albuquerque began to turn on, as if one by one, under the sky that grew darker as the sun sank behind the horizon of the West Mesa. Albuquerque was ready to dazzle the celebrities, all for the New Mexico Children's Hospital and Peanut Butter and Jelly Family Services.

A loud chime announced the first guest. Megan looked at the clock on the wall. It was past 6:00. Of course, she thought. No one would be on time.

The wait staff dressed in black and white– matching the black and white of Barry's kitchen as if it helped them to blend in– took their places and Megan slid her first batch of cookies out of the oven. She adjusted her apron, making sure it was secure.

"That's all you need," Julie joked, "someone untying it as if he is undressing you."

Stephanie nearly spit out her wine and the three of them laughed.

"Thanks for that happy thought," Megan told her friend, arranging the cookies on a platter and setting up another batch.

"Those will be gone in two seconds," Stephanie said.

"Look," Julie hissed, her head poking into the dining room from the kitchen. "It's Marcia Stevens."

"*The* Marcia Stevens?" Stephanie hissed back, trying to run her overweight body in heels to the doorway. "It is!"

Both of them scattered though, heading outside to the pool, leaving Megan in the kitchen by herself. While she waited for Marcia, who owned a home in Santa Fe, to waltz into the kitchen, a group of men did instead.

"This must be That Cooking Girl," one of them, the bald one, said to his bearded friend. He smiled at Megan and stopped in front of the counter, the side with the stools.

"That's me," she said, wondering if she should know who they were.

"Maria told us we needed to try these."

Megan waved her hand over them. "They certainly aren't here for me to eat," she joked.

As they took a bite, she poured out the ingredients for the next batch. Small batches worked better, she had learned. And so she would be baking all night.

"Don't worry," Maria had reassured her. "Showing how you do it will be part of the presentation of the cookies. I know these people and they'll love you."

The house was beginning to feel full. Megan could hear the voices increase while she stayed in the kitchen to keep cookies rolling out of the oven. After she had several batches finished, she switched over to dipping some of the peanut butter cookies into a melted dark chocolate.

"These are the cookies I heard about!" A woman exclaimed, waltzing into the kitchen with a black poncho draped over tight jeans and a black tank top.

"I guess they have a reputation," Megan laughed, holding the platter out in her palm.

The man with her picked up a napkin for each of them while the woman picked up two cookies.

That's when it hit Megan: Marcia Stevens.

Megan tried to act like they were any other people she encountered, especially like the people at the grocery store who had seen her on television.

"Your audience is much bigger now that people can DVR your segment and watch it at any time rather than having to be home whenever it's on," Barry had said.

"And we have them on YouTube," Kevin had piped in. "I saw someone from Australia commented on the cookies."

"Oh my God, these are incredible," the woman said, her eyes bulging out. She looked at the man with her and he nodded his head. They both chewed, looking at Megan as they did, waiting to swallow so they could speak.

The oven beeped and Megan turned to take another batch out.

"You need to keep those coming," the man said. "I might not leave this counter the rest of the night."

"I can't imagine there's anything else here that can top this," Marcia said, taking another one and putting her finger to her lip, motioning for Megan not to tell anyone.

Megan laughed and smiled, scraping the latest batch off the metal sheet. "Actually, there is something here that might be better."

"I can't imagine," the man said, leaning forward on the granite counter. "Unless it was made by you."

"Of course," Megan said, walking over to the oversized stainless refrigerator and pulling out the half-dipped cookies.

"Dipped in chocolate?" Marcia looked as though she might leap over the counter and grab one before Megan removed them from the cookie sheet.

"Yes," Megan said with a laugh. "Peanut butter cookies dipped in dark chocolate."

"Is this really carob?" the man asked as he inspected another cookie that he picked up.

"You have to eat it now," Marcia nudged him, teasing him. "Or you can give it to me."

"No way," he said. "It's mine." And he took a bite.

As they kept eating, a few people came over and then Maria arrived. "Are you enjoying the cookies?" she asked them, shaking her hair off her shoulders.

"Divine is the word that comes to mind," Marcia told her.

"That's a good word," Maria laughed, looking at Megan. "No one makes a better cookie than Megan."

"Then how you did you discover her?"

"She works for Barry and one of the morning shows here needed a new cooking segment so he got her on."

"You need to take her national," Marcia said, peering over the counter. "Is that an apron I see?"

"Isn't that great?" Maria laughed. "We've got the total modern girl here."

Megan felt a little like she was on the outside of the conversation even though it was about her. She began to mix up yet another batch as people walked by and kept taking more cookies. "We heard these are great," they would say and Megan would smile and wave.

The kitchen had filled up so much that Megan had no idea what happened to Julie or Stephanie nor did she see Barry and Kevin. Everyone seemed to be wearing black with high heels.

"You're the most colorful person in this room," said a salt and pepper-haired man, sliding into one of the metal stools opposite Megan and nodding at her dress and apron. "No one can miss you in this sea of black."

"You think so?" she asked him. "You don't want a cookie and then run?"

"I will take a cookie," he said, holding it up in front of him. "But I think I might stay a while."

"Sure," Megan said, smiling and sliding yet another sheet filled with cookies out of the oven.

"And I think I want one of those," he said, eyeing the cookies that Megan was carefully slipping a spatula underneath on the baking sheet.

"What if I tell you that you can't have them until they cool off?"

He laughed and Megan looked up to see big smile. "I didn't think you were my mom, but now that I see the apron, I'm beginning to wonder if she sent you."

"Where is your mom?" Megan asked setting the new platter of cookies in front of him.

"Vermont."

Megan shrugged her shoulders. "I don't know anyone in Vermont so you're good."

People milled around them, but mostly it felt as if Megan and the man were in the conversation by themselves. "These are great," someone would say, stopping to pick up a cookie, and eat it as he walked away. Or, "I heard I need to try these." Except for the one skinny woman who waved them off. "I'm not allowed to eat any carbs," she said, before walking away quickly, her whispy figure in a black dress disappearing into the crowd.

Megan would look up, smile, and return to her conversation with the man. Once she looked up and saw Julie and Stephanie standing behind the man with big smiles on their faces. And then, acting like high school girls, they ran off before they started giggling out loud.

"Hey, Nate," a man in a black jacket and jeans said, slapping him on the back.

That's when it hit Megan: this was Nate Matthews.

"Did you try these cookies?" Nate asked the man, holding the platter up to the other man.

"I heard the dipped ones are even more devilish," the man said with a twinkle in his eye. "And we know who the devil is in the house today."

"It's not her," Nate said, pointing at Megan. "And I don't even know your name." He stuck his hand out, "I'm Nate Matthews."

"You're That Cooking Girl, aren't you?" the man asked.

"I am." Megan wiped her hand with a dish towel. "I'm Megan Marshall."

"You need to live in LA so we can eat all your cookies," the other man said. And with that, he held one up as if to toast her and started to walk away. "Heck, there's a place in Beverly Hills that sells cupcakes for four dollars each. Out of an ATM, too. You could do the same with these."

"Maybe if I have a role I need to gain weight for," Nate said, rubbing his stomach.

"You're good," Megan said. "Lots of flax and oats. Good stuff."

Maria strolled over at that point and put her arm on Nate's shoulder. "I didn't realize you were such the cookie monster," she told Nate, looking at him and then winking at Megan.

"I want to know where you've been hiding this girl," Nate said. "I've been here two months shooting and you wait to introduce me to the best cookies ever? Why didn't you greet me with these the first day I arrived? This is your town, after all."

Maria climbed onto one of the other stools and laughed. "I didn't know about her either. Barry's the man on this one."

"You mean your man?"

Maria laughed. "You could say that."

Megan felt her heart skip a beat as she listened to Maria talk about Barry. And when someone pulled Maria away, Nate stayed in his spot.

"Don't you want to go mingle with everyone? I have to stay here and keep making cookies. Keep the oven warm, you know."

"I'm happy right here. Happy for a break. We had to shoot several scenes this morning." He shook his head. "I'm a little beat up." He looked around at the party. "There's a little bit of everyone here," he noted.

"I have no idea who all these people are," Megan said, dropping a cup of carob chips into the batter.

Nate leaned toward her. "They're Hollywood types. You aren't missing much."

"But these are your colleagues," Megan laughed.

"Let's just say I like some of them better than others."

"Kind of like extended family?" Megan suggested. "There are a few aunts, uncles, and cousins you just tolerate."

"Exactly." And he held his drink up to her. "To the best cookies ever." He made a face as he sipped his wine and said, "What I'd really like is a glass of milk."

Megan immediately turned and opened Barry's fridge to confirm what she thought: all beer and wine, no milk. "I don't think Barry's a milk kind of guy though. I hear your new show is about a guy who owns a motel," Megan said, trying to sound nonchalant.

"You're That Cooking Girl and I'm The Motel Guy," he said, his white teeth gleaming. "Jack Tepper of the Twilight Sands Motel."

"I love that name," Megan cooed, impressed. "It's on Central, isn't it? Route 66?"

She washed her hands and wiped them with a towel, taking a break by leaning against the counter, toward Nate. She had five minutes until the latest sheet was ready.

"Yes. We rebuilt it. Saved what we could. It'll be a motel when we're done with the show."

"Like you rebuilt the whole thing?" Megan asked, her eyebrows going up. "Not just the parts you needed? You saved the sign I hope?" She tried to remember the last time she had driven that way.

She tried to picture that motel in her mind, but so many of them were falling apart that they blended together. Except the ones that had pools. Those she remembered.

Nate laughed. "Yes. I bought it about five years ago– through a trust so no one knew it was me. I use my lawyer's name. But it took that long to get this to fruition. We shot a pilot last summer in Los Angeles, just to set the scene. Where Jack comes from, etc., how he ends up in Albuquerque. When it was picked up, we're going to start with the opening of the motel."

"Very nice. So you're contributing to the community as well."

Nate lifted his wine glass toward her. "I'm liking the community."

"How many years do you think the show can run?"

"I'll run it as long as the network will let me, but I'm hoping for about five. Things start to get stale and I might be bored. Then we'll wrap it up with the interstate changing the business."

Megan nodded, the oven sending off the high shrill of the timer.

"And the Twilight Sands becomes a real motel again?"

"Exactly."

Megan thought of Stephanie. "So is Jack like Mr. Rourke?"

Nate laughed. Megan watched, wanting to laugh hard simply because he was laughing hard. "No. And there's no Tattoo. No Hitchcock, either."

"But maybe Hitchcock comes through town. Pretty much everyone seemed to in those days."

"True," he said.

It had been two hours and the party was beginning to wind down. Barry made his way into the kitchen and sidled up next to Megan. "Are you doing okay?" he asked.

"Yes," she said, making the last batch of cookies. "Nate here has been keeping me company."

"Are you the one who's been hiding her?" Nate asked, sticking out his hand for Barry to shake.

"I had to figure out some way to keep her here so she didn't defect to LA."

"Oh please," Megan said. "I'd think you'd be worried about losing Maria to LA, not me."

"I think Maria is here to stay," Nate said.

"You do?" Megan asked, her eyebrows going up.

"He's the reason," Nate said, pointing his head at Barry.

Barry shook his head and walked away.

"He won't admit how much he's in love with her," Megan whispered to Nate, her eyes following Barry into the thinned-out crowd.

"Why wait to admit it?" Nate asked. "Life's too short."

Megan wanted to say something, but she kept her lips smacked together.

"I see you have an opinion," Nate said. "Everyone else has one, regardless of whether I want them to."

"I'm sure it's nothing new," Megan said. With the last sheet of cookies coming out of the oven, she stopped and looked around. She was done. Megan placed her hands on the counter and stood without anything to do for the moment. "I don't do much more than see the headlines while I'm waiting to check out my flax and oats at the grocery store."

"No more cookies?" he asked.

"No more." She found a plastic plate and placed a few cookies on it. "But you can take these home to remember me by."

She looked over on the counter by the sink and saw the bag of gummy bears she had brought and snagged a few since she hadn't had a chance to eat anything throughout the entire party.

"You don't eat your own cookies?" Nate asked as Megan dropped a few of the candies on the counter between them.

She laughed. "I love my cookies, but I had a few already today. I don't want to end up a Large Marge."

"And gummy bears are so much better?" he asked.

Megan laughed again. "They're comfort food."

"That's what people say about pizza, not gummy bears." Nate raised his eyebrows and Megan placed her elbows on the counter as she popped another one in her mouth.

"They remind me of growing up. My mom used to put them in my Christmas stocking. Mostly of junior high and high school." She paused and then, without thinking, adding, "And Duran Duran."

"Now there's a band I haven't heard anyone mention in a while," Nate laughed. "You were a Duranie?"

"Hell yes," Megan admitted. "Always a sucker for the lead singer." She shook her head. "That's embarrassing to admit."

"Such a girl thing," Nate said, clucking his tongue.

"I'm sure you were too busy listening to Def Leppard."

"Aerosmith was more my thing. And Guns N Roses."

Megan shook her head. "Such a guy thing."

He laughed and Megan looked up at the big windows. It had gotten dark and the lights of the city sparkled below them. "I haven't been outside at all. I'm going to go out for a moment."

"And I'm coming with you," Nate said.

"Don't forget your cookies," Megan told him, placing the last dozen on a platter to cool.

"I'll come back for those," he said, following Megan.

"Someone might steal them while we're away."

"I'll take that chance. I know how to find you to make more."

Barry had a yearly party at holiday time, but Megan hadn't ever been to his house during the spring or any of the warmer months. Nate followed her as she walked past the candles burning in the pool, giving the water a different look than if the pool light shimmered under the surface.

At the edge of the pool deck stood a stucco wall that surrounded the yard, as if to keep the desert that surrounded them out. Megan looked out into the darkness at the sage and tumbleweeds growing, then out at the city in front of her. A slight breeze filled the air and she shivered in her sleeveless dress and apron.

"Here," Nate said, taking off his black jacket, revealing a white long-sleeved button down shirt underneath. He placed it on Megan's shoulders.

"Thank you," she said.

"Are you from here?" Nate asked.

"Oh no," Megan said. "I came here after college from Colorado. I went right to work for Barry and here I am still today."

"I can see why people love it here. High Desert is a very unique place."

"Except that at such a high altitude the air gets cold at night!" she said with a slight shiver despite wearing his jacket.

They stood next to each other, Nate leaning his forearms on the brown stucco wall.

"It is. I like it. I rented a house in the valley," Nate said pointing as if he knew exactly where it was.

"The valley is nice."

"Did you always plan to stay here?" he asked.

Megan laughed. She took a look at him, his salt and pepper hair moving around in the slight breeze while the curl in hers was beginning to fall despite Maria's best effort using nearly an entire bottle of hairspray when she rolled it.

"I'll be happy if it holds until the last hour of the party," she had said.

Now that the party was over, Megan dared to touch it and put a finger through it as the wind blew it in her face.

"I always thought I was going to live between Los Angeles and London," she joked.

"Are you being serious or are you making fun of me?"

Megan shook her head. "I'm serious. I don't know much about where you live. I thought I was going to write these amazing novels and marry Simon Le Bon of Duran Duran." Megan laughed at herself, shaking her head, at the silly future she had created.

"Unless you're hiding something, I'm guessing you didn't marry Simon Le Bon," Nate said.

"Nor did I ever make it to LA."

"And the books?"

Megan shook her head. "I work in advertising and public relations. A different kind of writing. But cooking, there's my creativity."

"Probably like acting is to me," Nate said.

"I'm sure."

"Hey Nate, you promised to drive me home so I could drink," a voice called from the opened sliding glass doors.

"I did," Nate admitted. "It was nice to meet you, Megan."

They stared at each other for a moment. "It was nice to meet you, too," she said, not sure if she should say something. She pulled off his jacket and handed it to him.

"Keep it," he said. "You need it to get home. I'll get it later."

And with a quick hug, he ran off. "I'm coming, JJ! You're on my schedule now."

Megan stood out there for a moment and then went inside to help clean up the kitchen although the people in the white shirts and black pants had done most of it while she had been outside.

"You are so going to dish about this on Monday," Julie whispered as she ran out the door to relieve her husband from kid duty.

"That's double dish," Stephanie called, following Julie because they had driven together.

Megan walked back into the kitchen to retrieve her purse and phone from the cabinet with Barry's pots and pans where Maria had stuck it. "No one ever looks here," Maria had said. "But then we have to remember it was put here."

"That was great," Barry said, taking Maria by the hand and twirling her around the kitchen. Megan watched them, standing at her spot behind the kitchen island.

"We raised at least fifty," Maria laughed, stopping long enough to pick up a glass of champagne. "Thousand, that is."

"Are you serious?" Megan asked. "I was so busy doling out cookies I had no idea that was happening."

"You weren't supposed to," Maria told her. "Your cookies are half of what brought those donations in."

Barry walked over to Megan and hugged her. "She's right. Everyone spent the night raving about them."

Maria sat down at the glass-topped table in the kitchen. "Mission accomplished."

"We raised money while showcasing you," Barry said, loosening his shirt.

"And I think Nate rather liked you," Maria added with a sly smile.

"I doubt it. It seemed to me he was just glad to have someone to talk to who didn't live in LA."

The look on Maria's face changed. "Don't think you deserve any less than what he could give you."

Megan sat down on the opposite side of her at the table. "But I'm not one of those model types he dates. I'm just…"

"That Cooking Girl," Barry piped in, joining them at the table. "Who happens to be on her way to the top. Don't look back for Ryan. You've got something great ahead of you."

"Maybe even Nate," Maria said.

"She's had too much to drink to say that, right?" Megan asked Barry.

"I'm clear as a bell," Maria said.

Megan looked at the clock. "I better get home."

"Home to what?" Barry asked.

"My bed," Megan said, tapping the top of his head as she walked by.

Megan slipped Nate's jacket onto the table to Maria. "This is Nate's."

"What?" Maria asked, surprised, handing it back to Megan. "You keep it. He'll call you."

"Because you'll make him."

"I don't think I need to make him do anything," Maria laughed, looking at Barry. "Except give him your number when he asks."

Driving down the hill back into the city, Megan admired the lights and how lucky she was.

As she lay in bed, past being tired with all the events of the evening, she couldn't stop giggling when she thought of the time she spent with Nate. The last thought she remembered before she fell asleep was what Maria had said, "Maybe with Nate."

"There are plenty of men who would be happy to be your partner," Barry had told her. "Not one who doesn't give you the time of day."

"There are enough of those floating around LA," Maria had said while rolling her eyes. "They are so excited to be with the woman and then when their careers seem to 'get in the way' they become cacti and start to ruin things."

"No one is ruining this for you," Barry told her.

"Thanks, Dad," Megan had said.

Barry laughed and patted her hand. "You'll thank me later."

It was well past 8:00 am when Megan woke up the next morning, seeing the sun streaming through the curtains.

At least it's Sunday, she told herself, first curling up tighter under her green and blue duvet cover and then stretching when she realized it was time to get up, Sam staring at her where he stood on the side of the bed. Megan pulled on a pair of black shorts and a thin peach long-sleeved zip up, then went looking for her walking shoes.

For a brief moment she imagined life with Nate. Her and Nate. And then she stopped it.

"I'm no model," she mumbled to herself. "I think they all prefer leggy blondes than a petite blonde who gets on television and teaches people how to cook and bake. I'm too Martha Stewart for him."

And back to thinking about recipes she went.

CHAPTER 10

Monday morning Megan heard something, but it sounded like it was far away. She opened her eyes to darkness and looked around her bedroom, feeling fuzzy from a dream. Was it a dream? She wasn't even sure what she had been dreaming about. Sam was zonked out next to her, curled up in a ball at the foot of the bed.

She looked over at her phone and it had stopped ringing. Then started again.

Maria.

Megan glanced at her clock, rubbing her eyes, hoping she could rub away the fuzziness and saw it was 5:00 am.

"Why are you calling me at five in the morning?" Megan asked, her voice scratchy, worried something bad had happened. To Barry, maybe? Megan always worried his energy would catch up with him and he'd have a heart attack to slow him down.

"I need your help," Maria said, sounding frantic. "Well, we need your help. Some of the extras for the show didn't come today. Can you be on set all day? I've already talked to Barry and he says it's okay if you don't show for work today."

"I have to prep for my segment tomorrow," Megan reminded her, barely able to comprehend what was going on.

"You'll have plenty of time for that later. Please help us out. You're helping Nate out, too– after all, this is his show."

"Fine," Megan, said, sitting up. "What am I going to do?"

"I'll explain when you get here. Come down to the motel– there's a tent out back. That's base camp. Check in and come find me at wardrobe."

"I'll be there in thirty minutes."

"Hurry!" Maria said. As Megan began to wake up, she could hear voices in the background of the call as if people were milling around.

Megan drove straight up Central, yawning the whole way, wishing she had made herself a cup of coffee, and then realizing what motel Nate had bought and was using.

The Twilight Sands Motel once had a swimming pool that always looked green, she remembered, not able to see much from the street, but enough that she could see that, wondering why it wasn't important enough to keep the pool clean. The motel sat on the north side of the street, now sandwiched between a Walgreens (what corner didn't have one of those or a Starbucks anymore? Megan thought) and a small car dealership. The swimming pool was near the front of the motel and off to the left– with the lobby between– was the nightclub and a diner-style restaurant in the front.

Central was deserted until she reached the location. Megan didn't drive this way very often and she hadn't noticed the recent construction, but now she saw the Twilight Sands Motel sign lit up like a beacon in the nighttime sky– unless you looked beyond it and saw the Walgreens drug store. She drove around the back of the motel to find an empty lot where everyone was parking, several men standing in heavy coats and flashlights guiding everyone.

She spotted the big white tent that Maria had told her about, the kind someone might hold an event inside, large portable lights making it look important in the still dark hours. Inside, people were filling plates of food from a catered breakfast, most of them with half-sheets of paper in their hands or on the table next to them. Off to the left she spotted wardrobe: lines of clothes hung on racks.

She immediately saw Maria inside the tent, holding a stack of clothes in her hands and her hair pulled up in a loose bun that looked like it was about to fall apart. Megan wondered what they would have her doing, some part of her thinking it would be food related. A waitress, she figured.

A ploy to get us together? She wondered, thinking of Nate. Megan had left his jacket in the car from the party– this would be her opportunity to return it.

"I'm so glad you're here!" Maria exclaimed, talking a million miles an hour. Megan could see the thoughts in Maria's head jumbled, everything dancing around, no time for rest.

This was Maria in action, Megan thought, watching her in a white tank top and a light blue button down shirt, opened with the sleeves rolled up, and jeans, deflecting questions from every direction. No hat this morning. And Megan could see this was how she was happiest: making fashion happen.

"We need to get you checked in. Are you hungry? There's breakfast. But I need to get you to wardrobe. I'm sure we can make something work without your sizes. We always bring extras."

Sixty miles an hour, her hands flying everywhere now that she had handed off the stack of clothes to other people.

It was in a makeshift fitting room that a woman named Jolene brought Megan several options: bikinis.

"Esther Williams bikinis," Megan said, laughing, taking the first one.

"Pretty much. Let's see if we can get something to fit you. High waist, lots of coverage. You'll be at the pool. I'm guessing you figured that out though."

They were lucky, with some minor changes– in the form of tape and pins slightly pulling in what appeared to be a worn out elastic waist– Megan had her outfit. She grabbed her sweatshirt, unsure how warm it was supposed to get on the late April day, having forgotten to check the weather before she left home.

"Great!" Maria said, looking approvingly as Megan walked by her. From a pile on a table, Maria handed her a pair of large sunglasses and heels.

"Heels at the pool? Is that realistic?"

Maria laughed and pushed Megan to the makeshift makeup tables. "Hair, then makeup," she said. "It's television."

"No wonder she's so good at her job," Megan would tell Julie and Stephanie later. "She sends people off in the right direction, keeps them moving. But you can see her mind is filled with thoughts and she might explode at any moment."

As a woman curled and pinned Megan's hair, Megan stared at herself, watching the years fall back. She tried to remember all that Nate had told her about the show. Megan still knew very little though, yet she wasn't sure she would know much if she were just any extra. Like one who hadn't spent several hours with Nate just two nights ago.

Her mind wandered. So many people walking around. Nate must be in them somewhere. Megan tried not to look away from the mirror, to keep on task, but she kept thinking Nate must be back there.

You'll see him, she assured herself, Maria will see to that. If she hasn't already.

Megan peeked out the plastic windows of the tent. Light was beginning to come over the city, the sun now passing the top of the Sandias. People were starting to wander over to the set, just across the street from the empty lot where base camp was set up.

"You're all ready," said the young woman with long brown hair who did Megan's makeup. "I'm mostly concerned about having sunscreen on you. And that bright red lipstick they wore."

She and Megan giggled as the woman pulled the plastic drape away. "My fifties self," Megan joked, grabbing the sunglasses and following the others outside to the set. It was cold outside the heated tent and Megan started to pull her sweatshirt on, wondering if she was going to have to spend the day shivering. Couldn't Maria have come up with a better way for her and Nate to see each other again? And what about a nice swimsuit cover up?

"Megan!" She looked back to see Maria coming after her, her hat in her right hand. "Let me look!"

Maria looked happy as she came to a stop and surveyed Megan. In her element. "You look great! I can't wait to see this."

When Megan came around the corner with Maria, there was no green swimming pool. Megan wondered how long it took to clean it up. People were everywhere; it looked like a summer day in the 1950s, there just happened to be cameras, lights, and people wearing jackets and jeans everywhere, too. The motel had been completely transformed from its derelict status, right back to the late 1950s when it had opened.

Megan began to wonder what it really had been like. Maria was called away and she motioned Megan over to the tall man who was taking care of the extras, like a teacher on a field trip.

"Okay, gang, gather around," he said, Megan and her fellow extras walking over to him.

"I hope we aren't going to be in the pool," said a woman, wearing a similar bikini, falling in stride with Megan.

"Oh gosh, me too," Megan said, shivering from the thought. She looked across the parking lot from where they stood. The water looked inviting. But with the air temperature still remaining steady in the forties it wasn't that inviting. It would warm up, but not soon enough.

Megan surveyed the scene: she truly had been transported to the fifties despite the modern technology and outfits the crew wore.

"So today you're all going to be background for the life that goes on at the Twilight Sands Motel…," the production assistant said. There were men in Hawaiian shirts, some couples were dressed up as if they were arriving at the motel, several housekeepers, a maintenance man, and the list went on. Everyone had a specific task.

Megan listened, but she couldn't help but look around. It wasn't just about Nate. She hadn't ever been to one of these motels in Albuquerque; she'd only passed by them, knowing they had stories to tell, but so many had fallen into disrepair over the years.

All the history she thought, walking with the other woman to the swimming pool. Nancy, Megan learned was her name. She talked endlessly: about her experience as an extra, about working as a waitress in the evenings and weekends as she hoped she could make it big on the screen.

"Maybe someone will discover me here at the Twilight Sands pool," she giggled. "Just like in the fifties."

"It could happen," Megan said, trying to be hopeful for her.

"How about you?"

They sat down on the lounge chairs they were directed to, someone bringing them towels and straw bags–props– as if they had items to bring with them.

"I'm here as a fill-in," Megan admitted. "I have a job, but they needed someone this morning and I know the head of wardrobe."

"You're so lucky! You know people!"

Megan and Nancy– along with several other women and men– were placed at the pool by the production assistant– the PA.

"You," he said to Megan, and pointed at the diving board. Megan panicked that they were going to send her off it, forgetting that it would ruin her hair after one take. "You'll be sitting on the diving board sunning yourself."

Nancy, who was sitting by the pool ladder was instructed to place her legs in the pool for the scene.

"It's heated," the PA said, looking cold with his sunglasses on.

Nancy stuck her hand in and smiled. "Okay, I can do that."

"Camera's up!" a woman called. "Background!"

Megan slid her sunglasses over her eyes and looked over at Nancy who was flirting with a man in swim trunks and a Hawaiian shirt.

Maybe she can talk to him all day, Megan thought, enjoying being outside. At least the sun was warm on her bare skin.

"We're rolling!"

Megan had no idea what the scene was about, but she sat there for about thirty seconds, people milling out; one of the housekeepers walked by with a pile of towels in her arms, and the maintenance guy carried a hammer across the parking lot.

"Cut!"

Everyone relaxed, began to talk, and then they heard, "Let's do it again!"

This went on six times. Megan tried to remember what it was like to do this all summer, lay by a pool and sun herself. She thought about the segment for the next day– dark chocolate cookies made with rice flour.

"I don't get it," Barry said. "How's that different than the cookies you already make?"

"When you steal more than one off the plate, you'll understand," Megan told him.

"Nate! Maybe you should cross over to the left," the director called and Megan looked up to see him dressed in a Hawaiian shirt and black pants, looking his usual handsome self.

Albuquerque 1950s, Megan thought, watching him listen to the director.

"It was fun," Megan would tell Stephanie and Julie later. "For a while."

"Getting paid to lay by a pool all day?" Stephanie clucked her tongue. "Some people have all the luck."

After seven more takes– although Megan didn't keep track after that– they shuffled everyone around for another scene, keeping Megan on the diving board. "But this time, you're going to act as though you're going to go off it," the PA called to her. "Walk from the steps to the end of the board and that should be the whole scene where you'll be seen right there."

Megan nodded and saw Nate walk into the pool area with a woman in a green printed dress– with a full skirt– carrying a matching green purse and wearing green heels.

"Hey," he said when he spotted Megan standing at the diving board. "A little bird told me you were going to be here."

"So you know I didn't do this on purpose to be with you today," Megan told him. "I'm supposed to be prepping for my segment tomorrow, you know. But instead I'm playing a very small– minute– role in this TV show of yours." She took her left arm and swung it around the motel complex.

"She told me," he said. "I appreciate your pinch hitting."

"I got a call at 5 am."

Nate laughed and the director called for him. He waved and smiled as he walked back to the woman in the green dress.

Nancy came flying over. "You KNOW Nate Matthews??" Her eyes grew as big as globes.

Megan shrugged. "Not really."

"But he came over to talk to you, THAT was obvious!"

For the rest of the morning, Nancy clung to Megan's side, waiting for Nate to come back. When they broke for lunch, Megan filled her plate– in the tent– with fish and vegetables, grabbing a cupcake from the last serving dish at the table, glad to be out of the sun for a while.

She sat down at one of the tables by herself, hoping the guy flirting with Nancy (whose name turned out to be Mitch) would keep her busy. She figured at some point Maria would show up and checked her email on her phone in the meantime.

"Are you sitting alone on purpose?" a voice from her left side asked.

Megan instantly thought it was one of the other guys on the set. A few of them had been nearly as clingy as Nancy although not for the same reasons. But when she looked up, she saw Nate smiling down at her, a plate of food in one hand, a cupcake in the other.

"Yes, I'm waiting for my entourage to join me," she joked. "But you can sit here for now."

"I'm a little shocked to see you eating these low grade catering cupcakes," he joked, his plate filled with food, too.

"I'm desperate," Megan whispered. "I'm not that snooty, just because I cook on television."

"And I'm not that snooty to sit with the extras even though I produce and star in the show," he whispered back.

It didn't take long for Nancy– followed by Mitch who had turned into a puppy dog– to join them. Nancy slipped into the seat opposite Nate from Megan and Mitch looked disappointed that he had to sit across the table from her.

"My cousin worked on some movie," Nancy started to tell Nate. Megan internally rolled her eyes, knowing that Nate had probably heard a variation of that line repeatedly, just to get his attention. There was no room in the conversation for Megan so she turned to Mitch who looked sad that he'd been usurped by the star of the show.

"I thought it would be something fun to do," Mitch said. "I just finished graduate school and I'm looking for a job."

He seemed much more normal than the rest of the extras Megan began to realize. She wished Nancy would figure it out and give him a chance. When she was done eating, she checked her messages one more time, and got up, having heard a call that all the women were to stop by hair and makeup. And everyone needed another application of sunscreen.

"Hey," Nate said, when she started to pick up her plate from the table. "Where are you going?"

"I have to get my hair fixed for the afternoon," she told him. "And make sure I don't turn into a lobster."

"Let me walk with you," Nate said, grabbing his own plate, ignoring Nancy, who now looked hurt. Megan used her eyes to motion to Mitch to nab her while he could and quickly offered to take Nancy's plate.

"Walk with me across the tent?" Megan laughed. "It's such a long walk. I might need a map."

"Listen," Nate said, whispering. "I really wanted to talk to you."

"Nate! Nate!" A man looked frantic, running across the tent and flailing his arms. "We need you!"

"Oh geez," Nate said. Now it was his turn to look disappointed.

Megan smiled. "Go. You need to go. I know you're important."

She could see Nate wanted to say something, but the man was impatient. "Okay," he finally said to Megan, looking somewhat annoyed at having to leave. "We'll talk later."

"We have to," she called after him. "I have your jacket."

For the afternoon, Megan was still at the pool.

"When the show airs, everyone will think I live at the pool," she told everyone later.

It had warmed up nicely into the seventies and felt almost hot at times in the sun. Cases of bottled water sat in the shade around a corner, out of any camera shot, the labels reading, "NM Film Office," the water bottled in Santa Fe.

"You know him," Nancy insisted as they sunned themselves in lounge chairs next to each other– not Megan's idea.

"Not really," Megan said truthfully. "I just met him Saturday."

When they took a break, heading inside to the lobby to get out of the sun for a while, Nancy kept talking while Megan looked around at how well they had restored it to the fifties. She felt as if she were stopping in there to pick up a phone message at the front desk– vaguely remembering life without cell phones, or even answering machines and call waiting.

Megan slipped into one of the cushy brown chairs near the front desk, Nancy– and Mitch– across from her, settling in on the couch together– not Nancy's doing, but the fact that the other chairs were taken.

"There you are!" Maria called, coming out of nowhere to find Megan, her hat on her head. "It's a perfect day to film. Not too hot. And not too cold." She laughed. "Did you have to get in the pool?"

Megan shook her head. "Not so far. But the afternoon isn't over yet."

"Do you know everyone?" Nancy asked, looking at Maria and then Megan. "She's the head of wardrobe and you know her, too."

"She's That Cooking Girl," Maria said, to Nancy, making herself at home on the large armrest of Megan's chair. "Don't you know that? Haven't you seen her on television?"

"I knew it! I knew you were someone!" Nancy turned to Mitch and slapped his thigh. "See? Didn't I tell you? She is someone."

Megan shook her head and shrugged her shoulders.

Mitch leaned forward and scratched his chin. He was the kind of guy who had a five o'clock shadow by noon. "You're on TV at noon, right? You made those carob cookies?"

"Yes, that's me," Megan said, smiling, but feeling slightly uncomfortable.

"You watch the noon news?" Nancy asked, acting surprised that Mitch knew anything about television.

"I get up early. I work out and then I spend the rest of the day job hunting. I take a break at lunch and catch up with the world. What do you do all day?" he asked, turning the tables on her.

She laughed. "I'm a nighttime girl. Today was a stretch for me."

Megan watched Mitch back off after that comment. Instantly, Megan wished she knew a single girl his age she could set him up with. He looked like a nice guy, one who deserved a girl who would treat him well. Nancy hadn't been interested and now she knew Mitch was ready to be over her. His interest was quickly waning.

At least it turned the conversation away from her.

"All right, everyone!" the PA called, rounding everyone up. "We're going back to the pool! We have one last scene to shoot and then we'll be done."

"I'll see you later," Maria whispered, squeezing Megan's arm. Megan nodded and followed the crowd, the PA directing her back to the pool with Nancy and Mitch. However, this time, he kept them and several others in a group for a moment.

"So our main character, the motel guy," he said, smiling and clasping his hands together, "is going to be talking to a woman by the pool. We need all of you to keep doing what you were before. An afternoon at the pool at the Twilight Sands."

He pulled Megan aside and pointed back to the diving board.

"Everyone is going to think all I do is go off the diving board," she joked, knowing full well she had no idea how all the scenes they had filmed would play out. She knew they might be a matter of just a few minutes– that took all day to shoot.

"Maybe you're an Olympic diver," he joked. "Obsessed with the water."

Megan returned to the diving board steps and each time the director called "Background!" she waited a moment before starting her walk across the board.

Seven times.

She tried not to watch Nate as he interacted with the same woman. She couldn't really hear the conversation anyway.

Finally, as the sun was starting its movement across the sky and toward the west– Megan knew it was getting to be late afternoon– the director called, "One last time. We're going to wrap after this."

At that point, Nate called across the pool– from where he and the woman stood by the gate near the shallow end, "Dive in this time!"

Megan looked up and smiled, her hands on her hips filled with confidence. "You dare me?"

"I do!"

"You're on!" she called back.

By then everyone was at least smiling, if not laughing. And once Megan heard the word "Background!" she walked slowly, and then didn't stop at the end of the board to contemplate the water below her. Instead, she pulled up her arms, leaned forward, and did the smoothest dive in her life. Ever.

When she came up, they were still shooting and she pulled herself out of the water at the ladder and then tried to act 1950s sexy and walk back to the lounge chair where "her" towel was spread out.

"That's a wrap, everyone!" the director called.

Megan used her fingers to comb her hair, but the hairspray kept it in place so well she struggled to get her fingers through it.

"I didn't know Esther Williams was staying at my motel," she heard Nate say, his shadow covering the sun.

"Would you not stand in Esther Williams's sun?" she asked him, looking down the outline of his body in the concrete.

Nate laughed and sat down. "I can't wait to see that on film."

"That was great!" Maria called practically running by to get back to the tent and collect everyone's costumes.

"Nate!" a voice called. This time it was the director. "We need you!"

"A star's work is never done," Megan said, wrapping the towel around her head and beginning to shiver as the April air quickly cooled with the descending sun.

Nate looked at her arm. "You've got goosebumps."

"That's okay. I'll just use your coat to keep me warm," she joked.

The director called again and Nate waved at her. "Maybe I should have just produced the show and not tried to star in it, too," he sighed, shaking his head and walking across the pool area.

CHAPTER 11

"You can't avoid us, you know that," Stephanie said, following Megan down the hall to her office the next morning.

Megan sat down at her desk, placing her Humble Coffee to-go cup carefully where no one could accidentally spill it. Julie also had followed Stephanie in and they were staring at her.

"Oh, please," Megan said, yawning and stretching for a moment. "I'm exhausted."

"Oh please," they mimicked in unison.

"Barry told us you two were outside by the pool together at the end of the party."

"Staring at the city lights," Megan said honestly.

"One day you'll be on the cover of *People*," Julie said. "As the famous actress and cooking girl. And wife of Nate Matthews."

"And totally not our friend anymore," Stephanie said rolling her head to an uppity pose.

"Oh please," Megan said, waking up her laptop so she could check her email.

"You only have a few minutes to get ready," Barry remind her, seeming as if he were eavesdropping around the corner.

"I know, I know," Megan said. "I'll be ready."

He slyly walked into her office, eyeing the plate of cookies on her desk, the ones she had spent a recent weekend perfecting the cookie recipe and sharing it with the neighbors. And even Tom the mailman.

"Aren't you worried I could poison you?" Megan asked, when he greedily took three cookies off the plate.

"I'm starving," he said, scratching his chin. "I forgot my lunch today."

Before he reached next door, he'd devoured the cookies and looked back with a thumbs up while Megan was still in disbelief that he'd taken so many– and that she'd been worried they were too much like the cookies she made on her first segment.

"We'll let it pass this time," Stephanie said, "but when you get back we expect to hear all about it."

"Okay, okay," Megan said, shooing them off and sipping her coffee.

She looked in the mirror and quickly pulled out the concealer she always carried with her. Something had to cover up the bags under her eyes.

"I'm exhausted from television and I have to go do more television," she muttered to herself, knowing it was being in the sun all day that had worn her out. She pictured everyone gathered on the set again this morning– along with Nate– to film more of episode four.

Megan shut her eyes in Barry's car for the short drive to the studio, not really listening to what he was talking about. It was politics.

"I'm glad," Barry said, "that we have two of the mayoral candidates courting us, but ethically we can only do the campaign of one."

"Then pick the one whose politics you support," Megan said without thinking much about it.

"What if I don't support the politics of either one?" Barry laughed.

"She's a television star now," Barry joked to Janet when Megan forgot to remove her sunglasses as they walked through the building to the set.

"I was on a television set yesterday," Megan reminded him. "That hardly makes me a television star now." And forgetting she had her sunglasses on.

Mumbling to herself, Megan began to set up the ingredients, finally feeling like she was falling into a routine.

"We have someone who is appearing with you today," Janet said, Barry at her side.

She looked up, expecting to see Sally walking her way from the couch area only to see Nate strolling through the studio door. Like he owned it.

"Hello," Nate said, wearing a long-sleeved blue button-down shirt and jeans with cowboy boots.

Maria then appeared behind him laughing. "I love this!" She laughed, grabbing Barry's arm. "The look on Megan's face is priceless."

"Hi," Megan said. "Are you really good friends with her?" she asked, pointing her head at Maria.

"I have stories," Nate said, leaning forward into a whisper. "Stories about her no one else has."

"Then I think you need to share them with me because I need some material to get her back," Megan said, her right hand on her right hip, and then seeing the mic guy standing next to her.

"We're a minute away," he said, casting his usual frown on his red face.

"Lighten up, Carl," Janet said. "We're good. Everyone is ready."

The crew snuck away into the darkness behind the lights, including the host, Sally, having swiped a cookie herself.

"Let me take you to dinner Friday night," he said.

"Thirty seconds!" the director called.

"I need an answer," Nate said, smiling, looking at Megan.

"Yes," Megan said, trying to wrap her head around her cookies.

"I only agreed to do this because I wanted more cookies," Nate said, changing the subject, trying to grab one before Megan slapped his hand away.

"Sorry," she whispered. "It's habit because someone is always trying to grab them. Like Sally just did."

"And we're live….," John the director called, the lights on the cameras going bright.

Suddenly Megan found herself on television with Nate and she realized no one had told them what to do. Who was supposed to lead who? They looked at each other and Megan did exactly what she had done that first day back in January: she jumped right in.

"I'm here with Nate Matthews." Megan looked at him as if she were thinking and then back at the camera. "But I don't need to say more. We all know who Nate is. I think he's on the cover of *People* magazine at least every other week."

"So you must be a subscriber if you know that?" Nate teased her. "I want some cookies," he said, eyeing the plate in front of him.

"You and my mailman who took three when I let him taste them over the weekend," Megan joked.

"Then hurry up and show me how to make them," he said.

Megan quickly put together the dough, telling the story of how the original recipe came about in college where she had stumbled on brown rice flour in a health food store. "It was one of those places where everyone thought only the weird hippies shopped."

As she pulled out the plate from behind her of the ones she had made the night before, she added how her college friend Sarah had married a guy named Aaron, getting engaged around the same time she had created the recipe. "And they became the Marrying Off Cookies."

"You know next week I'll be on the cover of *People* again," Nate joked, Megan not slapping his hand away as he took one off the plate.

"Why's that?"

"Because the word 'marry' and the name Nate Matthews never go together."

"Maybe you'll find love filming in New Mexico," Megan said, the words slipping out of her mouth without any meaning to it.

"Maybe," Nate said. "New Mexico. Cookies. What more could I ask for?"

"And we're out!" John called, the lights going back up around the studio, the cameras getting pulled back.

Everyone rushed up to grab the cookies, Megan stepping away to avoid the rush.

"That was great!" Janet exclaimed, more to Barry than to Megan or Nate. "I didn't think it could get better, but it just did! We need to do more of this!"

"It was those two," Maria said, staring at Nate and Megan, her hands on her hips. "You won't replicate that."

"I have to get to the set," Nate said, looking at his watch. "But I believe I have Maria stories to tell you."

Megan waved at him, gathering up her baking supplies. "Friday night."

"Would you take me somewhere authentically New Mexican?" he asked. "I keep getting sent to nice places, but they feel so…"

"Touristy?"

"Yes," he said. "And Maria hasn't been much help."

"What haven't I been much help with?" she asked as everyone paraded out of the studio and down the hallway.

"Finding Nate good places to eat here," Megan said.

"You never asked," Maria reminded him. "You were too busy filming to spend any time with me."

"And you didn't tell me about Megan," he said.

Megan felt her cheeks turn red. The conversation wasn't supposed to be about her. She felt Barry put an encouraging hand on her shoulder, just like her dad might do.

"You know about her now," Maria said, the group reaching the front doors of the building, Janet having long been pulled aside for something, and Maria placing her hat on her head.

Nate walked with them to Barry's car, Maria and Barry climbing inside and leaving Nate with Megan. "I'll give you my number and you can text me when you're ready. I'll give you authentic if that's what you want."

Nate smiled. "I'll even impress you with my knowledge of Albuquerque streets and pick you up."

"It's not hard!" Maria called from the car. "The mountains never move!"

"The ocean doesn't either," Nate called back to her.

Megan felt as if she were making date plans and her parents were listening to the entire conversation.

Driving back to the office, Nate long gone to the set, Megan asked, "You did that on purpose didn't you? Not telling me?"

"It worked, didn't it?" Maria laughed.

"Made for a great segment, too."

"I feel as if you're all planning my life without including me in the planning."

Unable to believe she had dinner plans with Nate Matthews, Megan didn't tell anyone. Someone else did.

"What's this we hear about you having a date with Nate Matthews?" Julie and Stephanie asked, Stephanie stepping away from her desk, holding her headset close to her ear so she didn't miss anything.

Megan looked up and rolled her eyes. "Is that what you heard? How do you know it's a date? What makes it a date?"

"Where are you going?" Stephanie asked. "I'm going to show up."

"Then I'm not telling you." Megan scratched her head.

"We have a birthday party anyway," Stephanie said, Megan unsure if she should believe her.

Julie rocked back and forth on the chair where she was sitting. "This is so fun. Sure beats dealing with sick kids."

"Or life in general. Someone should be having all the fun," Stephanie added.

The next evening, Megan kept peeking out from behind her white living room curtains, hoping that no one would see Nate. She wanted to make a clear getaway from the house without being sidetracked by everyone else.

He arrived in a non-descript rental car. A sedan just like all the others. Megan waited a moment before she opened the door, letting him think she was on the other side of the house.

"Hi," she said, walking outside before he could go in and Sam could get out. Sam looked disappointed as Megan shut the door, almost on his nose.

"You don't want me to see the inside of your house?" he asked, chuckling. Megan was too busy noticing his jeans and white shirt, how tanned he looked.

"Sorry," she said, opening the door again, feeling slightly embarrassed.

"Megan!" a voice called, and there was Mrs. Rosales practically running down the street in her brown polyester pants and canvas shoes. She waved her right hand and cradled something in her left arm.

"My neighbor around the corner," Megan said, walking down the driveway, Nate following her.

"Hi," Megan said.

"I have a new apron for you." She didn't even notice Nate behind her. Mrs. Rosales unfolded the new apron, white with large vintage-looking pink and orange flowers on it. "It's actually old fabric I had from a dress my mother made me. Probably the fifties."

Megan smiled, wrapping it around her sundress. "I love it."

"Oh, I'm sorry," she said, seeing Nate. "I didn't realize you had a friend here."

"It's okay," Megan said, waving Nate off.

"I'm Nate," Nate said, sticking out his hand to her.

Mrs. Rosales took it and for a moment Megan thought for sure she knew who he was. "You look familiar," she said, eyeing him. "Are you on the city council?"

"No," he said, amused. "I don't live here."

Mrs. Rosales waved goodbye and turned to walk back to her house. Sam barked in the window at Megan's house as they walked back toward the door.

"I love your neighborhood," he said, walking through the door, his boots clicking against the tile.

"It's really cool," she said. "A lot of character."

"And characters," Nate said.

"Don't let her fool you, she's just upping her best friend by making these and the best friend seeing them on television."

"I really want to see the kitchen because that's where all the magic takes place," he said.

"It sounds like you only like me because I make food," Megan joked.

Megan looked up at Nate, who was perusing her cookbook collection, and watched him. Nate Matthews is in your kitchen, she told herself.

In that moment, Megan thought about her mom. If there was one person she wanted to share it with, it was her mom. Instead, she pictured her in a rocking chair, looking out the window at…nothing.

"Where's yours?" he asked. "I heard a rumor you're working on one."

"What else did Maria tell you?" Megan laughed, fixing the strap on her light brown heeled sandal. When she stood up, she adjusted the top of her orange sundress.

"Barry tells me just as much," he admitted. "Maria tells me the girl stuff. Barry tells me the professional stuff."

"That sounds right."

"So where are we going for dinner?"

"Where the natives eat," Megan said, smiling. They faced each other in the kitchen. "I hope you like tacos."

"I love tacos," he said.

"Not the kind we grew up on," she reminded him, "made with a seasoning packet from Old El Paso."

"You, too?"

Megan laughed. "Once a week."

"I was eating Mexican in the late seventies."

"It'll be easy to get where we're going," Megan said. "It's on Central."

"66."

"Yes."

Megan's house was several blocks from Central and the drive took them straight through downtown and skimmed the University of New Mexico campus.

"It's on the east side of Nob Hill. Taco Toté. A chain with more locations in Mexico than the United States."

When Nate saw the sign he asked, "Taco Tote? Like a tote bag?"

"Toté," Megan said.

"What does it mean?"

Megan shrugged her shoulders and helped him look for a parking spot, his rental sedan next to all the big pickup trucks. "You can ask inside. All I know is that it's one of my favorite places to eat."

Taco Toté sat on Central Avenue across from several antique malls filled with nostalgia of old Route 66. In the parking lot, Nate stood and looked around. "I drive by this every day to the set and I never noticed it," he admitted.

"And I admit I don't know much about what you're filming," she said. "I learned that being on the set doesn't mean I get to learn the story."

"That's kind of a good thing," he said in a lowered voice. "We wouldn't want all sort of crazy people on the set seeking autographs."

"Hence the code words on the yellow and black signs with the arrows all around town?"

"Exactly," he said. "There's a balance of people knowing a potential blockbuster television show is filming and of the privacy so we can finish the project."

A big board greeted them on the left inside the restaurant with a Hispanic woman, her hair piled high top on her head, standing at cash register, waiting to take their order. A big dining area off to the right was filled with mostly Hispanic couples and families.

"When we walk by, you'll notice most of them speaking Spanish. Or even Spanglish. I don't speak enough of the language to know the difference."

"What do we have?" Nate asked, squinting as he looked at the board.

"You can't see that?" Megan laughed. "Movie stars are afraid to let anyone know they need reading glasses?"

Nate stared at her as he pulled them out of his pocket. "They're really good– like reverse to Clark Kent and no one knows Superman is in the building." And then he changed the subject. "What do we order?"

Megan was relieved he'd made it easy. "I'll take care of that."

"Hola," she said to the woman, ordering a platter of al pastor meat.

"What are we having?" Nate whispered when they walked to the salsa bar and the beverage center. "Should I be scared of what I just paid for?"

"Pork," Megan said. "If you don't like it, I'll eat it for lunch for the next week. I'll grab the chips and salsa," Megan said, putting her drink on a table.

"You're on," he said as he as he slipped into a red vinyl booth along an east-facing window.

By the time she returned, a waitress had taken their number and left an oversized plate with bits of meat with warm tortillas, rice, and beans.

"You're lucky I waited for you," Nate said.

"You're lucky I got the salsas."

As they filled the soft corn tortillas with meat and a green tomatillo-avocado salsa, Megan sat back and sighed. "I don't come here often, but when I do, it's like paradise for my stomach. Comfort food."

"And your life seems to be all about food," Nate reminded her.

"You know it's only recent, right?"

Nate shook his head. "Every overnight sensation has been working at it for ten years. I know."

"But I haven't been," Megan protested. "I filled in for a chef who went on a Twitter rant and got himself fired from the restaurant– and thus the television spot he was doing weekly."

"So this isn't what you dreamed of doing? Making up recipes?"

Megan shrugged her shoulders and filled up a second taco. "I cook for people, yes. I bake for people, yes. But dinner parties. Not on television or in a book."

"Or in a restaurant."

"No way in a restaurant. That's hell. The quality usually goes away. Food is about sharing with a group– and the preparation." She paused to take a bite and they both looked out the window at darkness beginning to set on Albuquerque– complete with the Sandia Mountains showing off their watermelon color as the sun began to dip below the western horizon. "But I'm guessing you always wanted to be an actor."

Nate laughed. "I grew up in Vermont. Maple syrup. Skiing. But I did some theater to keep warm in the winter and that's how it started."

"The weather is better in LA," Megan laughed.

"And they import the maple syrup."

"Your mom probably sends it to you."

"She does. Once a year. I think I still have some from two years ago."

"Then you aren't eating enough pancakes."

"Or too much eating out in general. I like waffles better anyway."

"I have a waffle maker."

"I thought only married people had those."

"I was married. Once." They stared at each other. "A long time ago."

Megan looked out the window for a moment, watching the endless line of cars filter through the drive thru of the Dion's pizza restaurant next door.

"Can you tell me more about the show?"

Nate laughed as he filled a soft corn tortilla with the al pastor meat and a dollop of the red smoky chipotle salsa on top. "You were on the show the other day," he reminded her. "I like how you change the subject from talking about your former marriage."

"I felt like a kid on a field trip," Megan said, speaking honestly, "being ushered around by the production assistant. There's nothing to say about my marriage. We ended up housemates. It lasted longer than it should have, but I've heard everyone say they stayed longer than they should have. And that's kind of sad considering how short life is."

"You didn't feel like a star? Even when you made that bold move off the diving board?"

Megan laughed. "I hope that didn't get me in trouble with the producer or anything."

"I think you did it so the producer would notice you," he suggested, looking up briefly and then back at his food.

"Because I have grand dreams of being a Hollywood actress," Megan added, watching a young Hispanic family– mom, dad, and two kids, a boy and a girl– sit down at one of the tables near them.

"This cooking thing is just a cover."

"Am I that obvious?" Megan asked.

"You have bigger plans than most people."

"They aren't my plans," Megan reminded him.

"But it seems to me someone has plans for you."

"Why do we keep coming back to me? I want to know more about the show. I told you about my marriage. Now you tell me about the show." She waited while Nate chewed, taking part of a tortilla chip and dipping it into the smoky chipotle salsa. "I don't ever remember a show about a motel. Well, unless you include 'Fantasy Island.'"

"You figured me out!" Nathan exclaimed, throwing his arms up. "I want to be Mr. Rourke!"

"And I've never heard of anyone with a childhood dream to become Mr. Rourke," Megan laughed. "Besides, didn't we have this conversation the other day?"

"My dream that I never told anyone about," Nate said, leaning forward across the table. "Until now."

"How did I get so lucky?" Megan asked.

"You dove into the pool."

"Oh, please." She shook her head. "Still, I want to know where the idea came from. I mean, no one ever talks about who started all these places." She flipped her left hand to the right as if across Central Avenue to the motels on the east side of the restaurant. "You only see them in the news about how rundown they are, the drug deals and prostitution, and the families that can't afford anywhere else to live and move into them."

"But they had incredible lives when they started."

"That's my point," Megan said. "They were incredible places at one time."

"When we went on family vacations," Nathan pointed out, "as kids."

"I wonder who the people were that started them," Megan said.

"That's exactly why we're going to tell Jack Tepper's story."

"But you don't know who really owned the Twilight Sands, do you?" Megan asked, feeling surprised.

"And you forget that I work in Hollywood."

"Yeah, right," Megan reminded herself. "Nothing is real there. Not even the faces."

Back at her front door, Megan hated to say goodbye. She knew it wouldn't be cool to invite him in. No matter who the man was, she could hear Stephanie's words echoing in her ears. "Don't reveal too much at once. Give him a bone to gnaw on and then leave the room."

"Can I see you again?" Nate asked.

"I thought you were here to film a television show," Megan laughed. "Not date."

"I will say one thing," Nate told her. "No one said anything to us at Taco Toté," he said, saying it like a tote bag.

Megan laughed. "You're such a gringo. That's because they don't speak English. Don't you think I did that on purpose?"

"I know you're lying," he said. "They were looking, but they didn't say a word. Besides maybe it's a taco tote bag. It's not like you know what it means."

"Not a peep." Megan looked around. She saw Sam in the window watching, like a protective parent.

"I'm sure Maria will arrange something if we don't," Nate reminded her.

"You know she's been trying to get us together," Megan told him as he kissed her on the cheek and squeezed her arm, starting to walk away.

"That's why I'm going to the car to get the disclosure for dating me. You'll need to get it notarized."

"That's why I'm going in the house."

"I had fun tonight," he said, resting his hand on top of the silver sedan in the darkness. "And, hey," he added, looking a little nervous. "I'm not keeping you from knowing about the show. I've been burned on ideas before. From Starbucks baristas, no less. My ability to trust has been squashed. Please, give me a little time to build it up with you. It's not you, it's me."

Megan swallowed hard, at first feeling insulted and then realizing she didn't really know much about Hollywood. She took a deep breath. Understand, she told herself, understand. "I had fun, too," she called, letting it go, as she stood on her front porch, her arms wrapped around her chest in the cool desert breeze. "Dinner party here at my house Sunday," she added. "Be here or be square."

"I'll be here." With that, he waved and climbed into the car and drove away.

She went into the house, kept her phone in her hand, and flopped onto her bed, Sam jumping into it with her as if he wanted to know the details, too.

"We want to know!" Stephanie had texted, including Julie in it.

"How'd it go?" Maria also texted. "Call me!" Megan pulled herself out of the bed to brush her teeth and wash her face, changing into a pair of pajama shorts and a pink tank top. She climbed back into the bed, Sam long snoring, and sighed in disbelief.

She had just spent the evening with Nate Matthews, a known entity. A man who was kind to her, who made her laugh, who laughed at her jokes.

Megan texted all three women, "It was great!" she said. "More tomorrow! Need some sleep!"

She knew they wanted details, but those could wait. Maybe even until Sunday.

CHAPTER 12

When everyone arrived for dinner on Sunday, Zeke was already there, ready to photograph the evening.

"Is this going to be in *Martha Stewart* or does he work for the *Enquirer*?" Nate asked, walking into the house with a bunch of sunflowers in his hand, kissing Megan on the cheek. "Usually second dates don't involve a group of other people."

"Depends on where you got those," Megan told him as he slipped them into her hands. "If they came from the neighbors' front yard, it might be the *Enquirer*."

"Those look like ours," Josie teased, taking them from Megan, knowing where she kept the vases. "But he'd have to get the plastic somewhere."

"Plastic from Smith's," Jim said. "Just the plastic. Then the sunflowers from our front yard."

"Yours are nicer," Nate said, making himself at home on one of the stools after all the introductions.

Maria went up behind him and hugged him. "I found you a new girl," she laughed.

"Maria thinks we like each other," Megan said to Nate as Jim handed him a beer.

"Where does she get that idea?"

Megan shrugged her shoulders. "Not really sure."

She set bruschetta on the counter and everyone devoured it. Except Barry. "I want pizza," he admitted. "I've been waiting months since the last time we had this," he admitted to Nate.

"So this paper bag thing is a big deal?" Nate asked.

Zeke snapped photos as Megan slipped the first pizzas into the oven. She had spent part of the day cleaning her patio furniture, making room for the group of them at the oversized glass and wrought iron patio table she had found at an estate sale several years ago.

"Don't you think this is a little big?" Ryan had questioned her when Jim and Josie had transported it home in their truck for Megan from Four Hills on the other side of the city. It had six chairs and she had found two more, close, but not the same. Not that it mattered to her. This night was why she had bought it. "It's not like you have kids or anything," Ryan had said.

Megan had kept her lips zippered shut. And now when she looked back, she wondered why she kept him around at times like that. It wasn't even sarcasm. It was envy that she had friends and parties. And he didn't. Nor did he ever show up to something she invited him to.

As Megan stood in the kitchen, having set the timer on the oven, she watched her guests laughing and joking with Zeke in the background, catching it all. This was what she imagined her life to be. And later as they sat outside, the sun setting to the back of the yard, everyone laughing and joking and just enjoying themselves, it was like déjà vu. She had seen this before. Maybe this was her dream.

"Seriously, I can't believe you baked this on a paper bag," Nate said, leaning back in his wrought iron patio chair, his fingers wrapped around his glass of red wine that sat on the table.

"I was seriously doubtful the first time," Josie admitted, leaning on the table. "I thought for sure it would catch on fire."

"She's talking about the time she put the pizza box– with the pizza in it– in the oven to warm it up and it did catch fire," Jim said, teasing his wife who sat across the table from him.

"I was trying to feed my family," she said. "You can't fault me for that. I thought it was a great idea."

Jim leaned forward toward Nate. "Since no one has asked," he said, looking around at the others and then back at Nate, "I'm going to be the one. How did you manage to score dinner with That Cooking Girl?"

"You are way too nice," Megan said, stacking up several plates in front of her.

"I'm the lucky one here," Nate said, leaning forward toward Jim. "I'd be eating takeout if it weren't for her."

"He is," Barry concurred.

Maria raised her glass for the second toast of the night, this one again directed at Megan. "For bringing two people together."

"Shouldn't we be toasting you?" Nate asked Maria, lifting his glass.

"I'll just add it to the tab of what you owe me," she said.

Nate was the last to leave, helping Megan clean up what Josie and Maria hadn't finished.

"Everyone is really good at helping," Megan told him.

"I'm a little shocked Maria did any dishes," Nate laughed, a dish towel on his shoulder, his sleeves rolled up to his elbows, up to his arms with soap suds, helping her wash wine glasses by hand. "I don't think I ever saw her cook in her kitchen. It was beautiful, but it was perfect, as if she had a photo shoot there and never wanted to ruin it so she just ordered out."

He placed the rinsed-off wine glasses on the light green and white striped dish towel Megan had spread out on the tile counter and Megan picked them up to finish drying them, making sure they left no water spots.

"It would be easier if you put these in the dishwasher," Nate told her.

"Why would I do that?" Megan asked, inspecting a glass.

"Okay, Martha Junior."

They stopped what they were doing and stared at each other. Later when Megan thought about it, she couldn't describe the scene. A director couldn't have brought it together better. The energy was perfect.

Nate leaned over, his arms still wet with soap suds, and kissed Megan, not just on the cheek or the forehead. Right smack on the lips, she would tell Stephanie and Julie later, the only detail she would reveal about what happened in her kitchen.

"So romantic," Stephanie sighed.

"You're a lucky girl," Julie added.

"He's probably just acting," Megan joked. "He can turn a scene into anything he wants it to be."

"I don't think so," Julie said thoughtfully.

"I don't want you to leave," Megan admitted when the kitchen was cleaned up. She rested one hand on the counter, leaning her body onto it. "But I don't think there is anything else for us to clean."

"And I can only stay to clean?" Nate asked, raising his eyebrows.

Megan laughed. "I guess that doesn't sound good, does it?"

He wrapped his arms around her and they embraced for a moment. Megan felt herself rest in his arms, it felt safe. She could feel his breath in her hair. He wasn't Nate Matthews the actor to her, he was Nate the man who treated her well, how she deserved to be treated, and who liked to laugh with her. He just happened to be an actor.

"I need to go," he said, pulling away and kissing her on the forehead. I have an eight a.m. casting call in the morning."

Megan nodded.

"After all, I did come here to film a television show."

"The Motel Guy thing."

"I just happened to meet That Cooking Girl while I was here."

"Thanks to The Hollywood Stylist."

"And The Public Relations Man."

They both laughed, Megan watching him drive away, Sam looking up at her, wagging his tail.

"You approve, too?" she asked him, walking down the hall to her bedroom and Sam walking right along with her.

It was already 7:30 Sunday morning when Megan stirred from her sleep. Sam snored next to her. Megan stretched and lay in bed for a few minutes, recalling the events of the past few days. Two evenings with Nate Matthews.

She thought back on all her dreams about having a life with Simon Le Bon, about how she had– as a preteen– thought adult life would be married to a singer of such a popular band. But now? Maybe it was because they weren't in Los Angeles and people in Albuquerque seemed good to leave stars alone. Or how many people at Taco Toté cared that a celebrity was in their midst when they were busy enjoying a night out with their families after a hard week of work.

It didn't matter. Megan sat up. She didn't know what was next. Maybe it was just supposed to be for the weekend. It didn't mean they had a future together. And she wasn't leaving Albuquerque. She'd worked too hard to build a life there. Megan shook her head as if those thoughts would fall out. She didn't need to be thinking them.

After taking Sam for a walk, she came home to find a text on her phone.

From Nate: "Thanks again for last night. Getting some rest to start shooting again tomorrow. Lines to memorize!"

*****

Monday morning back at the office, Megan took a deep breath, knowing she had to work on the cookbook.

For the moment she opened the notebook and looked at the recipes she had written down and began to categorize them. In the office supply closet down the hall, she found the colored sticky notes they sometimes used for projects and pulled out several colors for categories: green for appetizers, pink for desserts, blue for main dishes, orange for drinks, yellow for sides. Then she began writing down the recipe titles and sticking them on her office wall in the categories, taking down the poster for Indian Market in Santa Fe that had hung there since she started the job. She choked when she saw the date of it: ten years before.

Had she really been working for Barry that long? She'd gotten the job not long after she and Guy divorced, coming from a smaller group where she knew she would never move up the ladder. It was the one thing Barry promised her, "I'll make it so one day if something happens to me, you can take this place and run with it."

He had lived up to that promise, and now he'd done even more for her, she knew. He had bigger plans for her than running his PR business.

"Nice," she heard a voice behind her say approvingly.

Megan looked around to see Barry standing quietly in the doorway with his hand under his chin.

"Good morning!" his voice called and Megan knew better than to get lost in her thoughts before Barry interrupted her.

"Great visualization!" he exclaimed, looking at the wall.

She turned around, perched her reading glasses on her head and watched him waltz in, look at the wall, and then fall into one of the chairs.

"You know, I was thinking this morning on the drive in how lucky I am," he said.

"Oh?" Megan sat on top of her desk, crossing her legs as she pulled down her pencil skirt to her knees while it slipped up as she climbed onto the desk.

"This whole thing," he said, his hand shaping an imaginary circle, "is because of you. Not just what we're creating with you but Maria coming back into my life, too. And then watching you and Nate."

Megan waved her hand. "The guy is here to film a TV show. He's not looking for a girlfriend." She shrugged her shoulders, acting like it wasn't a big deal, as if she were entertaining a friend of Maria's as a favor. "It was a fun weekend. We have fun together."

Barry laughed. "Maria would beg to differ with you. And she knows him pretty well since they were neighbors." He paused as if to transition the subjects. "But we need to talk about work."

"I was working when you walked in," she reminded him.

"About that…," Barry said, lounging back in the chair and looking at the board. "I need you to pick up the pace a little bit."

Freaked out. That was the phrase Megan would use later. "What? Why? Why are we in a hurry?"

"You're a lifestyle brand. It's not just about the food but the entertaining, too. The photos Zeke took show something bigger than the food. I mean it's still the food, you're still…"

"Now you want me to be That Lifestyle Girl?" Megan asked.

Barry laughed. "No, I just think we need to broaden it out to include the entertaining aspect. You do it well. You know that. But you know how many people are afraid of it?" When Megan gave him a blank stare, he continued, "It stressed my ex-wife out. She worried for days about a dinner party. Well, sometimes weeks. But you do it effortlessly. You and Martha."

"I'm not as anal as Martha," Megan protested. "I don't think…"

"You're not. There's a casual sense about you. People come in, they look around at your house, they get a good meal, they enjoy conversation with others. They feel at home with what you've collected and how you've decorated. We want to capture that."

"But why the hurry?"

"The holidays."

Freaked out. There it was again. "You want me to switch gears and write a holiday entertaining book?"

Barry laughed. "No. We want to release the book at the holidays. That way it can be a gift to the people who are faced with hosting a party– they don't just get the recipes, but they also get the hints about making it easier."

"And you have a publisher? Shouldn't I have signed something?"

Barry waved her off again. "I'll worry about that. You keep writing and think about adding this other piece. It means more writing for you."

"Obviously."

After he left, Megan pulled out a new notepad from her drawer and began to take notes. She had written one line when Julie walked in and sat down in the same chair Barry had occupied just moments before. "I wanted to come see you earlier, but I had those campaign meetings this morning," she said, rolling her eyes.

"Campaigns are still the bread and butter for Barry," Megan said, letting her pen slip onto the top of the notepad and knowing– although she wasn't ready to admit it to herself– that Barry was starting to groom Julie for the job that Megan currently held.

"I want to know about the dinner party! I wish we could have been there. My kids need to stay well. Our bodies should be born with better immunity," she sighed, leaning forward. "Well? Was it fun? What's he like? Barry won't tell me anything other than everyone had a good time. And the pizza was great, of course. He talked more about the pizza than Nate."

Megan smiled, shaking her head. "It's hard to put it into words." She shrugged her shoulders. "It was fun. I don't feel like I'm with some big actor guy when I'm with him. He's Nate."

"You need to have him come by the office. I want to meet him."

"And tell him how he got you through grad school?"

Julie shrugged her shoulders this time and a smile lit up her face. "Why not?"

Megan turned her chair and looked out the window at the northern part of the city. She thought about her parents, mostly her mom, wishing she could call and tell her she had been out with Nate Matthews. But she could already picture the conversation. And the disappointment.

"Who is that?" her mother would ask. "And whom am I talking to?"

Her dad didn't know enough about popular culture. He would care more about what kind of guy Nate was, not what he did for a living. If she brought home a PGA golfer it would be different.

No, she thought, I'll wait until I talk to him next.

But as she sat there, looking out the window and rolling her pen across the yellow note pad, she remembered the time her mother took her and her best friend Terri to a mall in Denver– not the one by their house, but another one– to meet some soap opera stars. The sad part was she couldn't even remember what soap opera they were on. Was it "Days of Our Lives"? she wondered.

It had been a zoo of not just teen girls, but also young women, probably college age and older women– housewives who had no lives and lived for the soaps. A mass of female energy screaming everywhere.

"I'll park and come find you," her mother had said, letting them off in front of the packed shopping center. "No, you'll find me on a bench here," she decided, pointing at the inside doors where a wooden bench was placed next to the directory of stores.

No cell phones, no way to get a hold of someone. What a different a time, Megan thought, remembering the throngs of people. And realizing today that many gay men might show up, unlike the girls-only crowd then.

They had stood in a long, winding line outside Dillard's, like a yellow brick road that was supposed to lead them to their stars. But two hours later, the line had barely moved, several women had gotten hurt fighting over 8 x 10 photos of the stars. And Megan had decided it wasn't worth it.

They found her mom sitting on a bench, as promised, a paperback Harlequin romance in one hand. "Well?" she asked.

Megan shrugged her shoulders. "We never got close. Seems sort of stupid now. Can we go get pizza?"

That was the end of her dream about Simon LeBon. She decided then that if he was going to enter her life, it would happen. But she would focus on school and the adulthood that lie ahead of her.

Now as she watched the sun move over the city slowly, the day wearing on, she realized that it must have been the end of her road of dreams. She worked hard, she knew she wanted to enter something creative– just as she was doing now with Barry's company– and chose public relations because it seemed interesting.

She lived each day for what it was, never thinking back far or too far ahead.

And that's the same attitude she gave to Nate. It was fun, but perhaps that was all it was going to be. Besides, Barry had just doubled her current workload.

Megan turned her focus back to the book and the social media, finally getting used to posting photos of what she was making. Kevin kept up with her followers– although sometimes he still did a few posts for her. "Keep posting, commenting on what people are saying, and I'll take care of the rest," he had said. And so she did, not looking at how many people were following her.

CHAPTER 13

Wednesday night she had just climbed into bed, happy to have time to read the latest issue of *Vogue*– feeling like a luxury after being so busy– when her phone buzzed.

An unknown number in a Los Angeles area code.

Nate? She wondered.

"Hello."

"Hi!" he said. "I hope I'm not calling too late. I'm just leaving the set and this is the first chance I've had to call."

"It's okay," Megan assured him. "I'm in bed reading a magazine."

"You know what?" Nate laughed. Megan could tell by the sounds he was in the car. "That sounds like heaven to me."

"Yeah, me, too," she said. "It's been a busy week."

"If you're not too busy, how about dinner tomorrow night?" Nate asked. "I won't ask you to cook."

"Great!" Megan joked. "That means you're going to make us Swanson TV dinners! Do you have TV trays? My favorite was the fried chicken."

"You like fried chicken?" Nate asked, ignoring her comment. "We can go to KFC."

"I can make better fried chicken than KFC," Megan taunted.

"I might put you up to that."

She could tell he had pulled into something. A parking lot? It sounded like the car was running over gravel.

"I'm home now. I'll come get you at seven tomorrow night. Is that okay? I know we'll be done shooting by then."

"Sure," Megan said. "Should I dress up?" she asked, sneakily wanting an indication of where they would be going.

"Casual," he said.

Megan laughed. "I don't know you well. I'm still going to dress very nicely."

"Then wear a swim suit. Ask Maria to get you something Esther Williams wore again."

"We're going swimming?"

"I have to go. I have another call."

Megan could tell someone was beeping in. "Saved by the bell," she said.

The next afternoon as she stood in front of her sticky-note wall for the cookbook, Maria swished in.

"I heard you have date tonight!" she giggled like a high school best friend.

"Does all of Albuquerque know this, too?" Megan asked.

"Nope, just me."

"What's going on?" Barry asked, walking by with a single sheet of paper in one hand.

"Megan has a date with Nate tonight."

"And now that's two of you who knows. Don't let Kevin know or it might be Instagram it or gram or insta or whatever it is out to my thousand or so followers that I think I have."

"What do you want me to post?" Kevin asked, popping his head into the office.

"Go back to work," Barry told him. "She's being her usual sarcastic self."

At 5:30 Megan changed her dress five times, finally looking in the mirror with a big sigh. "Why do I feel so nervous?" She asked herself out loud, looking over to see Sam was ignoring her. "He's just Nate. Really."

Despite the way she played it off to everyone, that it wasn't a big deal, that she knew Nate didn't come to Albuquerque looking for a girlfriend, Megan enjoyed her time with him. And the attention.

The doorbell rang and Megan, having barely zipped up a navy blue gingham shift dress, almost tripped over Sam, who lay in the hallway waiting for her to make up her mind on what to wear.

Together, they opened the door where they found Nate smiling.

"Hi," Megan said, knowing she didn't look as put together as she would have liked. She held her sandals in one hand, the other one opened the door.

"That's a cute dress," Nate said. "You look like you're going to a picnic."

Megan stepped aside to let him in, wearing khaki pants and a white long-sleeve shirt that he had rolled up to the elbows.

"I thought it was appropriate for KFC," she joked.

"We could still go there," Nate suggested, petting Sam, as Megan slipped her shoes on her feet.

"I'm guessing you have something better planned."

"I do," he said, guiding her back out the front door and turning his car east on Central.

"I did hear on the John Tesh radio show today that sushi is good for a first date."

"Really?" Nate asked, sounding interested. "Why would that be? Does raw fish have some sort of sexual power?"

Megan laughed. "That really is all men think about. Nooo. Well, maybe." She thought for a moment, remembering exactly what she heard. "It's partly the idea of trying something new. Of course, if sushi is new for you. And then the whole sharing aspect."

"Then maybe we're going for sushi," Nate said.

"Hmmm. Then I wore the wrong outfit," Megan said, looking down at her sundress.

"You have no idea," Nate said, Megan feeling like she was playing some sort of hot and cold game.

Finally, he turned into the Twilight Sands. She waited for him to tell her that he had forgotten something, that he would be right back. Instead, with just a smile on his face, Nate turned off the car and walked around to open Megan's car door.

He guided her through a fence gate in the back.

"Do you have this thing locked?" she asked, surprised when it opened right up. "I thought movie sets were top secret places."

"They are."

Around the corner, into the main parking area of the Twilight Sands, Megan saw the lights around the pool lit up and then– when they had gotten even closer– a table set up for two with candles set on top of it, the place settings shimmering in the candle and water light.

"Oh," Megan said, stopping in her tracks.

"But we could still have KFC," Nate said, taking her hand and leading her to a chair at the table.

Megan couldn't speak. All this for me, she thought, looking around. As Nate sat down, a man dressed in a white shirt and black pants appeared from the lobby area of the motel.

"Hello," he said, taking a slight bow in front of them.

"Megan, this is Tony. By day he's my assistant."

"It's my job to pick up the pieces that Nate drops."

"I expected a cute girl to be your assistant, not a handsome guy," Megan said as Tony pretended to model, running his hand across the side of his head to the man bun he'd formed for his growing brown hair.

"Did you cook for us?" Megan asked, anxious to know what Nate had worked up.

Nate laughed. "We've been on set all day. During breaks we cooked."

"That means catering made the meal," Megan surmised, sitting back in her chair, enjoying the banter and feeling right at home next to the darkened pool. The lights bounced off the surface, making them look distorted even in the calmness of the May evening.

"I told you she was smart," Nate said, turning to Tony.

"Yeah. Catering." Tony walked back toward the lobby and returned a moment later with guacamole and chips. "Rosa," he said. And then left again.

"Who is Rosa?" Megan asked, confused.

"She's the housekeeper at the house where I'm staying. She made dinner."

"Oh." Megan was impressed, dipping a chip into the chunky mix of avocado, tomato, onion, garlic, salt, and lime.

Shortly after, Tony returned with a casserole dish filled with red chile enchiladas. "I didn't think to ask Rosa to cook for me until you asked me what I had been eating recently. Only then did I realize what I was missing out on."

After they each had been served, Tony disappeared and it was quiet, only the sound of the traffic on Central traveling by, as they ate.

"I'm hungry," Nate laughed. "I didn't get much time for lunch today."

"It's okay," Megan said. "We don't have to talk all the time."

But as she sat there, comfortable in Nate's presence, her mind began to wander. She looked around at the darkened motel, the lights by the doorways of the rooms lit up, but the parking lot empty of cars, the ones for the set having been given back to their owners until Monday when they would use them again, Megan thought about the Twilight Sands in its heyday.

"Do you ever think about who owned this place?"

"You keep asking," Nate teased her.

"I know. It's because I can't stop thinking about it. There must be a story behind this place."

"That's the story I'm telling," Nate reminded her, taking another helping of the red chile, cheese, onion, and corn tortilla mess on his plate.

"You're telling the story you want," Megan told him, leaning forward and eyeing the casserole. "Not what really happened."

She knew it was the beauty of fiction, but as she looked around her, she couldn't help but wonder about the history. Who came through there? Living in Albuquerque she heard about Route 66 all the time. And Hollywood was all about fiction.

"I guess you're not going to be writing novels any time soon then," Nate laughed, waving to Tony to come out and take their plates.

"Probably not," Megan said, watching Tony take her plate and replace it with a dessert plate.

"Rosa made flan for dessert," Tony said with a grin.

"Does Rosa really exist? Maybe she should replace me on television."

With the flan finished, Megan and Nate looked at each other for a moment, the candle light making their faces glow like jack o'lanterns at Halloween.

"What are you thinking?" Megan asked. Before Nate could speak, she added, "Unless I don't want to know."

"I really like being with you," Nate said. "You're the first woman I've been with who doesn't act starstruck around me."

Megan laughed and placed her forearms on the white tablecloth that covered the table. She leaned forward and said, "I wouldn't have known who you were if I stepped over you."

"That's why you didn't have a problem diving into this pool," he said, motioning to the diving board.

Megan just laughed, following Nate's lead to stand up. He took her hand as they walked across the concrete onto the pavement and back to his car.

"I'm not sure if you turn into a pumpkin at any point," Nate said, turning the ignition of the car.

"Oh, I guess I should have told you that before," Megan realized, looking over at the clock and seeing it was just after 8:30.

"I was hoping you could show me more of Albuquerque. I don't feel like I've seen much other than the set and my place."

"Have you been to the top of the mountain?" She asked, pointing to the Sandia Crest, the outline barely visible in the darkening sky.

"No. Isn't that where Barry's house is?" he asked.

"It's not nearly that high up. I'm sure you have a better view in LA," Megan said with a cluck of her tongue. "Besides, the readers of the *Albuquerque Journal* voted it not only most romantic place for a date, but the place you should go on a first date. And we know that the readers of the local newspaper know all."

"Then we better get up there." He pulled out to Central. "Which way?" he asked.

Megan directed him to the freeway and through Tijeras Canyon. Then a left on NM 14 (still called Route 10 by old timers) until, turning left again, they drove up the hairpin turns to the top of the crest where she grabbed her sweater and they braved the winds at 10,000 feet, one mile above the city.

Only a few other cars sat in the parking lot, the little café and gift shop closed for the day. A few people looked like they were coming off one of the trails along the side of the mountain. But Megan guided Nate to a lookout on the crest where they could see the entire city.

"It's like Barry's view times ten," Megan joked and pointing to the darkness behind the shimmering lights in front of them. "You can see the edge of the city where the Sandia Pueblo land starts."

"And the rain clouds sitting over somewhere."

"At least someone is getting rain," Megan said, rubbing her arms.

"At least you have a sweater with you," Nate said, stepping behind her and wrapping his arms around hers.

Megan leaned into him and let herself rest for a moment.

Rest.

It was the appropriate word she would think later. How long had it been since she'd been able to do that? She couldn't answer it and she realized she didn't want to answer it. But for a moment she could do that.

Megan felt Nate breathing, his heart beating, just glad to be there with him. And to feel connected. She didn't have to worry about anything in that moment.

Then a cell phone rang.

"I'm sorry," he said, pulling away. "I forgot to turn the sound off." He took it out of his pocket, glanced at the number and shoved it back into the pocket.

"It's okay," Megan said, starting the walk back to the car. "I know you're a popular guy."

"That was my publicist," he said, slipping his hand into hers. "He's always got something for me to do."

"Need to keep you in the spotlight."

"He thinks he's a good matchmaker for me," Nate said, shaking his head, as they started the drive back into the city. "But he has some of the worst taste. Or maybe it's not taste so much as he doesn't know what to look for in a woman. He calls me at all hours telling me about women he's met in various places like the woman in line behind him at the grocery store."

"Is he married?" Megan asked, grateful to be in the warm car.

"Divorced. Three times."

"That explains a lot," Megan laughed.

A silence ensued between them. Megan tried not to let thoughts of recipes come back into her mind. This was the most fun she'd had in a long time. The recipes would be there for her tomorrow. She glanced at Nate, who seemed not just intent on making sure they got down the mountain, but also lost in his own thoughts.

"I'm thinking about buying a house here," Nate finally said.

"Really?"

"If the pilot gets good reviews and we get enough viewers for the first season."

"You really like it here?" Megan asked.

"You must," he reminded her. "You've been here a while. I do. But I don't have the big dreams you do."

"The pace is relaxed. I like the culture. The food. Traffic is easy. No three hours in a parking lot on the freeway." Megan nodded and thought for a moment as he traveled the interstate west toward downtown and her house. "I don't know that I see myself living anywhere else. But if you'd told me twenty years ago that I'd be living in Albuquerque, New Mexico, I might have laughed."

"And I thought I'd never get out of Vermont and get to California," Nate said.

"Somehow you found your way out from those maple trees."

"It wasn't easy. They trap you in pretty good. The pines are pretty thick, too."

Once at her front door, Megan pointed. "Do you want to come in?"

Nate looked at his watch and then took her hand. "Please know I do, but I have to be on the set in the morning. We have two scenes we didn't finish. Can I take a rain check?"

"I have a cookbook to write," Megan said. She tried not to hide her disappointment, knowing she really did have work to do herself.

"But I want to show you a house I'm looking at. Are you free Sunday morning?"

She nodded and Nate kissed her lightly on the lips.

"Does that come easily because you do it on television?" she asked as he pulled away, his keys in one hand.

"Not when it's personal," he said. "You look more confident than I feel."

"I doubt that," Megan laughed, opening her front door and greeting Sam, who was dancing around, his nails clicking on the tile floor.

"I'll pick you up at nine," he called, climbing into the car.

CHAPTER 14

Saturday morning she walked the mile and a half to the office, giving her time to think as she traversed the streets of her neighborhood, crossing from the Country Club area with houses, mostly stucco, to the tree-shaded more Victorians and bungalows. And finally into the downtown area of office buildings. She stopped at Humble Coffee on Central Avenue for her favorite brew, and happy her favorite barista, Sergio, was working and started it when he saw her walk through the doors of the coffee shop.

As Megan climbed the metal circular staircase to the second floor to catch the elevator to the sixth floor of the Simms Building, she tried not to think about Nate. It was quiet and nearly dark in the building. She waved to Gene the security man who never seemed to go home.

No one was in the office when Megan walked through the double-glass doors, for which she was kind of thankful.

I have to get my head back into this, she thought, feeling as if she had been on vacation lately with everything that was happening with Nate, let alone the job Barry had hired her to do in the beginning. It was causing her to lose her focus on the recipes and cooking. Everyone has invested so much, she thought, turning into the doorway of her office where her eyes immediately turned to the wall of colored sticky notes.

Life had taken on a frenetic pace lately. It wasn't bad, Megan knew, but it was different. She had gotten used to her time alone in the evenings and on weekends, whether that be good or bad. But the last week had left her feeling a bit depleted.

And wanting to see more of Nate.

Tomorrow, she reminded herself, diving into her recipe for the next week, mint brownies. Not black bean, dark chocolate. But with a minty flavor.

"It's not that easy," Megan had explained to Barry and the rest of the crew in a meeting on Thursday, just a few days before.

"You just throw some mint extract into the recipe, right?" Julie asked.

"That's what I thought but they taste more like Listerine that way," she laughed. "You need crème de menthe."

"What?" Kevin looked perplexed. "What is that?"

"He's so young," Barry laughed, spinning his chair around. "We drank a lot of it in the seventies."

"That makes you sound old," Julie laughed.

"It's an alcoholic drink," Megan explained. "You need it for the flavor. The alcohol bakes off in the process."

She could see Kevin was Googling it, but nodding at her, as she spoke.

"The secret ingredient is out of the bag," Megan had announced.

Megan glanced up at the calendar and happened to see Mother's Day was coming up. She ignored the conversation buzzing around her and wondered if she should send her mom a Mother's Day card even though she wouldn't know whom it was from. Megan found a wave of sadness rush over her. How she wished she could share the fun she was having with Nate with her mom. She could see her Googling him, watching all his movies, telling her when she saw him on the cover of *People* magazine at the grocery store while she waited to check out.

"This is the life you deserve," her mom would say, always the supportive one, always proud of Megan. "He's handsome and he's good to you. It's a rare combination you know."

Focus, Megan told herself, writing up the ingredients for the brownies in the quiet of the weekend office. She'd have to run home to get the car to go to the store later because there was no grocery store downtown, just the small market near her office that usually didn't stock much of what she needed.

For a while, Megan worked organizing the cookbook into new sections to add the entertainment component that Barry had decided they would include. They planned to have several dinner parties to photograph and she also started notes for those. At least it was spring and they could easily do them.

A text buzzed in and startled her.

"I hope you're having a great Saturday! Maybe we'll be done by dinner! I hope so– I really could use some sleep."

"I'm working hard in a darkened office building," Megan replied.

"Trying to make me feel better while I repeat my lines sixty times because Marty the director doesn't think I'm getting it right?"

"Yep. But at least you're out in the sunshine. I just see it from my window." She looked out at the north side of the city that lay before her, knowing that while it was quiet in the office, everywhere else people were enjoying their Saturday, or catching up on life.

"We're all crowded into one of the motel rooms. We probably should have shot this at the studio. Sometimes you realize you've made a mistake when it's too late. And the window is covered to keep out the sun."

"Oooh. Mimicking night time while shooting in the morning," Megan replied.

He didn't reply, probably because they had resumed the scene and Megan went back to her notes for the entertainment section. She heard the door to the office swoosh open and footsteps come down the hall, not looking up until Barry was standing in her doorway.

"Shouldn't you be doing something?"

"Like working on the cookbook you've decided I should write?" she asked.

Barry fell into the chair closest to Megan. "Yeah. You're right. Where's Nate today?"

"Shooting scenes for that little TV show he's doing. But why do you think I would know?"

"You act like there isn't anything between you two," Barry laughed, sitting up and leaning forward. "Everyone can see it. We're going to put him back on TV with you."

"That's nice," Megan said. "The Nate and Megan Show?"

"The Megan and Nate Show."

"Don't you think it's a little weird?" she asked, tapping her pen on her pad of paper.

"What?" Barry stood up.

Megan looked around for a moment before she spoke. "What if things do work out between him and me. Don't you worry people are going to think I'm using his popularity to advance my career?"

Barry looked at her and Megan knew he thought she said the wrong thing. "Why are you worried about that? This was taking off before you met him. Enjoy the ride."

After he had left, Megan sat for a moment. She was glad, no thankful, for it all. But at the same time, there was a part of her that worried. Never did she want anyone to think that Nate was part of advancing her career. But if she couldn't get Barry to see her perspective, no one else would.

That afternoon, she made the grocery store run, stopping at the Smith's a little further from her house– near the university campus– but where she had bought the crème de menthe before, realizing she had run out of it after a holiday party where she'd made frothy, snowy-looking drinks with it.

Pushing her cart to the checkout line, none of them looking like they were moving quickly, she stopped and found herself looking at the tabloids.

I don't ever want to be there, she thought.

"I'm sorry," a woman said, interrupting Megan's thoughts. "Are you the cooking girl on TV?"

"Yes," Megan said, feeling as if the only time anyone recognized her was at the grocery store, then she realized apparently she never went anywhere else. "I am."

"You had Nate Matthews on with you not too long ago, didn't you?"

"I did." Megan smiled.

"Is he as handsome in person as he is on television?"

"He is," Megan said, trying to sound calm, but really wanted to break out into a song and dance about how much she had come to like him. And about how…normal…he was.

"I hope he finds a good woman to be with," the woman said, readjusting the butter, broccoli, and milk in her arms. "I believe life is meant to be shared." She shook her head. "But it must be so hard to be someone like him and find someone who doesn't ogle over him. I could never be famous."

Megan started to say, "Me, too" before she realized that was a crazy statement for her to make and quickly shut her mouth.

It was her turn, but before she left the store, she waved to the woman behind her and wished her a good day.

See, she thought. Nothing about cooking, all about Nate.

Where do I find the balance in this? She wondered.

And she continued to ask herself that question through the next morning when she took Sam for a walk, then waited for Nate to pick her up.

He pulled into the driveway a few minutes after 9:00. "I know you people in California are never on time," Megan said, coming out the front door.

"I got stuck in traffic," Nate said, adding, "Oh wait, I can't use that excuse here."

As they walked to his car, Mrs. Rosales drove by in her white Ford sedan. "Hello! I'm on my way to church," she said. Then she spotted Nate and squinted. "I know I know you. Are you sure you're not on the city council?"

Nate laughed and held up his hands as if to surrender. "I'm not a politician," he declared.

"But he might have played one on TV!" Megan chimed in.

"Oh, that's funny," Mrs. Rosales laughed. "I remember those commercials." She quickly changed the subject. "I'm going to be late." She looked at Megan. "I was going to have you over for your second tortilla lesson, but I see you're busy." Before Megan could say anything, she then said, "You can bring him, too. I'll make lunch."

There was no room to say no. Before either of them could protest, Mrs. Rosales looked at her watch. "Dios mio! I won't have time to light a candle for Our Lady of Guadalupe. I'll see you both at noon."

With that, she drove off.

Megan looked at Nate and was ready to apologize when he said, "That's great! Now I don't have to take you to lunch."

"And maybe better than Rosa's dinner the other night at the motel. Is that okay?"

"That's more than okay," he said, opening the passenger seat of his rental car and inviting her into it. "I'm looking forward to getting to know Mrs. Rosales. Do you think she would teach me how to make tortillas, too?"

"If you want," Megan said.

He drove north on Rio Grande Boulevard from Old Town, the touristy area crawling with the first tourists of the late spring season. Soon the area turned into stuccoed houses and then into sprawling former farmlands now McMansions, filled with green, the trees having budded out not long before.

"Tell me about this house," Megan asked, having no idea where they were going.

"It's not on the market yet. It needs a ton of updating, but some well-known architect here, who is so well-known that I don't remember his name, designed it. Don Schlegel, I think was his name."

"Do you want to live here?" Megan asked. "I can't see how someone from Hollywood would want to live in Albuquerque."

"I'm not *from* Hollywood," Nate reminded her. "I just happen to work *in* Hollywood. I'm *from* Vermont."

"So I should be making you maple ice cream, maple smoothies, maple brownies…"

"That would be a good start. I'm still waiting on the waffles."

They pulled up to a stop sign. "I love what I do, but I get tired of living there. I have a place in Mexico, but I think I'm going to sell it. I love it there, too, but it's a lot of work to go between both places. I've thought about buying a place in England, but I'm not sure how much I time I could spend there."

"And Los Angeles-Albuquerque is a better commute?"

"Yes. And if the show takes off– which obviously I hope it does– then this would be easier, to have a house that's mine rather than a house someone picked for me. It's my fault, I should have rented something on my own. But Rosa is great."

"As long as you make us look better than 'Breaking Bad,'" Megan joked.

"But it was a great show," he reminded her.

"Showing all the wrong places in this town."

Nate made a right onto a long gravel driveway with a large field where alfalfa was just beginning to grow on his left. On Megan's right a line of trees kept the long driveway shaded. Ahead she saw a squarish-shaped house morphed by all the green in front of it. And the mountains off in the distance behind it.

"The owners have both died." Nate pulled into the carport near the entrance of the house. "They haven't updated it recently– or ever– but it has an incredibly cool energy to it."

"Jack Tepper-ish?" Megan asked.

"Exactly."

"You know," she said, undoing her seatbelt. "I don't think his name is ethnic enough."

"What does that mean?"

Nate met her on her side of the car, reaching into his pocket for a key.

"People had really ethnic names in the early sixties."

"Please," he said, unlocking the front door. "There were a lot of Smiths then, too."

"Who gave you the key?"

Nate smiled as he let Megan through the doorway first. "The very people who are hoping I buy their parents' house."

Megan walked up the few steps just inside the front door and stood in the empty foyer, unable to move past it. "Wow," she said, looking around. The space was open with the back wall filled with windows to let light in and showcase the jutting Sandia Mountains in the background. They were surrounded by rock walls everywhere and built-in planters. "This is so sixties."

"Isn't it great?" A big grin spread across Nate's face. "I love this." He walked to the left where a built-in couch faced the mountain view. And where a swimming pool sparkled right outside the windows and a set of sliding glass doors.

Behind the large rock fireplace, a set of stairs led to the second floor.

"I'm not a huge fan of the wood paneling," he said pointing at the walls.

"But it works in here," Megan said, still barely into the house and unable to believe what she was seeing. She stood at the glass doors and looked out at the pool. A lone patio table stood with four chairs, looking like the only furniture left behind. She turned back and said, "I'm not a huge fan of the brick floors either, but they work, too."

Before Nate turned to take her to the kitchen, he pointed to the right. "And you noticed the bar over here, right?"

"You mean, as soon as your guests walk in the door, you can offer them a drink?" Megan asked, amused.

"Exactly."

"A total period house," she said nodding.

"The kitchen needs a lot of work," he admitted, walking backward into the large room with another set of built-in benches surrounding a square table.

"You don't need much furniture," Megan joked, running her hand across the blue-green vinyl.

"But it needs new cabinets," Nate admitted, tapping the wood.

"I'd save those tiny tiles," Megan cried, pointing to the backsplash. "They are totally back in. My house didn't even look this cool when I got it."

"You remodeled?" he asked, his eyebrows going up.

"Room by room." She laughed, thinking of the process. "That was all I could afford. I tried to do a room a year and I had to give up everything else, including travel, to do it. I wasn't making the big bucks at Barry's yet."

They kept walking, both thinking their separate thoughts as Megan ran her hands across counters, opened cabinets and doors. "It's so hard to decide what to save, what to let go."

"You want to keep the integrity of what was originally created, but make it functional in today's world."

"Exactly." He held his hand out. "Let me show you the funkiest thing about this." Megan followed him. It was if the house went on forever. He led her into what appeared to be the master bedroom. And then the master bath.

The same tile and old wood cabinets were in there. Then he pointed to the bathtub in the ground.

"What?" Megan asked, looking confused.

The pink bathtub was sunken in, with a showerhead on one wall. But then on the other side of it hung a chain curtain.

That was visible from the living room.

Megan looked at the tub. Then she looked back at the bathroom. Then at the tub again.

"Am I seeing this right?" she asked, then looking at Nate who started laughed.

"I know. I'm still trying to figure out the thinking behind that."

"Either everyone watches you take a bath or you can't take a bath unless you're home alone." She shook her head. "If you get it, are you planning to leave it that way for a conversation piece?"

Nate shook his head and led the way back into the master bedroom. "But it makes for easy shower access."

They walked back to the living room and then outside to the pool area that had a good-sized wrap-around of concrete.

"This needs some work," Nate said, pointing. "The pool is good but the concrete needs to be replaced and covered with the cool deck stuff." And he continued, as they stood there admiring the water and the automatic pool cleaner roving across the bottom. "My dad was a contractor. I grew up in new houses. I actually like doing this kind of work."

"Putting in new tile? Replacing toilets?"

Nate smiled and shook his head. "All of it. There is this rumor I guess you would say in Hollywood that all I do is chase women who work at Starbucks. I hardly ever go to Starbucks, but the one time I do, because I desperately need caffeine, it ends up in the *Enquirer*."

Megan raised her eyebrows and followed him inside where they sat down on the blue and white striped vinyl couch. She let her brown sandal slides fall off her feet as she dangled her legs from the edge of the couch. "So I shouldn't believe everything I read in the tabloids at the checkout in the grocery store?"

"Believe only what I tell you." He looked at her and touched his arm.

"I'll remember that," she said.

"So should I buy it? What's your expert opinion as an Albuquerque resident and fellow remodeler?"

Megan looked around and shrugged her shoulders while smiling. "The money isn't a problem. It's a good investment because it's on Rio Grande in the Valley. And once you replace the pink bathtub, you've got yourself something that I'm sure someone will want. This is a great piece of land to sit on."

He nodded and they both looked out at the mountains. Nate glanced at his watch and then said, "We have about an hour until lunch. How about you show me around some more?"

"Depends on what you haven't seen," Megan said. "It seems to me you've seen more than you let on. I think you just want to act like you haven't seen anything so that I can show you around."

"You figured me out," he said, standing up and reaching for her hand. Megan slipped her feet back into her sandals and stood up. For a moment they were facing each other.

Megan broke the gaze. Later she kicked herself, but at that time she just wasn't quite there.

"I wasn't ready to admit it," she would tell Julie later.

"Admit what?" Julie gave her a blank stare.

"How much I was starting to care for him, how happy I was to be part of his life."

"Oh please," Julie said. "You're a lucky girl. You've got everything going for you after years of emptiness. Enjoy the ride."

They walked out of the house together quietly although nothing seemed lost in the silence. Back in the car Megan directed him to drive south and they hit Montano and then back through a busy part of the valley on 4th Street.

"This is where you'll probably grocery shop," Megan said, pointing out the Smith's. "It's not Whole Foods, but it does probably have everything you need."

"Swanson TV dinners?"

"Of course."

"Then I'm good."

He parked his car at Megan's and they walked over to Mrs. Rosales's house.

"Hello!" she said, the door flying open and Martino running in circles and barking. "Welcome!"

Megan led the way to the kitchen where something was once again bubbling on the stove.

"I'll show you how to do the tortillas and then we'll eat. It takes lots of practice. Have you ever made tortillas?" She looked at Nate. "I don't even know your name."

"Nate," he said, sticking out his hand to her. "Nate Matthews."

"Why do I know that name?" She stood for a moment with her hands on her hips, examining her tile floor. "You aren't on the city council…" She looked up and her face brightened. "You're in the movies!"

Megan dropped her face into her hands, laughing. "Have we been playing hot and cold?" she asked.

"Yes," Nate said. "I am in the movies."

"Then why are you here? Why aren't you in Hollywood? Are you here to be with Megan?"

"Megan is an added bonus," Nate said. Megan felt her cheeks turn red. "I'm filming a TV show. At the Twilight Sands."

"Oh! Roberto and I used to go dancing there." Her face brightened again. "Oh what fun we used to have. And then we had the children and we couldn't afford to go out anymore." She waved her hand and walked over to the stove. "Movie star or not, maybe it's good you learn how to make tortillas. You never know, Hollywood might not call you again."

"It is," Megan agreed, giving Nate a smug look. "You never know what might happen to your career and you'll have to go work in a tortilla factory."

Mrs. Rosales ignored the banter and motioned them both to stand behind her, starting her dough lesson from before. "I'll start all over again, just for Nate." Then she laughed and said softly, "Wait until Jean hears about this."

She showed them how to mix the dough and roll it into the perfect-sized balls to fry the tortillas. "I'm sure you don't have a *comal* either," she said to Nate, pointing at the tortilla pan. "Mine was a wedding gift."

"I don't," Nate admitted. "I've never been married so no wedding gifts for me."

"Where did you grow up?" she asked, rolling out the dough before flipping it into the pan. "No one from Hollywood is from Hollywood."

"Vermont," he said.

"Oh, then you should be able to make pancakes really well. Maybe we should have had you cook today." She looked back at Megan and winked.

"I can make you pancakes someday."

"For now let me see you make a tortilla." She handed the rolling pin to Nate and Megan watched over his shoulder, anxious to see how well he did rolling it out.

Somehow it ended up as an oval.

"Is that an *ovalilla*?" Megan asked.

"*Dios mio*," Mrs. Rosales said, taking the rolling pin back and rolling the dough back into ball. "Maybe you should go back to the movies," she suggested.

"It's television now," Megan corrected her. "He's hoping his show takes off so he can be here longer."

"Well, if you want to learn to make tortillas, then you will need to be here longer," she sighed, ushering them to the kitchen table.

After finishing the tortillas, she once again made them each a dish of huevos rancheros.

"Why did I ever eat out when I got here?" Nate asked, shaking his head.

"That's what happens when you don't know all the cool kids."

"You'd think Maria would have been help for that. She sent me to all the expensive places."

"The touristy places."

"Yeah."

"*Dios mio*. You poor thing," Mrs. Rosales said, shaking her head. "You've been missing out. You can come back. Of course, you need to come back with Megan."

Megan smiled as he looked at her. "Yes, of course," Nate said, standing up with his dish in his hand. Megan looked at Mrs. Rosales, who immediately jumped up.

"No no no," she said. "I'll do the dishes. You go on with your day. Thank you for spending time with me. I'm sure you have some movie star things to do."

Nate laughed and pushed his chair in. "Actually, I have lines to work on. We shoot again tomorrow."

As she walked them to the door, Mrs. Rosales was practically singing, Martino bouncing around at her feet as usual. "Jean will be so jealous," she said with a cluck of her tongue. Then she took Megan's hand and held it in both of hers. For being eighty years old, Megan felt a lot of strength– and in her brown eyes and weathered face that looked at Megan. "Thank you for coming into my life. You've made such a difference."

Megan smiled. "But you've made a difference in mine," she protested.

"You'll never understand," Mrs. Rosales said. "I think you're not just a gift from God, but a gift from Roberto." She patted Megan's hand, looking at both of them, and said, "I hope you understand what I mean one day, the love that two people have for each other."

"Me, too," Nate said, letting Megan out the door first.

They walked quietly back to Megan's house where Sam greeted them in the doorway.

"I guess you need to go work on your lines," Megan teased him.

"That was true, you know," he said.

"I don't doubt it." She opened a cabinet for a glass. "Do you want some water?"

He nodded. "I believe you have a cookbook to write anyway."

"I do," she said. "I have the wrath of Barry waiting for me at work tomorrow."

Nate slipped into one of her kitchen chairs. "How long will you work there?"

Megan shook her head. "I don't know. I'm not really sure where all this is going to go."

"To the top," Nate said, taking the glass that clinked with ice in it.

"That's what everyone says. We'll see what happens."

"Don't you see it?" he asked, looking at her as she sat down at the table.

Megan tried to explain, but she wasn't sure if she could. "Did you always have dreams of being an actor?"

"Not quite," he admitted.

As Megan watched him, she understood why woman found him appealing. While she knew it always had something to do with the characters he played– she much preferred this real person who was sitting across the ice cream table from her– his face was warm and inviting. Everyone who met him easily felt comfortable with him. He made it easy to be with people. She knew it wasn't just her, this was how he was with everyone.

"I wanted to be an athlete," he said.

"So you must have a sport you played?" She wondered why he didn't say which one right away.

"Baseball."

"How much baseball can you play in Vermont?"

"Exactly. And I could never convince my parents to move somewhere warm like California. I moved to Los Angeles for college and auditioned for a commercial on a dare from a friend."

"And I take it that you got the part?" Megan raised her eyebrows as she took a drink of the water, feeling thirsty after the heavy meal Mrs. Rosales had made.

"I was hooked. It's a different kind of high than getting a home run."

"Not one that renders you out of breath."

"When you're done jumping around maybe."

"You jump on couches when you get parts?" she was feeling very amused.

"When you get one of every fifty you try out for. Things are little different now. I have more control."

"What was the first commercial you did?"

"McDonald's."

Megan started to laugh and held her stomach when she couldn't stop. "Seriously?"

"I was the guy behind the counter. I didn't have any lines though because there was a jingle. I just had to look good."

"In a McDonald's uniform."

"They didn't even let me keep it."

"Please. Like you wanted to."

"As a monument to my rising fame I did," he said, looking serious.

Nate looked up at the clock and then at Megan. She wanted to look away. The stares were getting a little long. Gazing, she thought. We must be gazing into each other's eyes.

It's good, she reminded herself, yet feeling slightly uncomfortable.

"I need to go," he said. "I don't want to go, but I'm the head guy and I can't make the production run behind."

"Never, Mr. Tepper. You have to keep the Twilight Sands running. And all its adventures." Megan leaned forward toward him. "Any sneak peek of what you're filming this week? Harboring a mass murderer who's on the lam?"

"What kind of show do you think this is?"

"Aren't all shows like that now? A little murder and a lot of sex. Or a lot of sex and a little murder?"

"Not mine. I'm still into good, all-fashioned drama."

"No reality show for you?"

"What have you been watching?" he asked, getting up.

"I don't watch much TV," Megan admitted.

"Then that's the problem. We need to change that." He thought for a moment. "Do you watch yourself?"

She laughed. "I haven't. And no one has suggested I watch."

They were at the door and Megan opened it, using her leg to keep Sam from running out to a dog that was walking by.

"Maybe one day we'll watch the greatest hits together," he suggested.

She knew it was coming.

"It took him long enough to give you a real kiss," Stephanie would say later.

"Don't listen to her," Julie would whisper to Megan. "She slept with her husband the first night she met him."

"I didn't know this was a contest of how long it would take," Megan laughed, looking at them both.

But in the moment, she was excited and scared at the same time. Was it about who he was or was it about who she was and how she felt about him? And how he felt about her? It was that jumble of emotions one felt with a new relationship, wondering what would happen, but wanting it to work out– whatever that meant.

Megan tried to stop the thoughts in her head and enjoy the moment. This was the first time she had found herself feeling that way. Mostly she had felt very nonchalant about the whole relationship– despite everyone's excitement around her.

In her life, Megan hadn't been the kind of person to get too excited about much. Maybe it was because after high school, things hadn't quite turned out how she had thought they would in her mind. Or maybe it was because she learned that if she didn't plan things, there was no disappointment.

That was definitely true about her relationship with her mother. She'd always been there for Megan, always happy when she called, even if she called at ten at night, taking the cordless phone to another room so Megan's father could sleep. The descent into dementia had been quick and with Megan living away, she'd been spared most of it. But she'd also missed out on the last times her mother might have remembered her.

Megan flopped down on her couch, knowing she needed to get to work on the cookbook, but giving herself a few minutes to decompress.

All is well, she thought, knowing that life was good, no matter what happened ahead.

"Lines lines lines!" a text from Nate said.

"Recipe recipes recipes!" Megan typed back.

That was the biggest question in her head.

Could they balance two big careers?

No one seemed to doubt it– Barry saw Nate as an asset to everything Megan was doing– but Megan wasn't so sure. There hadn't been a conflict yet. And at some point there would be one. And then what would happen?

CHAPTER 15

Summer began to settle into Albuquerque. With Memorial Day passing, the traditional tourist season had begun. No one around Megan doubted the importance of the film industry, Megan finding herself paying more attention as she and Nate spent more time together.

"Did you just shave?" Megan asked him when he picked her up on Friday evening, Nate's face looking like he was ready to start the day.

"I had to look a bit scruffy for these scenes," he admitted.

"What is Jack Tepper up to?"

"I can't tell you," Nate laughed, turning out of her driveway. He stopped the car where the curb met the street. "Where are we going?"

"Is it always my job to decide where we go?"

"Then we can go to LA and I'll take you to my favorite taco stand."

She ignored him and pointed. "I have an idea. Head east on Central. You'll make a left on the other side of downtown, at Edith."

Nate turned left, looking at the building directly in front of them as he made the turn. "Albuquerque History Collection" read the sign in front of a low, adobe building.

"It's the original public library," Megan explained as he did a u-turn to park the car on the street in front of the library. "Now it houses the history of Albuquerque and New Mexico."

"You've been here before?" he asked, taking her hand as they walked into the building together.

"They also filmed some scenes from 'Better Call Saul' here," Megan whispered, acting sarcastically knowledgeable.

"As a library?" Nate asked, raising his eyebrows.

"When is there a library in Saul?" Megan asked, waving him off. "It was a law office in Santa Fe."

Once inside, Megan felt as if she were entering a piece of history. The building was a hundred years old and had recently been restored. The ceilings were high, the windows large– filtering in significant amounts of light– the furniture made of heavy wood that looked that it belonged in any sort of Southwestern home.

And then there were the materials. Stacks and shelves of history, much of it hidden behind closed doors.

"This is incredible. I wonder if our location scouts have been in here."

"Why would you need a library? Does Jack Tepper go to the library?" Megan asked. "That doesn't seem to be part of the show you're making."

Nate gritted his teeth and teasingly reached his hands out to her as if he were going to strangle her. "Enough opinions from the peanut gallery. I haven't seen you create a television show."

"I could do that," Megan told him as they walked toward the main desk where a tall slender woman with glasses and short brown hair sat.

"And get it past all the other ideas in Hollywood?"

"Ideas are a dime a dozen," she reassured him with a flip of her hand. "I know someone in Hollywood. That will get me past all the front desks."

"Hi," The woman said when they reached the front desk. She stopped typing on the computer and gave them her full attention.

"We need some help." Megan eyed the shelves of books behind the woman. "Could we start with the 1960 city directory? And you have a collection of postcards of Albuquerque, right?"

"Yes, we do." The woman held out one finger toward the back shelves and pulled the city directory, placing it on the counter. Megan motioned for Nate to pick it up.

"Did I fail to mention I missed lunch?" he whispered.

"They close at six," Megan whispered back, watching as the woman disappeared into the back and reappeared with a small box. "We don't have much time."

She pointed to the large tables near shelves of books, passing by several people using the computers, several looking like they might be homeless.

As they sat down, Megan opened the city directory and looked for Central. Then she moved her finger down the page from downtown, flipping the pages until she reached the Twilight Sands.

"Nicholas McLean," she said, tapping the text-filled page and looking up at Nate.

"So? Who is Nicholas McLean? The main character in your TV show?"

Megan leaned across the table. "He's the real Jack Tepper." She turned the city directory around to Nate– who sat across the table from her– and pointed to the spot where it says "Twilight Sands Hotel. 3323 Central Avenue NE." On the line below it, "Nicholas McLean, Proprietor."

"Oh," Nate said. "Wow." He shook his head. "I never thought about it."

"How could you not?" Megan asked. "There was a real person behind this place. Don't you want to know who built it?"

But she knew exactly what had happened: Nate had gotten caught up in the rebuilding, and of the story he wanted to tell, the story that he thought people would want to know.

She carried the directory back to the librarian, who placed it back on the shelf. Then Megan sat back down with Nate and pulled out her iPad from her purse.

"What else do you have in there?" he questioned, leaning over the table toward her.

"Wouldn't you like to know?" she asked, opening the lime green protective cover and launching the internet.

"If you won't tell me that, then what are you looking up?"

"Duh. Nicholas, of course."

"Oh." Nate sat back in the heavy wooden Southwestern chair and rolled the pencil he'd picked up at the desk across the table.

"Were you that really annoying boy in school?"

"Yeah. The one who pulled your ponytail." He made a yanking motion with his hand.

"Figures. No wonder you became an actor." She clucked her tongue. "Always looking for attention." She scrolled until she saw what she was looking for: useful information. His wife Eleanor's obituary. "Come here," Megan said, motioning to Nate, to come to her side of the table. "Look at this."

"That was quick," he said.

"Sometimes what we're looking for is easy to find." She felt her stomach flutter a bit as she said it. They caught each other's eyes and Megan quickly refocused on Eleanor, both of them reading silently. "I Googled him and he came up in her obituary."

"She was a doctor," Megan said, impressed.

"And he owned a hotel."

Nate sat back in the chair, this time the one next to Megan. She carefully laid her iPad on the heavy wooden table, both of them absorbing all that they had just learned.

"It must have been difficult for a woman to become a doctor then," Nate said.

"They both had careers. Big careers."

After a few minutes of thinking and not much conversation, Nate touched Megan's hand. "Are you ready to get something to eat?" She nodded, her thoughts still with Nicholas and Eleanor though.

"It's getting close to six, I'm sure they want to get rid of us," Megan said, watching the librarian start to pack up her belongings for the day.

For dinner, they continued east on Central, stopping at the Frontier Restaurant with its distinctive yellow barn roof, across from the University of New Mexico.

"You're never going to cook again for me, are you?" Nate asked as they stood in line to place their orders.

"Not at the rate we're going," she joked.

As they ate, they were silent, both tired from a long day of work, both enjoying the food they had ordered– enchiladas for Nate, the vegetarian burrito for Megan– "You get a better taste of the chile without the meat," she had explained. And the silence of just being together.

"Excuse me," a young woman wearing a short dress said, coming up to their table. Megan could see several giggly girls behind her, obviously college students, fully expecting they would want Nate's autograph.

Megan looked back at her food and kept eating.

"You're That Cooking Girl on TV, right?"

Megan looked up, surprised. Nate took his napkin and put it across his mouth, starting to laugh, and Megan knew he had caught her not thinking it was about her.

"I am," Megan said.

The girl motioned to her friends to come over. "We just wanted you to know how cool we think you are. We started watching you in the dorms, some of us missing class because your thingy is on at noon." She rolled her eyes at a dark-skinned girl with black curly hair.

"I can't help it. It was Western Civ or you. Which would you do?"

Megan laughed. "I think there are videos on the TV station web site."

"But it's not the same as all of us watching it together." They looked at each other and laughed. "On our iPads."

"Then don't schedule a class at noon in the fall," Megan suggested.

"I already took care of that," the girl said, standing tall and looking proud of herself.

"Well, some of us are getting an apartment in the fall and we've been collecting your recipes on our phones so we can try them." She pointed at her smartphone in one hand.

"That's great," Megan said.

"And we're hoping we can entice a boy or two with them." The redhead in the back giggled.

"You were on TV with her once, weren't you?" The main girl asked, peering at Nate.

"I was."

"Are you two together?" she asked, her head moving from Nate back to Megan and then back to Nate. Megan motioned at him since the girl was looking at him again.

"Yes, we are," he said.

Megan's heart took a leap. They hadn't discussed it. She'd been afraid to bring it up. Wasn't the guy supposed to bring it up? She had wondered, not knowing what to do. But here a college student had taken care of it for her.

"You make the cutest couple," the black curly-haired girl said.

"You do," the main girl added. "I hope we can find a boy as cute as you. And you're obviously really smart. Cooking isn't that easy!" She turned back to Megan.

"Didn't you learn to cook at home?" Megan asked, surprised.

"Oh no," the girl said, the others shaking their heads, too. "My mom did everything for me. Jeannie"– she pointed at the girl with the black curly hair– "had to teach me how to do laundry. My mom didn't even show me how to do that."

"But my mom didn't teach me to cook either," Jeannie piped in. "She made me do laundry, but she always cooked."

"We better go," the main girl said, looking around. "We've probably taken up too much of your time. We'll keep watching! Thank you!"

The other girls echoed her thank you and off they went, giggling as if they had met a movie star.

They had, Megan thought, realizing they didn't recognize Nate.

"I had no idea you were so popular with the college set," Nate said, returning to his enchiladas.

Megan's food was cold, but she didn't care, she kept eating anyway. "I didn't either. I think at this point I've had almost every age group of person come up to me. Except for young kids and I doubt that will happen."

"I felt a little dissed," he admitted, a smile underneath his sarcastic sadness.

"I thought they were coming for you."

"I'm getting old," he admitted. "They have those young guys they look up to."

"I don't know any of their names," Megan admitted.

"Me neither."

"Jack Tepper," Megan said.

"No, Nicholas McLean."

"They would be like Frank Sinatras to this group," Megan said, running her hand around the restaurant that was filled with college-age kids.

"Do they know who Frank Sinatra was?" Nate asked.

"I'm not sure they identify with that time in history at all." She shrugged her shoulders.

"More the reason to make a television show about that time."

"As long as you're real," Megan laughed and Nate waved a hand at her.

They drove back to Megan's house after dinner, taking the Central Avenue route once again.

She didn't think twice about letting Nate inside the house, Sam was happy to have a visitor, dancing around as Nate played with him. Megan led the way and sat down on her couch, Nate following her, Sam following him once he had retrieved his tennis ball.

At first they didn't talk, Nate placed his hand on one of her feet after she pulled them up on the couch cushion.

"Do you have to shoot tomorrow?" Megan asked, feeling a bit shy.

"I have a day off," Nate said leaning forward. "Can you believe it."

"I can't! Surely you have something to do."

"Any suggestions?"

Megan saw the opening to change the subject. "So we're together?"

He laughed and reached for her hand. "I didn't think anything of it. It rolled off my tongue."

"So it was inferred?" Megan knew she was messing with him. "But the improvisational actor in you didn't miss a beat."

Nate looked at her and squeezed her hand. "I guess so. But I guess now is a good time to check and see if that's okay with you."

"Do I have much choice?"

"Are you worried about anything?"

"It's been easy so far," she admitted.

"You mean because everyone has left us alone."

She nodded.

"Except, of course, the girls who knew you and not me."

"It's going to happen."

"And we'll deal with it," Nate said. He shrugged his shoulders. "It was different when I started in television. It wasn't so in your face all the time like it is now. That's probably one of the reasons I like it here. People are respectful, not like in LA where they dig through my trash and steal my banana peels. Then I read the next day how I eat overripe bananas."

Megan cringed.

"But I'm happy. I'm happy spending time with you. You've brought something to my life that is so different than anything I've ever had. I appreciate that."

"I'm not a Starbucks barista," she protested.

Nate laughed and pulled her to him. "Let's not go there. That was a mistake on my part."

"Every time?"

"All three," he laughed. "I have another month of shooting and then I need to go back to LA." She felt the words and his heart as she rested her head on his chest. "We'll figure it all out. Let's just enjoy this next month and see what happens."

"We both have work," she reminded him, pulling herself back.

"You have a cookbook to write."

Megan rolled her eyes. "Don't remind me. It's probably what I should do tomorrow."

"That reminds me," he said, sitting forward and pulling his phone out of his pocket. "Maria texted me and asked if we were free for dinner tomorrow night."

Megan shrugged her shoulders. "With Barry, too?" He smiled and nodded.

"Why not?"

"I'll let her know," he said, setting to typing a message.

Saturday morning, while Megan lay in bed thinking about going for a walk before she went to work on the cookbook, her phone buzzed. She fully expected it to be Nate, who had planned to do his laundry.

"Please don't let my mother know I haven't done it in a month," he had told Megan the night before

"As long as you have enough underwear," Megan told him. Then, "Yeah, that's more than I want to know."

"I can afford new underwear if I need it," he said.

"I'm not one to talk," Megan admitted. "I probably have enough clothes to wear for a month and not do laundry. Not that I wear half of them anymore."

But it wasn't Nate, it was Maria.

"So excited for dinner!" she texted. "I haven't seen you in two weeks! See you tonight! Wear something sexy and cute!"

Oh no, Megan thought, jumping out of bed so quickly she almost kicked Sam, who was happy for the morning snooze. What am I going to wear?

She opened her closet and realized she had no idea where they were going.

"Where are we going to eat tonight?"

Instantly the phone rang. "I've done two loads of laundry already. What are you doing?" Nate asked.

"Is it a contest?" Megan asked.

"No."

"Then nothing. I just got out of bed."

"I thought sleeping in until eight was late and look at you."

"Where are we going tonight?"

"Somewhere historical."

"Did Jack Tepper own it?" Megan raised her eyebrows.

"We're not going to eat at the Twilight Sands again. We're going to do something real tonight."

"Where? You're starting to annoy me." Megan felt as if she were talking to someone she had known a long time, not a man she'd just met several months ago. And found herself coupling up with the night before.

"Los Poblanos."

"Ohhhh."

Los Poblanos sat several miles south of the house Nate was thinking about buying. The property was a former ranch and one-time first home of the local Creamland Dairy. It had been reinvented into an historical inn known for its weddings and restaurant. And growing large fields of lavender.

When Nate stopped to pick her up, seven dresses lay on the floor of Megan's bedroom. She scooped them into a pile and threw them on a chair. She had chosen a deep purple sleeveless dress and a pair of low heels. Not too dressy, not too casual. Just right for the gravel parking lot and upscale dinner they were about to have.

Barry and Maria were already in the La Sala Grande when Megan and Nate arrived into the old adobe building, built like a hacienda, with a courtyard and a running tiled-fountain in the middle.

"What is it?" Nate asked, looking at the sign with the arrow that said "La Sala Grande."

"It's a fancy word for lounge," Megan said, letting Nate open the heavy door for her.

Maria and Barry had arrived and were sitting under the window in the former living room of the main house. A bar was set up off to their left and a woman bartending smiled as they walked in.

Megan almost didn't recognize Maria without her hat. No sun at night, Megan reminded herself, sliding on the couch next to Barry, who was already sipping a martini.

"Did you need that?" Megan whispered, Barry looking like he needed to wind down.

"I spent the day with Maria. It started with tennis and then lunch at the country club. And culminated with what was supposed to be a short shopping trip for her to buy a new purse for tonight. But that turned into two hours in Nob Hill when she couldn't find what she wanted."

Megan patted his hand. "If it's any consolation, I worked on the cookbook."

Barry turned and smiled, looking relieved. "You know exactly what I needed to hear."

As Maria began to talk endlessly– Megan wasn't sure about what because she quickly tuned her out and found herself nodding her head occasionally– her thoughts shifted elsewhere.

How life had changed, she thought, remembering Christmas just seven months ago and how she had spent part of it alone– the morning– and then had dinner with Julie and her family. Mostly because Julie felt sorry for her that she had nowhere to go.

"I can let my kids climb all over you and show you all their gifts," Julie had volunteered. As they sat at the dinner table that night, Megan had wondered if she had made mistakes with all the relationships in her life. Maybe, she and Guy could have worked things out. Maybe she shouldn't have pushed Ryan out of her life. She was beginning to wonder if she'd spend the rest of her life alone.

But all that changed in January by a twist of fate only worthy of something Nate's writers could have created in their Hollywood office. A chef having a nervous breakdown. Janet calling Barry. Barry thinking about Megan's cookies. Maria moving back because the film industry was taking off in New Mexico. And here they were.

"I did finally find a bag," Maria was saying, pointing at the red sequined evening purse sitting next to her on the chair. "So it was a good day."

Barry's eyes looked glazed over, as if Maria might be too much energy for him. Megan wanted to shake him and tell him to hang on, that Maria was worth it.

You two truly love each other! She wanted to shout making sure both of them didn't forget it.

Several thousand followers on Instagram, people posting messages on the Facebook posts that Kevin usually did for her, and here she was. Barry negotiating a cookbook deal, Maria helping her pick clothes. And Nate. She was dating a movie star.

No, actor, she thought. He's an actor. Give his profession some credit.

That's just what he did. It was interesting, but far more interesting was the way he found Megan interesting. And the time they spent together.

As she sipped the lavender margarita she had ordered and looked around at the books and photos on the built-in shelves, she wondered about the history that the walls could tell. She wondered if the people who lived there had a happy ending. She wondered what happened to Nicholas and Eleanor McLean. And she wondered if she, too, would have a happy ending.

On the drive home, Nate took her by the house. "Is it okay?" he asked. It was just dusk and there would be another half hour of light. "I just want to sit in front of it."

Megan nodded and when they arrived, he parked the car in front of it and they sat silent.

"Do you believe everyone has a happy ending?" Megan finally asked.

"What?" Nate shook his head as if to loosen his thoughts that had taken hold. He turned to her to give his full attention.

"You act, you write, you tell stories. Do you always believe in happy endings?"

"Is that a loaded question?" he asked. She could tell he was teasing. "I couple up with you and now you're asking me about happy endings? And here we are sitting in front of this house I want to buy."

Megan laughed, embarrassed. "I'm sorry. I didn't mean it related to the house. I've been mulling it over in my head and sitting there at Los Poblanos tonight, a place filled with history, I began to think about the people who lived there. And I thought about Nicholas McLean. And I thought about myself." She felt silly adding the last line.

Nate took her hand in his. "My movies haven't always had happy endings. But it's where someone is at that day. If the movie of our story ended right now, it would be a happy ending."

Megan raised her eyebrows. "Are you saying if we continue on after tonight it will be a bad ending?" She was working in her usual sarcasm, but something told her it didn't quite get through this time.

Nate laughed and shook his head. "No no no. You missed the point. It's wherever we are in this moment, where the story ends."

Megan nodded.

It was dark and the house didn't have any lights on so Nate turned the car back around and turned onto Rio Grande and they drove back to Megan's house.

She let Sam outside and Nate followed her into the yard, molding himself into one of the two lounge chairs on the patio. When he had found a comfortable spot on the lime green cushions, Megan joined him.

"Um, who said you could join me?" he asked, adjusting himself to make room for her. "There is another one. I assume you have two in case two people are here and we are two people."

She giggled. "I don't think it's happened since I bought them," she said honestly, curling as close to Nate as she could. He played with her hair, running his hands through it and pretending to be separating it for no reason.

It was quiet as they listened for the sounds of the Saturday evening: voices at a gathering in the distance, the crickets.

"We film the last episode of the season next week," Nate finally said.

"Oh," Megan said, knowing it was coming soon, but not having wanted to bring it up.

"I have to go back to LA when we're done."

"I figured," Megan said, not sure if she should let him know that the idea made her feel a little sad.

"I'll be back in the fall, but I have to go back for the editing and everything else."

"You don't have to explain," Megan said, rubbing her hand lightly across his chest and the light blue button-down shirt that covered it. "Your life is in LA."

Nate pushed her back so he could look at her. "But you're part of my life now."

"I know."

She didn't know what to say so she said nothing. They were in a relationship, but they weren't joined at the hip. And she had the cookbook that she knew she had to get her act together and finish so Barry could do the photo shoot for it.

"I was thinking," he said, drifting off, as if he were waiting for Megan to respond, "that maybe you could drive back to LA with me?"

"Aren't you flying?" Megan asked.

"Not with all the stuff I have accumulated," he joked. "I'll have to rent a bigger car for sure."

She sat up. "Sure. If Barry will let me go."

"Because he might not want to let you out of his sight," Nate said. "And I don't blame him." He paused before he spoke again. "Spend a few days with me and then you can come back here."

"Take me for your favorite tacos?"

"And milkshakes."

"It's a deal," she said.

CHAPTER 16

The milkshake comment had given Megan an idea for her segment that week. Somewhere she had read about a date shake and with the popularity of making smoothies and other drinks in the blender, she thought it was time for something different. And something cold for summer.

As she sat in her office adding the date shake to the cookbook notes, she heard Barry talking to Julie outside Julie's office about a campaign they were working on. While she didn't tell anyone, part of her missed the excitement of creating the campaigns. But Megan knew if she mentioned it, everyone would laugh at her.

"You have the best job in the world," they would say. "Television and a cookbook. You're on your way to your own show. And who knows what else. We'll handle the campaigns!"

But maybe it also was the sadness that Nate would be leaving in a few days. She was leaving with him, but she looked at her calendar and realized that in nine days, he would be in LA and she would be in New Mexico. Even though they didn't see each other every day– it was impossible with the shooting schedule– she liked knowing he was just a few miles away and there was the possibility that they might see each other that evening.

But with him in Los Angeles, she had no idea when he might be back.

Focus, she told herself. You had a life long before he came along. And you can't mess up all that everyone has done for you.

She didn't want to cause drama. This wasn't the climax of a movie. She had to remind herself that it didn't end here. She just didn't know how it would end. And for the first time in a long time, it bothered her that she didn't know.

"Hey!" Barry said, popping in and sending Megan almost out of her chair.

"You must have been deep in thought about the cookbook?" he asked.

"Yes," Megan said. "Date shakes next week. And in the cookbook. You know they're big in Palm Springs."

He slipped into his usual chair. "Hey, I know this week is the last episode and Nate's going back to Hollywood."

After feeling like her life had been in constant motion, something always happening, even if it was Barry or Maria flying into her office with their hysterical energy, things had settled into a steady pace with Nate and life.

But now they were about to change.

He sat forward. "Enjoy your time with him and we'll get the cookbook finished when you get back."

Megan nodded. "That's the plan."

After he left, she opened the internet. She didn't want to work on the cookbook. Her segment for the show was ready. No one would pay attention to what she was doing. So she did a Google search.

On Nicholas McLean.

It took some doing to find him because it had been over fifty years since the Twilight Sands was built, but finally she found his obituary. She started to read it, seeing again that he had a wife named Eleanor, but then Megan stopped herself.

Maybe she didn't want to know how it ended. Maybe she didn't want to know anything about Nicholas McLean. Maybe it was enough that he had opened the Twilight Sands that one day would create an opportunity for Nate to come to Albuquerque and renovate it and turn it into a television show.

Maybe all she needed to know was that it was a happy ending that he opened it.

Megan closed the tab of the internet search and went back to the cookbook.

I've always been okay with where things are, she thought. Enjoy them. Don't worry about the future.

With that, she sent Nate a text. "How about dinner with me one night this week? Whatever night works for you?"

He texted back an hour later, "Of course! Thursday– we have the wrap party Friday when we're done."

Green chile cheeseburgers, Megan thought. And milkshakes. She would do better than anything he could find in Los Angeles. And fries. She chuckled to herself.

And with that she also was set for her segment that they would film on Friday because she would be gone the next week.

*****

While Megan's week was fairly quiet, Nate's was frantic as they wrapped filming for the show and packed up everything in the house where he was staying.

"I was never there so I never put anything away," he admitted. "I kept throwing it in piles."

On Saturday, Megan helped him put some organization to his mess and on Monday morning, he pulled up in front of her house with the car packed, ready to head west.

"It's a bad omen for the show if I leave anything here," Nate admitted before Megan could say anything as she handed him her two bags and he kissed her.

Once they were in the car, driving west to the I-40 and heading to Gallup, Nate continued, "I had a friend named Andy who shot a first season on location in Chicago. So he left all this stuff in storage in Chicago and returned to LA."

"And the show didn't get picked up for a second season?"

"Exactly," Nate said. "Lesson learned. Don't ever assume. It's better to take it back with me and bring it all back."

"When you move it into your new house?"

"Hopefully," he said, patting her hand.

They crossed the Rio Grande River and passed through the west side of the city, neighborhoods popping up and filling the land as far as it could go until it reached the eastern edge of a small portion of the Navajo Nation. And then it turned to scrub, dotted with horses and cattle wandering their land looking for something interesting to eat.

Megan watched the land, slowly turning to a climb into the Laguna-Acoma Pueblo area. The bright July sunshine wouldn't let any clouds into the sky and it felt as if the land went on as far as they could see.

They stopped in Gallup for lunch, getting off the freeway early and driving the city's entire portion of Route 66. "Maybe Nicholas McLean did this, too," Megan suggested.

"Or maybe Jack Tepper does in season two."

"Why?" She was teasing him but she still wanted to know.

"Perhaps he wants to scope out the competition."

"I'm sure that's not it," Megan said, pointing at a rundown and sad-looking motel on their left.

"But maybe it was at one time," Nate suggested. "Any suggestions of a place to eat?" he asked.

"Because I come to Gallup all the time?" Megan asked. She thought for a moment. "I do know Earl's is supposed to be good."

With a Google search, they arrived and made themselves at home in a turquoise corner booth with paper New Mexico map placemats.

"I should get a stack of these," Nate suggested, running his finger along the scalloped edge.

"So you don't have to ever to wipe down a placemat again?"

"You whip out a new one and they always look perfect."

A Native American artist walked by, selling a variety of beaded items. And then another one. And another one.

"I didn't know about that part," Megan whispered.

"Might be something we could add to the show," Nate said quietly, looking as if a lightbulb popped on in his head.

But then a Navajo man with a goatee walked by with a tray of turquoise rings. At first Megan said "no, thank you" and he went on his way, but Nate called him back, taking out one in particular.

The turquoise was more teal than blue, and the silver edges were scalloped, like the placemat.

"Or like a flower," Nate said.

Megan noticed it wasn't like the other ones in the tray which had rounded or squared edges. Nate reached for Megan's right hand and slipped it on her ring finger. "It's a perfect fit."

"Like the slipper?" she asked.

The man laughed and Nate handed him the cash to pay for the ring.

"Thank you," the man said. "Are you two traveling through?"

"She lives in Albuquerque, I live in Los Angeles," Nate told the man, their Navajo waitress placing the drinks on the table.

"Or something like that," Megan said. "He might buy a house in Albuquerque."

"Ah, he likes you that much?"

"I'm just secondary in this," Megan laughed. "The work comes first."

"That's not true," Nate said. "The work happened to be the reason I came to New Mexico."

"Have fun," the man said, doing a slight bow of his head. "Thank you."

After he left, Megan looked down in her lap at the ring and rubbed her left index finger across the stone and the silver around it. "Thank you," she said, the meaning starting to hit, that Nate had bought her something. And not just anything, something she could wear all the time.

He reached around her and pulled her close to him. "Don't think leaving is easy for me. I have to make a great show so I can come back."

Megan nodded. She knew without a second season of "Twilight Sands," Nate would have to move onto something else, probably somewhere else. And it wouldn't be that it couldn't work, it would just be…more of a challenge. A challenge Megan wasn't sure she was up to.

"It seems like a great show to me," she said, still admiring the ring. "But I live there. I find it interesting."

"And you don't watch television," he laughed. "I'm not sure you're a good TV critic."

"I like a good story," she pointed out.

On the way out of town, Nate kept driving on Route 66 and they came across several more rundown motels. He pulled into one – The Desert Inn– and they stood in the large parking lot looking up at the large sign where half the letters that should have said "single and double rate" were missing. The C in "Color TV" was gone, too.

"Did they fall out or run out?" Megan whispered, afraid someone might ask what they were doing.

"Probably they ran out of money to buy new ones," Nate suggested.

Megan watched him as he stared at the sign for a moment, lost in some sort of thought. Her mind drifted back in time like it had with the Twilight Sands, wondering about the history of the place, of what happened there, of all the happy people who had traveled through, and of the motel's demise.

Looking over at the motel itself, a few cars in the lot, a maid's cart in front of the open door of a room, she wondered who stayed there now. And to her right, a chain motel with a modern sign. Obviously fairly new.

Why would you stay somewhere rundown if you didn't have to? Megan thought, but also feeling sad that at some point this had been a happy place. She walked a little ways toward the motel itself, forgetting that she cared what anyone thought. And that's when she realized that at one time there had been a swimming pool right there. Smack in the middle of the parking lot.

It had been filled in with looked like loads of rocks, but then nothing on top, just a fence around it.

Nate joined her and let out a soft laugh. "This was a pool."

"And they let it die."

"It was probably too much work," he said shaking his head.

"I guess the good news is the previous owners left the Twilight Sands in better shape," Megan said, attempting to be hopeful.

"They did." Nate took her hand and they walked back to the car together, silent, each in their own thoughts. But Megan grateful for the strength that walked beside her.

"There is something about these old places," Nate said as he shook his head, looking out the window, merging the car onto I-40 west. "We save so few of them. I know it's a lot of work. We did the best we could with the Twilight Sands. But I guess people don't think it's always worth it."

"I guess not." Megan thought about the swimming families at the Desert Inn. About the hope people had. About how they were happy in that moment. And maybe when they left the Desert Inn– or the Twilight Sands– at least it was etched in their memories as a happy place.

That's when she began to think it might not always be worth going back to see something. Maybe it was better to remember it as it was. To remember her mom as who she was before the dementia set in and she believed that Megan was her sister Marie, the one who had died at eighteen in a car accident.

Or to remember the motel one had stayed in as a child for what it had been at one time, not to return to it and see the pool filled in with rocks.

Don't look back, she told herself, glancing at the rearview mirror on her right. There is no reason to go back. Here's where you are today, it's a place to be happy.

She looked ahead at the highway that felt endless in front of them, never having driven to California, but knowing they had to traverse the entire state of Arizona to get there.

"Is it easier to look ahead than look back?" she asked randomly.

Nate turned down the music on the satellite radio. "Hmmm. It's comfortable to look back and see where you've been. But there's an element of fear of looking ahead."

Megan glanced into the rearview mirror again.

She'd had no choice about looking ahead for seven months because Barry had quickly turned her life upside down. No one expected it to happen, not even Barry, but once the first domino fell, no one wanted to stop the others. Why would they?

And yet it hadn't seemed as hard as it was now. Part of her wondered if Barry was handing her the falling dominos and saying, "Now it's your turn to run with it."

That can't be it, she thought. He didn't know Nate would enter the picture. But one thing was leading to another: the segment, Maria coming back, Nate. It was all connected.

She looked over at Nate, lost in his own thoughts, Megan grateful they could have silence and not worry there wasn't a conversation going at all times. But she had her chance now to ask about some things. A captive audience.

She looked down at her ring and rubbed the stone as if it would give her energy. And support.

"You know," she said, feeling awkward, as if her body were being bent in directions like she did with her Barbies. Just because she could. "Have you ever been married?"

"You know the answer to that," Nate laughed, switching lanes as they got caught behind a grocery store semi. "You've read everything online about me."

"But I don't know what's true."

Nate looked at her briefly. "I haven't been married, but not for the reasons you read about. I haven't been married because I like having a million women. I haven't been married because nothing has felt right. I haven't felt something where I've thought, this is the person I want to sit on the front porch with when I'm eighty and rock the day away, reminiscing about the times we had together."

"What about the baristas?"

He shrugged his shoulders. "It was fun. If I couldn't find the right girl, sometimes I just wanted someone to hang out with. I had to let go of the press a long time ago. It doesn't matter what I say or do, they're going to print what they want and how they view me with a girl on a beach in Hawaii even if she just stopped to ask for an autograph."

Megan nodded and looked out the window.

"Hey, are you worried you might find out something you didn't know about?" he asked. "When we get to LA, that is."

"No," Megan said. "Not really." She thought for a moment. "I think what's harder with this is that everyone knows you so…"

"…everyone has an opinion."

She laughed. "Yes!" And then, "But it's really not been that way for me. Everyone is really supportive and so far it's been easy. But I wonder if at some point it will get hard."

"It will," Nate said. "And that's why Albuquerque is a better place to be than LA. It's more private. Unless, of course, the paparazzi discover how to get there."

"As long as Bugs Bunny goes the wrong way, I think we're good," Megan reminded him.

"That's true." He patted her hand. "We'll have a great life in Albuquerque together."

Megan's stomach jumped and she almost looked back, afraid to see it go bouncing down the interstate on its way back to New Mexico. She couldn't speak for a moment, processing what he just said. Happy at first. Then surprised. And then she wasn't sure what she thought.

"You've thought about that?" she asked.

"Of course. Haven't you?"

"But we haven't really talked about it."

"Do we have to talk about everything we've thought about?" He patted her leg. "I'm just asking. I'm not judging."

Megan thought for a moment. He had a point. She didn't want to tell him she'd been too afraid to think about it. But what did occur to her was how lucky she was that he'd thought about it. After all, he was the movie star, she was just the cooking girl.

Using the Yelp! app, they found what appeared to be a decent motel on Route 66 in Barstow, California, to stop for the night before the final stretch into Los Angeles. The motel was small and quiet.

"And it has a pool," Megan said.

"Perfect. We'll pretend it's the Barstow Twilight Sands."

As they traveled through the desert, watching the temperatures climb on the car thermometer after they passed Flagstaff and came down from the mountain heights, everything became sparser. And as the sun began to set, getting in their eyes, they also saw what looked like a layer of clouds in the middle of the scenery on either side of them.

"Must be the heat," Nate said, pointing at the car temperature that said it was 115 degrees outside.

It was slightly cooler in Barstow although still hot.

"Why is the pool so cold?" Megan asked, sticking her toe in the water, surprised by the coolness, not the bath water she expected.

Nate put down the towels and keys and instead of dipping his toes in as Megan did– and as she thought he would do– he dove into the deep end.

Megan stood on the side of the pool, by the steps in the shallow end, waiting for him to come up. "Agghhh!" he called, jumping up out of the water. "Come in! It's perfect!"

"No," she said, having no intention of getting that cold. "I'll let you be cold for both of us. How can a pool in the desert be this cold?" she asked, looking around for a hot tub, and knowing full well an old motel like the Gas Light Inn wouldn't have one. "I expected bathwater."

"This isn't bathwater," he said, touching her back with his hand as he climbed out, using the steps near where she stood.

"That's cold!" she cried, jumping.

"I know." Nate laughed and Megan rolled her eyes. "Now I need to stay out here and warm up before I go inside to our air conditioned room."

"Too bad we can't keep the door open," Megan said, quietly. "It's a little stinky in there."

"You wouldn't believe what the Twilight Sands smelled like when we bought it," Nate laughed.

Megan wrinkled her nose. "Really?" And then she thought better of it. "No, maybe I don't want to know."

CHAPTER 17

Megan woke up, at first forgetting where she was. She opened her eyes and saw a glimmer of light coming through under the heavy curtain at the window. She looked to her left and saw Nate sleeping next to her, burrowed under the blanket, his arms wrapped around the very flat pillow, his attempt at making it higher under his head.

She rolled over and lay on her back.

Barstow.

The room still smelled a bit, but she found herself somewhat used to it. She quietly pulled back the covers, working carefully not to disturb Nate (after all, she wasn't sure if he was like Sam whom she could kick during the night, on accident of course, and Sam wouldn't budge). It had been their first night together, she hoped there hadn't been any kicking on her part involved.

Megan pulled back the curtain slowly, not exposing any of herself and saw the light was coming from the overhead fluorescents– the lighted walkway. It wasn't any sort of complimentary light, not the kind you wanted to look into a mirror when you stand under those lights.

But beyond the lights she could see the first glimmer of daylight coming from the eastern part of Barstow. Megan pulled on her workout clothes and walked outside into what was already a hot morning.

She stood in the parking lot for a moment, deciding where to go, her phone in one hand– aware that Nate would wonder where she was– so she walked to the pool and found the gate hadn't been locked that night. Megan wandered in and lay on a lounge chair, watching the light come over the darkened pool, the light in the water having been turned off some time during the night.

It's a new life, she thought. It's all good. We're together. Don't think about next week when you go home.

Her cell phone buzzed.

"Where are you? Are you okay?"

"I'm at the pool."

Not three minutes later, Nate, wearing shorts, a t-shirt, and his flip flops, joined her, pulling up another lounge chair after kissing the top of her head.

"Good morning," he said. "I was hoping to roll over and see you next to me. I was a little afraid something had gone wrong last night I wasn't aware of."

As he lay down, she took his hand. "All is well. But the room is stinky."

"So all is not well," he reminded her.

"All is well with us."

Nate squeezed her hand. "It's warm out here."

"So why is the pool so cold?"

He shrugged his shoulders. "It's the desert. I don't always understand the desert. Besides, don't you live in the desert, too?"

"Should we go for a walk?"

"After I change my shoes," Nate said, sitting up again. "You aren't going to let me sleep in, are you?"

Megan laughed and sat up with him. "I'll go with you and stand outside the door."

"You can guard me from the paparazzi. I know they secretly all live in Barstow."

The sun was beginning to heat up the air even more, but they kept walking down Route 66, seeing old motel signs in the distance each time they thought about turning around.

"Sad how derelict everything looks," Megan said, thinking the motels looked nice from a distance, but seeing, as they got closer, all the chipped off paint and letters falling off the marquees on the signs, just like Gallup.

"And at one time it was so nice," Nate said, jamming his hands in his pockets as they stood and stared at the Barstow Motel. Megan walked up and peeked between the boards of the fence to the pool.

"The pool looks nice."

"Until you smell the stinky room," Nate teased her, taking her hand.

"Exactly," Megan said, pointing at a restaurant ahead. "Looks like an old Denny's."

"Good because I'm hungry."

"Don't you want to check the Yelp ratings or something?" Megan asked. "How do you know it's any good?"

He glanced at his watch. "It's 6:30 in the morning and the parking lot is half full. It's good. And if it's not, I'll stop and get you an exotic smoothie made with kale when we get closer to LA."

Megan laughed as he took her hand and led her across the street between cars.

Jenny's Grill Steaks & Mariscos wasn't as full inside as it appeared outside.

A tall, thin Hispanic woman with her hair wrapped in a bun on top of her head greeted them and led them to a red vinyl booth along the window, where Megan slid to the window, Nate sliding in next to her so they could sit together. Men eating breakfast before work– most of them by themselves– sipped their coffee and ate their eggs reading the newspaper as Megan and Nate read the menu.

After the salsa and chips and two mugs of coffee appeared, Nate leaned over and said in a lowered voice, "You could advocate for chips and salsa at breakfast. Start a new trend."

"No," Megan said, lowering her voice and leaning toward him. "It would be quicker if the paparazzi saw you eating it here. Then Jenny would have more business than she would know what to do with. And everyone would see it as acceptable to eat chips and salsa no matter the time of day."

Two plates of food were placed in front of them and they began to eat quietly.

"Delicious, but simple food," Megan sighed, sitting back after finishing her plate of chorizo and eggs.

"No pancakes here," Nate said, finishing off his huevos rancheros. "I'll have to find you some lunch though. My fridge is empty I'm sure."

"You don't remember?"

"I don't remember," he said, shaking his head.

It was empty when they arrived although Megan let him check that, not her. She was afraid of pizza boxes or mold from something else.

The house sat on top of a hill overlooking the valley. He pointed out Maria's old house– directly across the street– although one couldn't see much of either one. Maria's went down a slight hill, but Nate's was blocked by a gate.

"I didn't always have it," he admitted, using a remote on his keys to open it. "But after you catch that first woman looking into your kitchen window, you put one in."

Megan cringed and Nate drove gingerly through the gate and around a corner that opened to his driveway.

"Not much to see from the front," he said, turning the car off. "But you'll understand why I bought it when you see the view."

Inside, the house was as Nate had left it six weeks ago, the last time he'd been in Los Angeles, just for a quick trip to attend several meetings. A stack of laundry was stacked on the couch ready to be folded. He pointed at the laundry. "I did that because I was running out of underwear."

"Didn't that happen in Albuquerque? Why didn't you just buy more?"

"I did in Albuquerque," he admitted.

Megan didn't say a word, looking around and absorbing Nate's surroundings for the first time. They had been in her territory and finally she was in his. She wasn't surprised: everything was a little dark, "early nineties" he had admitted, when he was busy doing television. "I don't even have granite countertops," he had told her, acting embarrassed, prompting Megan to ask, "How do I know what's real if you're an actor?"

But she had come to realize she didn't see the acting side of him. To her, he was just Nate. He led her to the sliding glass doors that opened to a small backyard.

"No pool?" she asked.

"I have one in Mexico," he admitted.

She looked out and immediately spotted the Hollywood sign. "Oh," she said.

"That's it. I mean, I started making a little money, how else should I spend it? What more can you ask for than a view of the Hollywood sign. Isn't that why I came here?"

Megan nodded and looked around, houses all around him, trees, the Hollywood sign, a canyon below. This was Nate's life.

"Are you sure you really like Albuquerque?" she asked, feeling slightly mesmerized.

"When you experience the traffic, you'll wish you were back in Albuquerque," he reminded her. And he quickly changed the subject. "I really need to change the sheets on the bed."

Megan raised her eyebrows. "I might be afraid to ask about that."

Nate reached for her hand and squeezed it. "I've been gone for a while. It's nothing more than I think you deserve clean sheets."

"I'm sure your dirty sheets will be better than anything we stayed on last night."

Megan followed him to the linen closet in the hall. "Don't look," he said, holding the door just right so she couldn't see. "It's a mess."

"But you can afford someone to look after you," she protested, continuing down the hall after him.

"And she's been in Bolivia, visiting her adult children."

Nate's bedroom was sparse. As Megan looked around, reflecting on much of the way the rest of the house was, she thought about what a big life Nate had, how hard he worked. And yet his house felt so bare.

"What are you thinking?" he asked, swatting her hand away when she tried to help take a pillowcase off a pillow. "This isn't your job," he said.

"I'm thinking about how this house doesn't really look like you," she said, looking around again. There were a few framed vintage movie posters on the wall. "Your house is all solid colors, no stripes."

"No polka dots?"

"Yes. No variation."

Nate dropped the pillow in his hand and sat on the side of the bed. He patted the place next to him. Megan walked over to him and sat down. He took a deep breath before he looked at her.

He patted her knee. Megan had no idea what was coming, but she braced herself. She knew she had something wrong about his décor. Maybe that had been the last straw and he was ready to move on. She looked ahead of her at the closet doors.

"I love what I've done," he said. "All the acting. It's been fun."

Megan was perplexed. What could be such a big deal? She wondered.

He shook his head. She watched his gray eyes focused on the closet doors, too. It was as if they both saw something that wasn't there. "I've been lucky in so many ways. And I do believe that luck plays a part in it. But I don't want to be followed around all the time. That's not how it used to be. It's changed so much with social media. The paparazzi are like vultures now."

She stared at the closet doors, afraid to face him.

"I don't know that I want to continue to star in 'Twilight Sands,'" he said. Megan turned to him, ready to speak, but he squeezed her leg. "Let me finish." He paused. "I love writing, I love creating. I think when I look back on who I am, I always have been more about that than the acting itself. The acting has been a means to get here, but it's not the direction I want to continue to go."

She stayed quiet, still waiting for the point of it.

"And when I met you, I realized it could be different if I want it to be." He looked at Megan and she reached over to squeeze the top of his hand that he left on her thigh. "I don't have to be the movie star. I don't have to be *People's* Hottest Man of the Year or whatever it is." He shook his head.

Tears had already formed in Megan's eyes and now she started to laugh.

"I want to be creative, to explore life, to put out there what inspires me."

Megan had stopped laughing and gulped.

"And I want to do this with you."

"Is this all the stuff you didn't think you needed to say?" she asked, feeling a little nervous about throwing it out there.

"Yes," he laughed. "When we got here, I realized this isn't where I want to be. To some extent I'll always need to be here, but really what I want is what you and I had in Albuquerque over the last few months." He put his arms around her and pulled her close. Megan rested her head on his shoulder. "You inspired me with all your ideas. I know that probably sounds funny."

"I usually just inspire people to cook," she joked and they both laughed. "And eat."

She pulled away, tears welling up in her eyes again. Life kept changing on her. That in a sense scared her. This was good, she told herself, don't be scared. This is what it's supposed to be.

"But we have two really big things going," she reminded him. "Yours much bigger than mine."

He shook his head. "No, you're on your way to the top. Everyone can see it. Barry and Maria knew exactly what they were doing. It's a case of being in the right place at the right time."

"But won't that take away from us?" she protested, not sure what she wanted. Then remembering she never wanted the cooking thing. She'd been content with the way things had been. The thoughts were starting to spin around: without the cooking gig she doubted she ever would have met Nate. Not only were the thoughts spinning, but she couldn't tease them out anymore.

"No," he said, looking at her. "I've been where you are and I know enough of how to not let it happen."

"Maybe I don't want to go to the top," she admitted.

"Yes, you do," he told her. "You have an opportunity the majority of people will never have. Just get there and you can do whatever you want with it. I know they say there is no way but down from the top but, you can also disappear from the top if you choose. I don't think you should, but we can manage it. We'll make it happen."

Megan found herself crying. "I'm sorry," she said. "I don't know where this is coming from. It all happened so fast, it wasn't what I dreamed. I never dreamed. And now I have so much and I'm not sure what to do with it."

Nate pulled her to him and spoke into her hair. "Let's enjoy the ride. You aren't going to the top alone. That's what I did and it's not only a lonely trip, but it's lonely up there, too. I'm with you the whole way. At Christmas we'll figure out what's next. Let's get your cookbook out and 'Twilight Sands' premiered and then we can figure out what's next."

"Maybe in Mexico?" she asked, pulling away.

"I hope it's sold by then. But if you want Mexico, we'll do Mexico. I was more preferring New Mexico for Christmas. I heard something about paper bags filled with sand and candles on Christmas Eve."

Megan laughed. "Yes, luminarias."

Nate stood up from the bed, walking into what Megan guessed was the bathroom and returning with the box of tissues.

"Nate?" she asked after she blew her nose.

"Hmmm." He sat back down on the bed.

"How do I know you're not acting?"

And with that he began to tickle her and they both laughed. "There are no cameras," he finally said.

That evening they took a drive up to Malibu for a seafood dinner. "I feel like I'm watching some seventies movie," Megan admitted, leaning over the table in a whisper, looking around at the dark furniture and the large windows that faced the ocean, the tide lazily rolling in onto the sandy beach. "Do Jon and Ponch bring their dates here?"

Nate– who had been looking out the window– looked at her. "Like 'CHiPs'?" he asked.

She giggled.

"Wasn't one of them married?"

Megan shrugged her shoulders. "I'm sure Ponch wasn't."

"We might have to look that up," he said, glancing back out at the ocean, as if he saw something he wanted to focus on.

As they walked along the beach after dinner, Megan felt exhausted. She was relieved in many ways. She knew where she stood with Nate. But now they each had a road to travel before they would come back together.

*****

"How about going to a party tonight?" Nate asked, putting his phone on his chest as Megan yawned and stretched, looking around the next morning.

"Is that how you greet me in the morning?" she asked, turning up her nose at him. "'Not good morning, did you sleep well?' but 'Do you want to go to a party tonight?'" She curled up under his left arm, her cheek against his chest and resting in the quiet of the morning.

She felt his body shake as he laughed. "I guess it makes a better movie line."

Megan's eyes burst open and she sat up, mostly teasing. "That wasn't in a movie? Was it?"

He laughed and pulled her back to him. "No, I was kidding. But I might save it for something later."

"Like '*Twilight Sands*'?"

"Perhaps. So back to the party."

"Can't I have some coffee before you start asking me questions?"

Nate pulled back the covers and she watched him pad down the hall to the kitchen. Megan stayed in bed giggling, surprised he thought she was serious. After what sounded like a tornado in the kitchen, he returned with two cups of coffee. "I might recommend the deck though," he said, looking around at the darkened bedroom. "The view anytime is better than this."

Before Megan could start looking for something to wear, he handed her a bathrobe.

"I wasn't serious about the coffee," she said, watching Nate open the curtains and then the sliding glass doors.

"I wasn't serious about making it. It's instant."

Megan almost spit it out.

"Isn't it good enough for you?" Nate asked, raising his presidential White House mug for a toast.

"It's fine," she said. "But why all the racket in the kitchen? I would have thought you picked the beans off the tree and ground them."

"I couldn't find the coffee. Or a spoon."

"Or a mug?" she asked, looking at hers that was from Vermont.

"My mom sent that to me," Nate said, pretending to snap at her. "She was afraid Los Angeles would turn me into something weird and this was her way of helping me remember where I was from."

"Making you stare at a group of trees while you drank coffee?"

"Yep."

Megan looked out across the canyon that lay in directly in front of them and toward the city, the Hollywood sign to the left and life all around. It was quiet where they sat, but she knew Los Angeles was busy, a hubbub of energy.

"Back to the party."

"Can't I drink the whole mug?" Megan asked.

"No. Then you'll want another cup and it will go on all day. Do I need to tell you to stop acting?"

Megan burst out laughing. "Fine. We'll go to the party. I don't think I have a good dress though."

He clucked his tongue. "You're 'That Cooking Girl.' Hmmm. I might not want to be seen with you."

Megan gave him a snide smile. What he didn't know was that she had packed a dress, with Maria's advice. "You never know where you're going to go." She had suggested a white spaghetti strap dress with printed pink flowers on it. "Very much summer. Very LA."

On the way to Manhattan Beach that evening, where the party was to be held– this time they drove in Nate's SUV with the nondescript license plate. "Nothing to give yourself away?" Megan pointed out when she saw it in the garage.

"Heck no. I wasn't going to put something like 'Nate's Car' on it."

They were quiet as he entered the freeway.

"Kelly and I worked in TV a long time ago," he said, merging into traffic.

"Is he an actor?"

"Kelly Jones."

Megan laughed and shook her head. "You throw these names around like they aren't a big deal."

He shrugged his shoulders. "They're my friends."

"And any woman in this car…"

"Other than you who only laughs when I tell you anything like that."

She ignored him. "…would be fainting."

"And yet you don't seem to care."

Megan shrugged her shoulders this time. "Not really. It gives me a good laugh though."

"Obviously."

He pulled into an empty spot on the street that lined the ocean, houses keeping the water from their view as they climbed out of the car. "He bought this place a long time ago and his girlfriend Val moved into it about three years ago."

Nate took Megan's hand and led her to a gray beach house with white trim that stood three floors up, Nate explaining the bedrooms had been placed on the lower floors and living space above.

"Better view that way."

The sound of voices on a balcony drifted down as they walked up the stairs to the open door that led directly into the modern kitchen.

"Nate! My man!"

Megan thought it was Kelly although later she would tell Julie and Stephanie she wasn't quite sure.

"How could you not know?" Stephanie asked, rolling her eyes as if she were embarrassed.

"They don't look quite the same in person."

"I would probably faint."

"You would," Julie agreed.

"Is this Megan?" Kelly asked, turning to her and sticking out a strong hand. He was tan, wearing a long-sleeved striped shirt that was rolled up halfway on his forearms.

Megan took his hand, surprised at how firm he shook her hand.

"Obviously, you've been surfing a lot," Nate pointed out, noting Kelly's dark skin.

"And getting balder by the way," Kelly said running his hand across his bald head.

"Lucky for you, they seem to be casting for more bald men lately."

"Exactly." Kelly turned around. "Val is here somewhere. How long are you here?" He looked at Megan.

"She goes back to New Mexico on Monday."

"I have a cookbook to finish," Megan said, smiling.

"That's right. That cooking gig. And you? Are you staying?"

"For a while," Nate said. "I've got the editing room ahead of me."

"Text me if you need a snack. I'm not envious."

"But you will be on the final product."

"Way cool for you," Kelly said, folding his arms across his chest. "I'm happy for you. If I didn't want to keep up a lifestyle I'd attempt what you're doing. But I think you made the switch just in time."

"Seamless," Nate said.

Megan glanced around the room: modern and simple, very Los Angeles. She guessed a decorator did most of the work, knowing that Kelly did multiple films a year– only because Nate had told her, not that she really knew anything about his films. They stood next to the kitchen, the entire floor made up of one room, sweeping from one area to the next, the wood floors seamlessly running the entire expanse of the space.

And the living area that met the balcony at the deck– the ocean view right there. Megan looked past the people milling around between the open sliding glass doors and the balcony, coming in and out with drinks and plates of food, seeing the light of the late day sun bounce off the water.

"It's never a problem with people showing up, is it?" Nate joked with Kelly, looking at all the people in the room.

Kelly turned around and shook his head, resting his left hand on the corner of the kitchen counter. "You say you're going to have thirty and fifty show up." He took a look at the catered trays of pasta and salad on the counters. "Make sure you get something to eat. I have to go on a diet after this." He patted his already flat stomach. "I'm playing a pro cyclist in my new movie."

Nate laughed. "And growing some hair, too?"

"I hope not." Kelly ran his hand across his head. "Those plugs hurt when they take them out. I'd rather go bald. Or wear a hat."

Nate took Megan by the elbow and whispered, "And there you have the Hollywood I want to leave behind. He'll be making movies the rest of his life."

"Which will turn into TV appearances?"

"Probably. There's no 'Fantasy Island' for him now though."

"Hmmm. I would have pictured him more on 'Love Boat.'"

A woman in a red dress that left most everything out to be seen and a dark tan, practically came running up to Nate and threw her arms around him. At first Megan thought it was an old girlfriend the way she acted like she hadn't seen him in years. Her breasts and high heels pushed her body forward and she looked like she was going to fall down.

"Hi Nate! How are you?" She gave him a kiss on the cheek that left a slight smear of red lipstick on his cheek.

Nate looked uncomfortable, Megan's only solace as she watched the scene play out.

"Hi Val," he said, holding his hand out to show off Megan. "This is my girlfriend Megan."

"Hi," Megan said.

"Hi," Val said, clearly not interested in her– or probably any other man in the room.

After a few minutes of light conversation– clearly all Megan thought Val was capable of– he finally untangled himself from her arms. "We're going to check out the balcony," he said. "I hear it's quite a view."

"As if you've never seen it before," Val said, rolling her eyes and looking slightly disappointed.

"What the…," Megan whispered as they walked through the doorway to the outside.

"Don't ask. I think he found her working at the mall or something like that. Some store like Forever 21. More talent goes into working at Starbucks."

Megan raised her eyes as they stood by the glass railing, taking in the water, the sun, the beach, and the few people left on it in the late day. "Is she even capable of that?"

"About all she can do is post selfies on her Instagram account."

Megan leaned onto Nate and laughed.

Later, they ended up separated as Nate discussed "Twilight Sands" and Megan went searching for another bottle of water. As she walked in the door, Val– and what appeared to be her entourage– looked like they were lying in wait for the moment to pounce on Megan.

"So how did you snag him?" a blonde with just as much make up as Val asked.

Megan laughed. "I'm sorry." She shook her head, trying to grasp who these girls were.

"He's been single forever," Val said, her eyes traveling from one end of Megan to the other. "And you're pretty, but you're not drop-dead gorgeous."

Megan almost burst out laughing. She wasn't sure if she was back in high school or watching a high school movie. "Um, okay," she told them. "I didn't snag him. We snagged each other. I'm sure in time you'll find that out. And I did it by being myself." She took the opportunity to look Val up and down. "Not something I'm really not."

"Well…," Val started to say.

"Excuse me," Megan said, using the manners her mother had taught her years ago, and she backed out of the little circle and into the kitchen area where she spotted a metal bucket filled with ice and drinks.

She smiled at the girls, walking back outside to Nate who instantly wrapped his arm around her waist. When someone pulled one of the men– was it Chris? Megan tried to remember– away from the conversation, Nate asked, "Are you ready to go?"

Megan smiled and when they were back in the car, driving back toward his house, she knew she had been lucky that she'd been quick enough to make remarks. But her feelings were slightly hurt at the comments.

"I'm not as pretty as those girls," she said, looking out the window, as if to no one in particular, but really to Nate.

"What?" Nate asked, lost in his own thoughts. "Did you say what I think you said?"

She looked at him. "I think so."

"And you believe that?"

"When someone tells me it."

They were quiet as Nate merged on the freeway. "What did Val say to you? Was it about me?"

"I'm sure you can figure it out."

Megan didn't want to repeat it. As she watched the darkening evening sky and the Los Angeles traffic, she realized it was the first time anyone had said anything to her so painful since she had started the cooking segment. If there was negative feedback, no one told her. But this was Los Angeles, she knew, where everything was cutthroat and Megan told herself she needed to get used to it.

She felt Nate's hand on hers. "I can't reach over and hug you," he said, squeezing her hand. "And I can't make the sting of what she said go away. But remember she has no future ahead of her."

Megan nodded. Part of her wished she were back in the comfort of Albuquerque. She began to wonder if this was what she wanted, to be scrutinized like that. Maybe it was better to keep it local. She knew in the back of her mind that Barry would never let it fly though. She longed to be curling up in bed, the familiarity of Sam next to her and sleeping. She knew she'd feel better in the morning of New Mexico sunshine, that Los Angeles all would be a distant memory.

Tomorrow, she told herself, you're going home tomorrow.

She squeezed Nate's hand back, but she wasn't feeling it. How long would it be before he got bored with her. It was hard not to compare herself to what she saw on the internet. Everything was so jumbled.

Back at the house, she went immediately outside to the view, the lights of the city sparkling in front of her. Nate brought her a glass of water.

"I know this got you," he said. "Please don't let it. It's not worth it."

"I'm not sure I can do this," she said honestly, clutching the glass filled with ice and water in both hands. "Albuquerque is like a comfortable blanket. Los Angeles is like a dragon that wants to chew you up and spit you out."

"It's true," he said, "but you don't have to be here. You know I'm not interested in building a life with you here."

Megan looked at him, his face partly shadowed from the light that only came from inside the house. "But how do I know you'll always want me?"

"Isn't that the journey of faith this is all about?"

"It's why I never dreamed," she said, shaking her head.

CHAPTER 18

As the plane began its descent into Albuquerque, Megan looked out the window and watched her return to the desert. Just over an hour ago, the same plane had taken off, rounding itself at the Pacific Ocean where Megan could see Malibu to the north and the Santa Monica Pier below.

She wondered what Nate was doing, knowing full well he was probably already editing the television show.

"There won't be any rest for a while," he had joked, looking into his empty refrigerator. "I'll need to get groceries ordered because I'm not sure when I'll be able to get my head back above water."

Megan knew her life would be much the same way. They'd had so much fun, fun for which she was grateful, but there was a cookbook to do.

Barry met her outside, a wall of heat hitting Megan as the automatic doors opened and she pulled her rolling bag behind her. He was standing by his car when she walked up.

"Why don't you get in trouble for that?" Megan asked. "I would get in trouble. You've probably been there for ten minutes."

Barry laughed. "I have."

He loaded up the bag and zipped through traffic on the I-25 freeway, past downtown, onto the I-40 freeway, and into Megan's neighborhood, via Rio Grande Boulevard, patting her shoulder. "I know you're in a tough spot," he said. "You both have a lot on your plates."

"Is there anything you don't know?" Megan asked, looking away from the mountains and at Barry, who was focused on the road. She felt a need to be funny. She didn't want to be serious. That had been tough enough recently.

Barry laughed. "Not really. Maria is helpful to have around."

"I bet."

"Listen." He pulled in her driveway and left the key in the ignition for the moment. "You'll get through this."

Megan interrupted him. "I know. I know. Cookbook. Lifestyle. We have a lot to do."

"Hey," Barry said, a sternness to his voice. "I'm not taking you away from him. You two have very busy times ahead of you and we're all going to help weather this storm.

This cookbook is your next step and the show is his. I believe it'll all work out in the end. The two roads will come back together."

Megan nodded, not wanting to talk about it anymore. She was glad to be alone for a while, Sam happily greeting her when she walked inside the door, Stephanie and her husband having taken care of him while Megan was gone. She left her bags by the front door and walked to the couch where she flopped onto it, Sam jumping up on the couch next to her. He put his head in her lap and she ran her hand across the side of his face.

"Ugh," she said, talking to Sam, who was soon snoring. "Talk about complicated. I had no idea how much I was falling in love. I just enjoyed my time with Nate. I thought that's what you're supposed to do. But now I'm in deep and we're in different places." She was quiet for a moment, shutting her eyes. "And I'm not sure if we can make it work. So many unknowns. How do two people manage two successful careers?"

Megan knew it would have been easier if That Cooking Girl hadn't taken off, but she also knew– deep in her heart– that there would be no Nate without That Cooking Girl. He had become part of her energy.

She hadn't been there more than ten minutes when the doorbell rang. Having no idea who it might be, Megan glanced out the window to see Mrs. Rosales standing there– with something in her arms. Aprons, of course.

Megan opened the door and invited her in. "I wasn't spying," she said, holding her hand up. "I happened to be driving by and I saw you getting dropped off. I'm glad you're home safe." She clucked her tongue. "Los Angeles is a dangerous place," she said quietly. And then she looked around, "Where is the movie star?"

"He's in Los Angeles," Megan said, thinking she was going to burst into tears again.

"When is he coming back?"

Megan shrugged her shoulders. "In the fall. He has to edit the TV show he was here filming."

"Oh." Mrs. Rosales looked sad, too. "I'm sorry. You already miss him."

Mrs. Rosales thought for a moment. Megan wished Mrs. Rosales could take her sadness away. Someone, she thought, say something that will make me feel better. "Oh," she said. "Well, you two will be together again. God willing. Be hopeful. God willing."

Megan felt as if she were listening to a mixed message.

"Can someone explain God willing to me?" she would ask Stephanie and Julie in the office on Monday at which time Stephanie would burst out laughing. "If I understood it, I might be a churchgoer."

But right now Mrs. Rosales quickly changed the subject and stood up, unrolling the bottom apron. "I made this for Nate. Do you think he'll like it?" The apron was filled with small retro barbecue scenes: hot dogs, hamburgers, ketchup, mustard, a grill. "All men like to be grill men, I know."

Megan laughed and ran her hand lightly across it. "Yes, he will."

Mrs. Rosales folded it back up and handed it to Megan. "And I made you a matching one." She smiled as she unfolded one that had a ruffle at the bottom. And red ribbon to tie it rather than the white canvas.

Megan laughed and smiled, being reminded that she and Nate had been a team.

"You could wear them on television," Mrs. Rosales suggested.

"So Jean will see them, right?"

Mrs. Rosales turned her eyes upward and looked like she was going to start humming.

Megan laughed again. "You don't need to admit it. It's okay."

"I need to get home to Martino," she said. "He thinks dinner is at three in the afternoon." She rolled her eyes. "My kids said I turned him into a monster. But he's the only man in my life now." She started to walk away, Megan following her bun. Then Mrs. Rosales turned back. "Have faith. That's all we have in life. And I do know that everything works out."

Megan nodded as Mrs. Rosales turned back again to cross the street and walk around the corner.

Have faith, she thought. She held the aprons in her arms, clutching them like a pillow.

CHAPTER 19

The next day, she and Barry sat down and created a set of deadlines, both to keep Megan busy, but also to ensure the book would be ready before the holidays.

"It's not a holiday book though." Megan kept pleading with him, thinking spring would make a better release.

Barry waved her off though. "Let us handle that. Entertaining advice is good any time," he reminded her. "Besides, if we're out before the holidays, that gives us plenty of time to bump it up in the spring."

Megan slithered back in the chair in the conference room and nodded. She didn't agree, but Barry had made it clear he knew what he was doing.

"Two weeks for the first shoots. If we divide them up five at a time, that's manageable for cooking."

"And for the stylist to be ready," Maria said, waltzing into the room and looking for a place to put her hat.

She kissed Barry on the top of the head and then walked over to Megan and gave her a hug from behind. "Oh, I know how hard this is. He didn't have any idea how attached he would become to you either. Remember that. Soon. You'll be together soon."

Megan shook her head, as if to shake the thoughts out of it. If she left them in the conference room, they were less likely to bother her.

Quickly, her days were filled with prepping for the cookbook. All the text that needed to be written. Not just the recipes but introductions and stories to go along with them, too. Each night she thought she could work after she ate dinner, but found she could barely make it to bed.

However, one Sunday afternoon, about a week later, she looked up and knew she had reached a saturation point.

"How about a walk?" she asked Sam, who bounced up quickly off his four legs and wiggled his body around, his tail hitting everything in sight, knocking over a stack of magazines on the coffee table. "Okay, okay," Megan said, glad to see the exuberance over something as simple as a walk. "I hope I'm that excited when we get outside."

They didn't get far– turning the corner and walking into the park so Sam could sniff the grass. Megan looked up to see Mrs. Rosales once again flying out of her house, waving one arm to get Megan's attention.

Megan waved back and tugged on Sam to walk over there. "I just wanted to say hi," Mrs. Rosales said. "I lit a candle for you and the movie star at church this morning."

"Thank you," Megan said, appreciating the faith that the older woman held so close to her. "I know Roberto would have suggested I do the same. He loved to see happy couples. You should come over for a minute. You know the first crop of chile is in and I picked mine up yesterday. I've been putting it in baggies in the freezer. Let me give you some."

You don't turn green chile down, Megan thought, not wanting to say that she would buy the frozen plastic tubs of it. It wasn't sacrilege to buy it that way, but it definitely wasn't the traditional way of suffering in front of your grill while you roasted it and then peeled off the skin over the kitchen sink.

"Roberto always did the roasting," she said as she opened the front door, Martino barking.

"Are you sure it's okay?" Megan asked, Sam looking tentatively at the little dog and wondering if he would eat Sam.

"Oh yes. His bark is bigger than his bite. Oh Martino, knock it off." She clapped her hands and waved Sam into the house.

Before the conversation could continue, the two dogs sniffed each other, spending what seemed like several minutes chasing each other's back sides.

"They're fine," Mrs. Rosales said, clearly bored of watching the situation, waving them off, and walking through her living room to the kitchen.

"It's okay," Megan whispered to Sam, who still wasn't so sure and kept to Megan's side. She kept him on leash and Martino lost interest, disappearing to his bed in the corner of the family room while Sam stayed with Megan.

"Here you go," Mrs. Rosales said, opening her freezer and pulling out two clear plastic bags filled with frozen green chile. "And if you need more, just let me know." She sighed and left her hand gripping the freezer door for the moment, shaking her head. "I do miss Roberto. We had such fun together. Each day was a blessing. Even when life was dark, it was nice to know at night he was there next to me."

Megan swallowed hard, finding comfort in petting Sam, who was panting slightly still.

Just then, Mrs. Rosales turned around. "Oh! I have something to show you. Come, follow me." She again waved her hand and led Megan down the hall to one of the bedrooms.

The house was clean, but Megan could see it had been some time since it had been painted and the carpet had been replaced, leaving Megan wondering why Mrs. Rosales's children didn't help out more.

Inside the bedroom a bed sat in the middle of the room and several pieces of furniture: a dresser and a desk.

"This was my daughter's room. After she moved out, I made her take all her things yet she refused to take the furniture. But you never know when you might have a house guest," Mrs. Rosales laughed, sliding one of the closet doors to reveal a full length of clothes. She began to go sift through the clothes, obviously looking for something specific.

"Ah," she said pulling out a deep purple dress– plum– with a full skirt and sleeveless top. "Here it is." She held it out and admired it as if it were a diamond ring. "When I watch you on television, I see your style and it reminds me of how we dressed in the early sixties. Roberto and I were so poor, we hardly had anything. But somehow I scraped the money– with his help– for this dress so he could take me dancing. I remember when I saw it in a shop window downtown. I knew I wanted it. I didn't care that I wore the same dress every week. I loved being spun around in it."

She sighed, entranced in the memory. Then Mrs. Rosales looked at Megan. "It looks about your size. I bet you could wear it."

Megan laughed. "Where would I wear it?"

It was Mrs. Rosales's turn to laugh. "You remember that baseball movie– the one about the field?" she asked, waving her hand as if that would hurry the thought along.

"'Field of Dreams'– that one?"

"Yes! You have the dress ready, the opportunity will come." She held out the dress to Megan. "Try it on. Let's see how it fits."

She sent Megan down the hall to the bathroom, painted baby blue from the late sixties, Megan guessed, right down to the baby blue toilet. She pulled off her shorts and tank top and wriggled into the full skirt, laughing when she realized Mrs. Rosales's chest was bigger than hers. It wasn't a perfect fit, but with a nip here and there, Megan knew it would work.

Mrs. Rosales was pacing outside the bathroom, in the hall, when Megan made her grand entrance.

"Oh my goodness," she exclaimed. "It's the perfect color for you. Who knew a blonde could wear something that I thought was perfect for my dark skin and hair."

"It is," Megan said. "But where would I wear it?"

"Don't worry about that!" Mrs. Rosales called, nearly running down the hall. She returned with a pin cushion. "I'll fix this right up."

By the time Megan left Mrs. Rosales's house, with Sam and her two bags of thawing green chile, she felt a new sense of faith.

The opportunity will come, she thought.

But that night, as darkness set on Albuquerque, the days getting shorter as fall loomed near– and the start of the school year– a rite of passage for fall– Megan felt the sadness creep in.

That's when her phone rang, nearly sending her flying off the couch, Sam almost falling off the couch when she jumped.

Nate.

"Hi!" he called, wind blowing wherever he was. "I hope you can hear me okay. I'm standing on the beach and called to tell you how much I miss you."

Megan thought she was going to cry. The sound of his voice– even in the wind– and the very fact that he thought of her.

"Shouldn't you be editing?" she asked.

"I'm edited out. I had to do something else so I drove to the beach for a walk. Are you cookbooked out yet?"

Megan laughed. "How did you know?"

"When there's no distractions, it's easy to work. And crash."

She didn't say anything, just wanting to be in that moment, not wanting him to go anywhere, but at least be where she could hear him.

"Are you there? Did I lose you? Cell coverage isn't always so great on the coast."

"I'm here," Megan assured him.

"Tell me what's going on." She could tell he was walking on the beach. "How's Maria? Barry?"

"I've been drowning in the cookbook," she reminded him. "I haven't seen much of anyone. Except maybe Mrs. Rosales, whom I seem to run into all the time."

"Or she runs into you."

"That's a good assumption," Megan laughed.

"Agh. I have another call. Looks like I need to get back to the editing."

"Okay," Megan said, trying to sound hopeful.

And with that, he was gone. She slumped back on the couch, telling herself she could do it.

But how can *we* do it? She wondered.

As Megan brushed her teeth, she thought of couples who had two big careers. Actors and actresses or people whose careers were completely different than each other. She felt as if she were leafing through a card catalog of names, looking at who was most like them.

Still, she kept coming back to Nicholas and Eleanor McLean. There was something about them even though she knew nothing about them. Hotel owner and doctor. Did that work? When did one ever hear of someone owning a hotel and his wife a doctor. Of course, maybe that was handy if a guest became sick.

Megan's head swirled. She grabbed her tablet and climbed into bed, Sam jumping up to the other side.

"Good night, Sam," she told him with a pat of the head, and started a Google search.

Except that there was nothing to find. It's like hotel owners are elusive people, Megan thought, closing the tablet's protective cover and giving up. She turned out the light, thankful to be sleepy.

CHAPTER 20

"I think we have enough to do the first round of photography," Megan said, looking straight at Barry. "I have no idea how we're going to do this though."

Barry pulled out his phone and held it up. "That's why we have Zeke." Megan nodded. "And Emily the food stylist."

"Food stylist? Isn't my food good enough the way it is?" Megan asked, feeling slightly insulted.

Barry laughed. "She'll put it together with the dishes and everything else. That way you can focus on making it."

They had finally decided on thirty recipes and Megan had written some of the excerpts that would go with them. She didn't tell anyone– she didn't want to sound ungrateful– but she was a little burned out. Her life was a little too much about cooking. And she'd been doing a segment weekly since the year started. She was afraid to ask when she might get a break.

After everyone started to leave the room, Barry asked her to stay.

"Now what? I'm going to write the memoir of my life? Or maybe some fiction about my life with the movie star?"

Barry laughed and played with the pen in his hand. "No, we're working on a cable show for you. I know this must seem a little draining right now. Once the cookbook is out, you'll be moving into television. I mean, your own show on television. And at that point…," he sat back and she could tell he had something he was afraid to say. He took a deep breath, looking away from Megan. "You won't be working here anymore."

"What? Why not?" She realized after she said it that it sounded stupid. After all, what was she contributing at this point anyway? It was more that she couldn't imagine life without her office. And everyone. What would she do all day? How would she make a living?

He took another deep breath. "Look, by the end of the year, you'll be making more money without the salary I'm paying you," he explained, his face looking a little pained as he said it. "I don't want to lose you, but I know that at some point I need to let my chickadee fly away."

Megan felt some tears herself. She couldn't say it, but it felt like too much. Barry's office had been her life for so long. He was right, she needed to fly.

I didn't want this, she wanted to tell him. Can't I give it up and go back to the way things were? I can jump onto the mayoral campaign today.

But she knew they'd gone too far. Everyone had invested too much. It was time to move on.

"You'll stay until the end of the year. By then the book will be rolling and you'll be ready to shoot in January for the show."

"I understand," Megan said, quietly, getting up and going to her office where she did something she hardly did in all the years of working there: she shut the door, sitting down at her desk and crying as she looked around her.

It was early August and in four months she would be on her own. There was no string attached to anything: there would be no job to go to daily, no daily office relationships. She took a deep breath and did something she had been putting off, dialing the landline her dad still kept. "Just in case," he always said.

"Hello!" he called into the phone, the sound of the lawn mower coming to a stop in the background. He always kept the cordless phone on the patio in case a call came in.

"Hi Dad," Megan said, wishing she were with her parents, wishing she could crawl into the space of her past life in Denver. Looking back nothing seemed hard, it felt comfortable.

"Hi there! How's my favorite Megan?" he asked.

"You sound good. Mom must be doing okay."

He laughed. "She was in good spirits this morning. She didn't call me names or throw anything at me. Yesterday I had a doctor's appointment after I visited her and I had to go with spaghetti all over my shirt."

Megan wasn't sure if she should laugh or cry at the thought. If her mom hadn't been sick, it would have been funny. Megan knew well her mom would be embarrassed to know how she was acting.

She had so much to share and suddenly, once she got on the phone, the need was gone. She knew her dad would be happy for her. There was no doubt. He wouldn't care who Nate was as long as he was nice to Megan. But her mom. It wasn't the same without her mom with whom to share all that was happening in Megan's life.

What Megan really wanted to ask her dad was what his dream had been: had everything always included her mother? Did he have dreams for them when they were kids, about how their lives would be? And his dream for his life with her mother.

But as he talked about his beloved St. Louis Cardinals baseball team– when the Colorado Rockies were introduced he tried to follow them, but he couldn't tear himself away from his Cardinals– and how they were doing, she realized it wasn't the right time. Or maybe it was, but she didn't want to hurt him any more than she knew he was already hurting.

After the call ended, Megan tried to turn her attention back to the cookbook. The next month promised to be busier than any month before and somehow she had to be focused. A part of her wondered if she should start going to church. Then she chuckled and went back to what she was doing.

Her phone rang

"Hey!" Nate.

"Hi," Megan said.

"How are you? I'm barely awake. I probably shouldn't drive anywhere, but I'm hoping the coffee kicks in soon."

"Sounds like it already has," Megan laughed, knowing he was in the car driving to the studio.

"They've given us a premiere date," he said.

"Really?!"

"Yes– October 16."

"You must be relieved."

"Yes. And…drum roll, please!"

There was a silent pause.

"You were supposed to drum roll," he reminded her.

"I was waiting for you," Megan said.

"We're beyond the drum roll. We're going to have a big party in Albuquerque."

"Oh?"

"Do you want to guess where?" he asked.

Megan thought for a moment. "At the Twilight Sands?"

"Good guess. We have plans around that, but it's something more media centric. I meant the crew party."

"I don't know." Megan was trying to think why he was making such a big deal out of it.

"At my new house!"

She almost popped out of her chair. "You're buying the house??? Why didn't you tell me?" she lowered her voice, realizing the whole office probably heard what she just said.

"I am," he laughed. "I close at the end of August."

"Why didn't you tell me?" Megan asked again, feeling relieved that it meant Nate truly had plans to stay in Albuquerque.

"I wanted to make sure all the I's were crossed and T's dotted, er, you know what I mean, before I told you. But that's not all…"

"What could be bigger than that?" Megan asked, thinking.

"We're going to have the party there and I'd like you to do the cooking." Megan opened her mouth to speak and he got to it before she did. "Look, I know it's a lot of work and I know catering isn't your thing, it's the recipes, but I think we can find a way, find a few people to help, and then you and I are hosting the party together."

"Are you serious?"

"Would I not be?" She could tell he went through the gate, saying good morning to the security guard.

"How many people?"

"Probably about forty. No more than fifty."

"Okay."

"Pizza."

"Why are you one step ahead of me when you're an hour behind me?" Megan wondered.

"Because I've had several days to think about this. I need to go, but, Megan?"

"Yes?" She thought her brain was going to explode between the cookbook and now this big event.

For every door that closes a new one opens, she pictured Julie telling her when she would give her the news later.

And these are big double doors, Megan though.

"I love you."

Her heard skipped a beat. "I love you, too," she said, feeling as if the words didn't quite come together as they tumbled off her tongue and out of her mouth, as if it were a foreign language. Words she hadn't spoken too many times before in her life.

CHAPTER 21

"Life has a funny way of working out," Julie said one afternoon in the office, the cookbook nearly together thanks to Julie's layout work. "You never know what's going to come next."

"I'm starting to think that's a good thing," Megan admitted, her tablet in her hand with all the plans for the party.

With a break from the cookbook, she focused on the premiere party. Nate gave her free rein outside of asking for pizza and cookies.

Now there was the little detail of the house to deal with. Nate flew in for Labor Day weekend, closing on the house via overnighted paperwork, and arrived in time to pick up the key from his realtor Isabella before she went on vacation.

"Um, aren't you moving in?" Megan asked when she picked up Nate from the airport and he only had a carry-on roller bag. She looked at the back of her SUV and decided not to open it, pointing to the middle seat. "I hate for it to roll around and get lost."

"The house needs to be gutted. You know that. Besides, that's why I have your help."

"Aren't you going to stay there?"

She was starting to realized there was much they didn't talk about. Details, important, logistical details.

"I'm staying with you," he said, squeezing her hand.

"Oh, you don't want some big fancy hotel suite that's the size of my house?"

"When I can be with you?"

"And Sam."

"And Sam."

They stood under the covering of the lower level of the airport, a security guard watching them.

"I guess we should go," she said.

"Let's go to the house first."

With a trip to meet Isabella and pick up the key, they were on their way.

"I think you just made the day of every woman in that office," Megan giggled, watching the reactions of the sixty-some aged realtors who all at some point made a point to walk closely to Nate.

"I think Isabella told them all I was coming so they could be all there," he said.

"We should have brought coffee and donuts and done a meet and greet."

Megan drove her car north on Rio Grande and turned right onto the gravel driveway that led to the house. "So how many houses do you own?" she asked teasingly.

"This is the third, but I still think I'm going to sell the place in Mexico." He looked around, taking in everything he could about the land and house that was now his.

As Megan parked the car under the carport, she didn't want to ask. Now wasn't the time. Instead, she knew she should let Nate soak in all that was now his.

As he opened the passenger-side door of the SUV, he smiled, jingling the keys in his right hand. "Let's go take a look," he said.

Megan smiled and followed him, happy for him. It was all she felt– happiness for him and what was now his. And that in some way she was part of it.

"Should I carry you over the threshold?" he asked, his gray eyes sparkling, turning the key in the lock.

"I didn't know we got married? Does your buying a house mean you got married? So this is your third marriage?"

"I didn't have anyone in my life either time before," Nate said. He held the door open and motioned for Megan to walk in.

"Where do we start?" she asked, thinking back to their previous visit.

"I don't know." He laughed, his hand on his chest, looking around in awe. "Maybe we need a notepad and a list."

"Are you going to furnish it before the party?"

"I doubt it. Maybe that's where we should start. Figuring out how to make it party ready."

Megan walked over to the blue built-in couch in what she assumed was the living room.

"Let's go outside," he suggested, seeing the lone table with the umbrella and four chairs were still there. "They left me some furniture," he joked, slipping through the open sliding glass door.

Megan pulled out her tablet and set it on the table.

"Do you always carry that?" Nate asked, pulling his chair closer to the table and watching the pool cleaner run next to the stairs.

"I didn't used to but this cookbook thing…" she drifted off, shaking her head. "It's just been easier to get things done this way." She opened the file she had created for the party and sat back, pulling her hair up into a ponytail, then dropping it and looking for a hair tie in her bag to keep it pulled back. "So I'm wondering what you had in mind?" she tapped her finger to her lips.

Nate leaned more forward, Megan able to see every freckle and what looked like two small scars, on his face. "Like I said before, pizza and carob cookies."

Megan stared him down, a faint smile, the kind that was made up of just one's lips. Her mouth was a straight line with just enough upturn that it was obviously a smile. Then she burst out laughing. "And how do you expect me to make pizza for forty people? We have to do that then and there."

She had visions of herself running back and forth to the oven– taking one out, putting one in. The cookies could be done– that was easy. "This goes against everything about entertaining that I teach. And we're not having a party where everyone gets to make their own toppings."

"Don't you like disorganized people messes?"

"You've seen my house. You know how I live."

"And you've seen mine."

"And I know you're the total usual guy with only a pizza box in the fridge."

"An empty one, too," he admitted sadly.

Megan sat back in her chair and looked across the pool to the far end of the property where the previous owners had been growing alfalfa. And beyond that, the Sandia Mountains in the background. "Hmmm," she said, not looking at Nate, thinking out loud.

She'd gotten so used to Barry beating her to any ideas, always telling her what to do. And here she was with Nate, they were doing this together. "I can make the cookies early. That's not a problem. But I also could have all the pizzas ready to go before the party. Do you think you could get me help? I don't want to be in the kitchen the whole party. I'm not getting into catering."

"Exactly," he said. "You're the hostess to my host." He reached over and tapped the top of her right hand. "I'll have Tony round up whatever you need. You give me lists and I'll have Tony take care of it."

"How are you ever going to transform this place into something that looks more than empty for the party?" she asked, looking around, the pool looking forlorn, too.

"After the party I'll make it livable. I don't need much between now and then."

"And you're going back to LA anyway."

"Yes." His face changed and he reached out for her hand again, this time, holding it in his. "But I'll be back."

Megan nodded.

CHAPTER 22

As time flew toward the premiere, the cookbook was moving five steps forward and two back. Barry had hired a group of PR people in New York to partner with and engage the national media.

"We might be the biggest PR organization in New Mexico, but I think we'll have more luck if we let Madison Avenue handle it," he said in a meeting one day.

There was constant looking at the manuscript and the photos, scanning for errors, for typos.

"I swear they multiply when I'm not looking," Megan said, shaking her head after Barry had brought in the latest draft for her to look at, red pen marked all over it. A period missing here, a T not capitalized for Tablespoon there.

As life swirled around her, in the spare moments she had to think– which seemed to be few and far between– she noted how it was turning to fall, how the shadows were changing, how the smell of green chile was in the air as it was roasted in front of the grocery stores, and how the number of hot air balloons increased in the sky.

Soon it would be winter. Megan didn't want to think that far in advance. She had never been one to look too far into the future. Why would now be any different? She wondered. There was a lot going on, a lot of good stuff.

"I'm so excited," Maria would sing, dancing around the office when she stopped by, having found work on a film project in town. And having moved into Barry's house.

"It looks more like a girl lives there," she joked and then would add, "Does Nate still keep an empty pizza box in his fridge?"

"What's up with that?" Megan would ask, shrugging her shoulders. "Is it a badge of something?"

"Memory of when he was last home. If you look, the receipt is always on top of the box."

Megan was beginning to feel that way herself. She walked Sam daily, often taking him to the office so he could at least have people to be around because her nose was always in something.

It's good that things are this busy? she often asked herself.

*****

"Hellloooo!" called Mrs. Rosales from her car, leaning over the empty passenger seat to get Megan's attention.

Megan pulled herself out of the back of her SUV and put down the grocery bags she was pulling out, walking to Mrs. Rosales.

"I have your dress ready! You need it this week, right?"

"Yes," Megan said, having been so caught up in the cookbook and the party that she forgot about her dress. She said a silent thank you to the universe for Mrs. Rosales being on top of having it ready.

"I haven't seen you. You must be busy." She motioned with her hand as if to call Megan onto the stage of "The Price is Right." "Why don't you come down now? Do you have time?"

Megan thought for a moment. "Sure. Let me put the groceries in the house."

"No hurry," Mrs. Rosales said, lifting up a big candle in her hand. "I need to light my Our Lady of Guadalupe candle."

Once in the house, the smell of something simmering in red chile coming from the kitchen, Mrs. Rosales took Megan down the hall where the plum-colored dress hung at the top of the closet door, looking brand new.

"It doesn't look like it's been in the closet for forty-some years now," Mrs. Rosales laughed. "I had it hung in my daughter's closet all this time, my hope that one day she would want to wear it." She shrugged her shoulders, her arms hugging herself across her chest. "But she never did." Mrs. Rosales turned to Megan, who couldn't believe what she was seeing. "I had it steamed, too. I know there's a cigarette burn somewhere, but I don't think you can see it." Her finger wagged around the left side. "Oh, go try it on!" she finally said. "I need to stop talking."

Megan walked down the hall, the dress moving with her, like a wedding gown might, a happy noise, Megan thought.

"Unless it's Cinderella running from the pumpkin," she later told Julie.

She pulled the dress on and looked in the mirror, not totally recognizing herself. She thought for a moment about how little time she had spent thinking about what she looked like recently. Megan then saw she had changed since January.

"Are you okay? You're making me nervous," Mrs. Rosales called from outside the bathroom door.

Megan laughed. It's all good, she thought, reaching for the bathroom door and pulling it to her. "It's perfect," she said.

Mrs. Rosales began to cry, intertwining her fingers at her mouth. Megan walked down the hall, as she had before, then walked back to Mrs. Rosales. "It is," she said. "I'm so happy, *mija*."

Megan didn't know much Spanish, but she knew the term for "my daughter." Megan hugged her.

"Now take it off and come have a bowl of *carne adovada*," she said. "I put it in the crock pot yesterday afternoon and it should be about perfect by now."

While Mrs. Rosales served them each a bowl of pork cooked in red chile, Megan walked in to see a package wrapped in tissue paper, tied with a purple ribbon, at her place setting. She picked it up to scoot it out of the way, when Mrs. Rosales stopped her.

"That's for you," she said, sitting down with the two bowls of carne adovada, holding one away from Megan. "Open it."

Megan opened the package to see an apron. "No surprise," she laughed.

But Mrs. Rosales didn't show any emotion until Megan opened it up and saw the white apron had something printed on it with a deep pocket off to the right side.

The Twilight Sands logo, the neon sign. The very sign Nate had restored.

Megan laughed. "Oh my gosh! How did you..."

Mrs. Rosales looked the happiest Megan had ever seen her. "You won't believe what I kept in those closets all those years." She shook her head toward the hall and the bedrooms. "The waitresses at the Twilight Sands used to wear these. I found an old postcard and my son, he owns a printing shop, made this for me."

"Thank you." Megan said, shaking her head, unable to believe what she was holding in front of her. "I can't wait to show this to Nate." She turned to Mrs. Rosales. "You'll be there, right?"

Mrs. Rosales shook her head and took a bite of the meat. "Oh no. I don't need to be in the way of all you young people."

"But we want you there," Megan told her, not sure how to convince her, part of her wanting to say, "Because my own mom won't be there." Yet not feeling like it was something she could say. Mrs. Rosales did have a family.

At home, the dress hung on the back of the door in the guest room, the apron folded and put away where Nate wouldn't see it, Megan went back to work on the cookbook.

Sunday, she told herself, Sunday.

CHAPTER 23

Megan put her head in her hands.

"Take a deep breath," she muttered to herself. "Everything will get done."

She still wasn't quite sure how she was going to get twenty-five pizzas made for Saturday. She'd been baking carob cookies like there was no tomorrow, thanks to help from Julie. And her kids.

"At least you know the recipe is foolproof," Julie said, delivering another three dozen cookies to Megan on Tuesday morning.

"And good thing the previous owners left a huge freezer in the storage area," Megan said, putting a blue sticky note on her purse to remind her to take the cookies up to Nate's house after work.

"And, what, a million dozen to go, down from a billion?" Julie cracked, handing Megan a receipt for the ingredients.

"Exactly," Megan told her, putting it with the stack of others she had for Nate.

"Cookies? Did I see some cookies walk in here?" Barry asked, sticking his head in the door.

"No," Megan said. "Julie carried some in, but they're for the party."

"One? Please let me have one?" he begged.

"Under normal circumstances, you know I would say yes," Megan said, feeling slightly agitated, "but in this circumstance I'm not sure how I'm going to get them all made so the answer is no."

At that moment, Maria and her hat magically breezed in.

"My Cinderella has arrived to go to lunch anyway," he said, looking relieved that he could eat soon.

"You need to stop thinking about cookies," Maria teased him. "There's more to life than cookies you know."

"But cookies are the reason for That Cooking Girl's success," Barry said, pointing at Megan who was looking at Julie who had a look that said, "Can you believe we work for him?"

They were gone twenty minutes when Barry came flying back into the office, Maria calling behind him, "Slow down! I'm wearing heels!"

"You won't believe what happened!" he cried out, snapping his fingers and dancing around the room to a song only he could hear.

"Um, no," Megan said, looking up from a list she was making. "Shouldn't you be at lunch?"

"He forgot about that," Maria said, her hair looking slightly out of place, as if they had run all the up to the sixth floor. "We were in the car when he got the call."

"What call and why do I care?" Megan asked.

"Because," and Barry stopped and stood in front of her desk, "you've just been booked on 'The Today Show'!"

It took a moment for it to register. "You're not kidding, right?" she asked, her eyes shifting back and forth between both him and Maria.

"I was there," Maria said. "I heard the phone call."

"Really?" Megan's face broke out in a big smile. She wanted to jump up and dance around with Barry, but she realized she was too tired. Instead, it felt like relief. All their hard work on the cookbook was paying off.

"It'll lead off your cookbook tour," Barry said.

"When?" She opened her calendar on her tablet. "When am I booked?"

"On Tuesday, October 18."

And that's when Megan saw it: the day after the premiere. Her face fell. "Didn't you realize what date that is?" She stared at both of them.

"What? What's wrong with it? We're adding a New York City book signing." He shrugged his shoulders.

"That's two days after 'Twilight Sands' premieres."

"Oh," Maria said, quietly, dropping into the chair, keeping her hands in her lap, as if it would protect her from any anger. Or other emotions Megan might be preparing to spew out.

Barry looked at Maria and she looked at him. Megan looked at Maria, afraid to look at Barry because she couldn't understand why he didn't get it.

"Oh," he finally said, scratching the back of his head which caused his tie and shirt to move with his hand. "Oh oh oh."

"Can you change it?" Maria asked quietly.

Megan knew by the tone of her voice– Maria knew how these things worked– that there would be no changing it. The book signing was in the works. All the dominos were lining up and there was no moving them around.

"I'm sorry," Barry said, his face scrunching up. "You'll just have to leave the morning after the premiere."

Megan sat back in her chair. She was so tired she knew she might burst into tears. She wanted to call Nate and talk to him. She needed someone to tell her this was okay. But what she saw was a storm hovering overhead and she wasn't sure how to manage it. It was getting out of control.

"I'm sorry," Barry said again. His cell rang. "That's the travel people," he said, looking at the number. "I'll get you the latest flight out of here."

"I think there's a red eye," Maria told him, kicking him lightly in the shin so he didn't miss what she said.

"Hello, Barry … here." He nodded and left the office, his voice trailing down the hall until they couldn't hear it anymore.

Maria got up, put her hat down, and shut the door quietly. "Cry, "she said. "Don't stop until it's all out."

Megan looked at her.

Maria shook her head. "Come on. Do it now. Don't let it fester."

It took Megan a moment, thinking about how crazy things were, how she missed having Nate around, how she felt like life was out of control. How life was good. But out of control. And then the flood began.

Megan turned her chair to face the window, seeing a storm forming over the Jemez Mountains north of Santa Fe, and she let the tears fall.

She wasn't sure how long it lasted but when it began to subside, she turned back to Maria, who had picked up the box of tissues that Megan kept across the room and handed it to her. "I know," Maria said. "This isn't what you signed up for. Your life is a million miles from where it was a year ago this time. And it's good. But it's scary. You're on the verge of being a star. You're dating one of the handsomest men ever. One who absolutely adores you. And you're trying to figure out how to manage your two big careers."

Megan looked at her. "How do you know all this?" she asked, blowing her nose several times.

Maria sat back down in the chair. "Because you know I work in Hollywood. I see it. But I see something different with you two. Usually two people come together to double their star power. You and Nate are doing that, but your relationship isn't about that. It's just going to take some doing to get it figured out."

Megan nodded. "I'm so tired," she said.

"I know. And you will be for a while. Once the premiere is over and Nate sees what his future holds and you do your book tour and you see what your future holds, you two can begin to weave your lives together. But for now you have to reside in two separate places."

Megan nodded again.

Maria took a deep breath and placed her hands on her knees. "In the meantime, we need to discuss your outfits."

"Yes, of course," Megan laughed. "It's all about the clothes."

"It is," Maria said. "Clothes can make anyone feel better. As long as they're good clothes."

CHAPTER 24

On the morning of the premiere party, Megan looked out the large windows in the kitchen eating area of Nate's house that she faced from the counter where she was making pizza dough, and saw several balloons coming closer and closer to the house.

"Nate!" She called. "Come see this!" Nate and Tony came running from the other half of the house and Megan motioned them outside to the field.

The yellow and red striped balloon – with the wicker basket holding five people drifted slowly closer to them.

They stood by the swimming pool, their hands shielding their foreheads so they could look up and watch the balloon. It drifted closer and closer– and lower. The flame lit inside the balloon, making a loud sound and sending Sam into a full bark from where he stood next to the trio. Megan held his collar and the pilot yelled out, "Can we land here?"

"Sure, man!" Nate yelled back, motioning with his hand that they could come down.

The pilot waved back and continued the balloon's descent into the field. "We didn't need the alfalfa anyway," Nate joked as they watched the basket make several light bounces and then the big, heavy balloon start to fall to the ground, trailing the basket. Everyone clapped and the five riders began to climb out.

"Thanks for letting us land here," the pilot said, the chase crew in a pickup truck arriving. "Can they drive in the field?" he asked, scratching his beard as they had already entered the field.

"A little late to worry about that," Nate said, shrugging his shoulders. "I just bought the place."

"You did?" The pilot asked, his eyes opening wide and looking around. "It's quite a spread."

Then he was interrupted by a woman looking at Nate. "Aren't you Nate Matthews? You sure look like him."

"I am," Nate said, shoving his hands in the pockets of his jeans.

"Oh yeah," the pilot said, nodding his head. "You have a new series coming out."

"Premiering tonight as a matter of fact," Tony said.

"That's right- that hotel thing?" The woman asked. "Or motel. Or what's the difference in them anyway? Can we get a photo?"

And with that, the five people and the chase crew formed an informal line to take the photo, some of them visitors from North Carolina. It was several minutes before they got everything they wanted and started the process to roll up the balloon.

After the balloon people left, and as the trio walked back into the house, Sam free again, Nate laughed. "That was way cool."

"I might move here, too," Tony smiled, shaking his head. "When does that ever happen in California?"

"Never," Nate laughed.

Megan felt a little smug, proud of her town, wishing she could pat Albuquerque on the shoulder and say, "Job well done, my friend."

But she had pizzas to make and a party to prep for.

*****

Everything was ready and in place, just in time for the first guests to arrive that Sunday evening. Nate had employed plenty of people to help with the food serving. And whom Megan educated on how to make the perfect pizza. "If it's not done enough," she teasingly warned, "I'm coming after you."

Her biggest hope though was that the oven would survive the night.

"I can't replace it until we remodel," Nate said, holding his hands out in front of her.

"I know," Megan said, her hands on her hips, wearing the dress Mrs. Rosales had given her– and the Twilight Sands apron– biting her lip, staring at the 1970-something almond-colored wall oven.

Somehow everything fell into place that night, including Mrs. Rosales showing up, looking elegant in her navy blue pant suit. "I'm so nervous," she whispered to Megan, looking more excited than nervous. "I'm not used to being around celebrities."

"But you're around him," Megan reminded her, pointing at Nate, who was pouring a beer into a glass for someone. "And he's almost as big as it gets."

"He's your boyfriend," Mrs. Rosales said, waving him off. "He's not a celebrity to me." She changed the subject. "The dress looks perfect on you."

"It does look perfect doesn't it?" Nate asked Mrs. Rosales, coming up to her and giving her a quick hug. "And that apron! I heard you're behind that, too. We'll have to add that to the show."

"Oh," she laughed, waving her hand. "I'm just a little old lady. I'm happy to be of help when I can."

Megan chuckled inside, waiting for her phone alarm to remind her the pizzas were ready. While the ovens worked, the timer didn't and she didn't have a watch on. "Use your phone," one of the twenty-somethings said.

"It's so annoying when they're helping make our lives easier," Megan said to Nate with an eye roll. "How did so much time go by that I'm now old?"

Megan pushed Mrs. Rosales into the party, someone asking her if she was Eddie's mother (she wasn't) and another person asking if she had ever taught school somewhere in Albuquerque because she reminded him of his third grade teacher.

"I dropped my children off at school," she laughed, "but they're much older than you so I'm sure it wasn't the same time."

The staff Nate hired kept Megan's pizzas moving. She placed them in the oven and there was always someone else watching to take them out, getting Megan's approval for doneness.

"I'll never be a caterer," she would lament to Barry later at the party.

"No no no," he agreed, taking a drink of his micro-brewed beer from the bottle. "You'll create the recipes. You're the personality behind the recipes. That's a big enough job."

By the time the party came to a close, the premiere ending, the first indication that it was time to break it up, Megan was exhausted. She had longed to lay on the couch and watch the premiere, to absorb it, but there wasn't room– not that she could have laid on it during the party– there wasn't even room to sit.

"There's a lot of background set," Nate had told her. "We'll re-watch it together."

"Everything looks so different on the screen, after all the editing," Megan lamented near the end of the party, leaning against the counter in the kitchen, ready to remove her heels. "You can't even tell what the big picture is."

"That's the beauty of the screen," he reminded her, and still laughing at her debut diving scene that sent everyone into a fit of applause.

"Ten! Ten!" they had yelled.

And when the last guest had left, the wait staff had finished cleaning up and had long gone themselves, Megan looked at the clock and saw that it was 11:30. She wasn't sure where Nate was, talking to someone in front of the house, she thought, so she opened the sliding glass doors from the kitchen and walked outside into the Albuquerque evening. The nights were cool, the days warm, but it had yet to cool down on this night, no breeze in the air.

Megan stood– in her heels– on the concrete pool deck, staring at the water with the lights shimmering in it, and then looked up at the stars. In between, she could make out the lights at the top of the Sandias where the tram stopped.

She looked around, realizing she was all alone, and how silent the valley was, surrounded by trees and acres of alfalfa. First, she kicked off her heels and then wiggled out of her dress and underwear, not caring that she had no swimsuit to put on or a towel for later. She walked onto the diving board, looking down at the darkened water below her, took a breath and did a shallow dive– just like that day into the Twilight Sands pool– and came up in the shallow end near the house.

When she got her bearings and found her breath again, she heard a voice. "Is that what you do after parties? Go skinny dipping?"

Megan swam to the middle of the pool to tread water. "I double dog dare you to join me."

"That's not a hard one," he said, pulling off his shoes first.

When he dove in, the water swung from side to side, almost like a wave pool. Nate came up for air and swam to Megan, taking her in his arms and held her for a moment in the middle of the pool. She could see the outline of his face from the lights that streamed outside from the house– and from the pool light.

"You put on quite a party," he told her.

"I just made the food," she reminded him.

"And looked stunning in that dress."

Megan laughed. "Thank you. You created the occasion."

"With you in mind."

"That's a lie."

"Not at all," he said seriously. "I've never had such a big premiere party."

"You never had your own show before," she reminded him, splashing him lightly in the face.

He leaned toward her for a kiss, taking Megan by surprise, but she quickly jumped in.

"That's just the beginning," he said.

"Of what?"

"Everything."

CHAPTER 25

It was dark in the morning– fall was definitely starting to show, Megan thought– as the plane rumbled up the east-west runway, heading toward the Manzano Mountains. Megan looked out the window of her first class seat at the lights of the airport whizzing by and then the ascent into the air, the lights of Albuquerque below them.

Leaving Nate at the airport, forcing herself to walk away from his embrace, from his smell, had been hard. She wasn't going to lie. She didn't want to leave. She wanted to be with him, the end of the party just hours old. She knew it didn't make sense though– in the afternoon, he would lock up the house and board a plane to Los Angeles himself. He had his own media ahead of him for the show.

"We'll be together soon," he had promised, being the one to pull away.

It was made worse for Megan to see the magazines in the stores in the airport terminals: all the Hollywood gossip, mostly about breakups and divorces. She cringed, knowing that people were apt to enjoy hearing about the demise of the relationships of others. Why couldn't there be more stories about the enduring marriages like Paul Newman and Joanne Woodward? Instead of feeling hopeful, Megan walked by the stores with a boulder filling up her stomach.

Megan rested her head against the back of the leather seat and sighed, hoping she could sleep all the way to Chicago, and then another ninety minutes or so to New York City from there.

"They'll take great care of you," Barry had promised, handing her several sheets of paper folded and held together by a shiny silver paper clip.

"None of it matters," Maria had laughed. "The important part is that you'll look great."

"It's going to go so fast," Megan said, seeing she was flying out Monday morning and then on Wednesday she would return to Albuquerque.

"New York City should always be a whirlwind," Maria reminded her, waving her hand. "Then you never see the bad of it."

A morning show, a book signing, a trip home. Alone.

That afternoon, having arrived– she looked out the window of her hotel room overlooking Central Park and opted to go for a walk under the cloudy skies rather than sit in the room alone.

"And you have dinner with some executives of the publishing company," Barry said.

"Shouldn't you be there?" she asked.

He shook his head. "They want to meet you, get to know you. Just have fun."

"And don't drink too much," Maria warned, Megan started to feel like Maria was playing the part of her mother.

"One drink," Barry suggested.

"How about none? I don't really care," she reminded them.

"Sure," they said, looking at each other and then nodding simultaneously.

Megan walked across the street, having turned down the offer of an umbrella from the concierge. "It's okay," she had laughed. "I'm from New Mexico. We never carry them. It usually rains ten drops."

"But you might need it," he warned.

"I'll be fine," she assured him, knowing she was going to have to shower and fix her hair before dinner anyway.

She crossed into the park near the Metropolitan Museum, people everywhere. Megan looked around, seeing a little bit of every culture, every group, every age– right down to school kids clearly on a class field trip– people standing on the sidewalk, people sitting on the steps, everyone exploring the city just like her.

And then she walked south, finding more silence and fewer people, and finally the pond with the little sailboats. Megan sat down on a concrete bench and looked around, the leaves ready to turn color and fall to the ground, the buildings that made up the skyline placed all around her, a few people walking by. But mostly she was alone in Central Park with low hanging clouds threatening rain above her.

Megan thought back nine months. Was that how long it had been since this had all started? Sometimes she wasn't sure. It all blended together. So much had changed. Nine months. The time it takes to have a baby, she thought. Maybe she had birthed her own version of having a baby with the cookbook.

That meant Barry was the father.

Megan quickly put that thought out of her head.

She wished she could share her happiness with her mom, but knowing that wasn't going to happen. It was going to be like the time she called after getting her first job, after getting the job at Barry's firm and her mother sounded confused on the phone, like she didn't know who Megan was. For Megan it was the first sign that something was wrong. Presently, her dad had emailed her some photos recently– from her mother's seventy-first birthday. They had a cake for her at the place where she was living and everyone was gathered around her singing.

"Not that she knew what was going on," he said in the email, Megan hearing the chuckle in his writing, knowing that was how he was coping. "But I think she thought it was her tenth birthday. She kept asking where her presents were. And when she opened up the few things she was given, she said, 'I thought I was getting a new doll.' I should have thought about that when I bought her a new robe."

The email had brought Megan to tears when she read it and now as she sat alone in Central Park– although she was in what she always believed was the center of the universe– she began to cry. For all she had now, she felt as if she had lost something along the way. Her mother.

Just then her phone rang. Megan dug into her purse looking for it and then realizing it was Mrs. Rosales– someone who had never called her before.

"Hello," she said, clearing her throat and taking a deep breath.

"Hi!" the familiar voice called, sounding as if she were standing right next to Megan. "Can you hear me? I never use my cell phone. I should have called you on my phone in my kitchen, but I'm never sure if I have long distance or not. The kids are always asking me and I don't know. Maybe I should call the phone company."

Finally, she stopped talking and by then Megan had forgotten her sadness. But after a quick pause, Mrs. Rosales said, "Are you in New York? I thought you said that's where you were going, but I already forgot. I want to make sure I don't miss you on television tomorrow. And I need to tell Jean, of course."

"Yes," Megan said. "I'll be on 'The Today Show' tomorrow. I think I'll be on around 8:15 your time."

"Oh good. Okay. Enjoy New York for me. I've never been there. I'll see you when you get back."

The call ended, Megan was back to being alone. She felt a rain drop and wondered if she should have listened to the concierge.

"I've been living in the desert too long," she muttered, starting a quick-paced walk back to the hotel, after she looked up and saw an extra dark cloud hovering over her.

This is why everyone wears black here, she thought, looking around. All they see is gray.

*****

There were three people at the upscale Italian restaurant waiting for her when she arrived that evening, looking as if they had just sat down. Two women and a man. The man reminded her of Barry, almost like his long-lost brother. Everyone was dressed from the business day.

"Don't worry," Maria had told her. "You won't be dressed like them, but you'll be dressed as you. That's what's important."

She and Maria had picked out a burnt orange shift dress. "Not summer, not fall. Somewhere in between. Just like September."

"Finally, we get to meet you!" the three of them seemed to say in unison, smiling and holding out their hands.

Millie, the woman, wearing the pink and white vertical striped jacket and a long gold necklace was the first. She was the assistant publisher. Then Karl, the man, the publisher. Karl was missing more hair than Barry, but there were times Megan found herself stopping in almost mid-sentence, realizing it wasn't Barry she was talking to. And Denise, the editor, had long brown hair she wore in a ponytail that whipped around as she talked, her head seemingly in constant motion.

"We're so excited to meet you," they said again.

Megan sat down at the table and everyone watched her, constantly smiling. She looked at them, waiting, not sure what was next. And not used to doing anything like this without Barry.

They all tried to ask questions at once, not giving Megan a chance to say anything. What she really wanted was something to drink.

"Beer? Wine? Mixed drink?" Karl asked, when he was finally able to interrupt.

Megan waved her hand. "Just water. With lemon."

"Don't you drink a lot of margaritas in New Mexico?" Millie asked, her eyes opening wide.

"That food. Oh my goodness," Karl added.

Denise, having been the editor of the cookbook, laughed and looked at Megan.

"Maybe you should come visit," Megan suggested. "I don't think margaritas are appropriate at all meals. Like before church."

Millie shook her head. "I've been to Arizona so many times, but never New Mexico. Maybe Bob and I should go."

When dinner was over and Megan was back in her room, while she felt like a fish out of water in the suite that she thought might be bigger than her own house, she was relieved to be alone again. She turned out the light, knowing she had an early morning, and lay there wondering if it had been what she really wanted: to take That Cooking Girl national. Maybe being local wasn't a bad thing. It would give her a better life with Nate.

But Megan knew what Barry would say if she told him. "You can't come back to work here as if nothing happened." She could see his flailing arms. He would get up from his desk and pace the room. There was no going backward just so she could feel comfortable again.

"You'll be great," Nate assured her, calling ten minutes later, still only 7:00 pm on the west coast. "You know it's no different than the Albuquerque studio."

"Except that they're doing my hair and makeup," she reminded him.

"You should wear your 'Twilight Sands' apron," Nate said thoughtfully. Megan could tell he was sitting outside.

"Are you paying me for product placement?"

"Maybe I should," he said.

"Just like Albuquerque," she muttered to herself, as she was checked in at security and escorted to hair, then makeup, and then to the green room to wait, her apron in hand, and her fingers and toes crossed that they had all her items ready for the cooking segment. The halls were endless, filled with people who didn't notice her and pieces of camera and studio equipment they didn't seem to have a place for. Instead they stuck them in the hall, reminding her of a visit to the emergency room once when Julie's husband was in a car crash and all the beds that were lined up in the hall, people in various states of sitting and laying in them, but no room for them otherwise.

Megan took a deep breath.

"Megan?" a woman with black cat-eye glasses asked, poking her head in the door, a bun of dark hair piled high on her head and baby blue scarf wrapped around her neck.

"Hi," Megan said, standing up and having no idea who the woman was. The woman walked into the room, revealing her long-sleeved black dress and black boots, and extended her hand to Megan.

"I'm Tina, the assistant producer."

"Break a leg!" Barry texted at just that moment, Megan happening to see it with her phone in one hand.

"Break both legs!" Maria texted right after him.

Megan pictured them on the couch together at Barry's, Barry saying he was texting first, Maria not wanting to be outdone.

Tina escorted Megan to the set and the cooking area she would be using. "I know you need to get a batch in the oven and we've timed it so they'll be ready at the end of your segment." Tina pointed at her watch. "You need to have them in the oven at forty-four past the hour."

Megan nodded, Tina still talking, Megan eyeing the ingredients and thinking about getting the cookies made quickly. She would have been happy if they had decided to just let her serve the cookies, as if they were having a chat in a living room.

"It's about the process," Nate told her. "That's more interesting than doing what everyone else does: sitting around a couch talking."

"Like you?"

"Exactly. I'm not capable of anything else," he joked. "Just put me on a couch to make conversation."

Megan knew that wasn't true, especially as she thought about the day they filmed her segment together.

"You'll be great," he texted for the eleventh time.

As she was escorted into the studio, her part to take place in a nook around the corner from the main set, Megan felt the rush of cold air that kept the cameras cool. She followed Tina behind the cameras, filming Tory Davis and her co-host Dan Mildrew, sharing about their respective weekends with their families. The cameramen, all wearing heavy puffy coats as if they were going to be going out in a snow storm, looked bored as Megan walked by.

Once in her place, Tina gave her some last words of advice. "It might be a problem if you drop something, but otherwise they probably won't hear it on camera. If you need anything, Tim over there"– and she pointed to a tall skinny guy wearing glasses– "is your go-to. Flag him down and he'll help resolve it. I'll be around the corner."

Megan tied her apron on and didn't think about anything other than making the cookies. She heard bits and pieces from the main set– they were interviewing an author, something about a book that followed several former beauty queens in a reality television show.

That's what we've been reduced to, Megan thought about the state of television and belief that Nate had something far more interesting, at least to the "non-trash" crowd as she called them. She opened the oven and slipped the cookie sheet inside it and then she said a silent prayer that everything went correctly, that she hadn't forgotten the baking soda like she did one time before a party, finding her guests arriving as she was hurriedly placing a new round of cookies in the oven.

"Give me anything you don't need," Tim whispered when she turned back to the counter top. "There's your second round of items for the live segment."

She was placing the last bowl in the exact spot she wanted it when she heard Tory say, "We've got cookies baking in the studio after this break."

"And I'm a cookie monster," Dan laughed.

"And we're out!" The director called.

Tory and Dan wandered over to Megan, Tory's red heels that matched her red dress, clicking on the floor, Dan wearing his usual suit.

"These smell incredible," Tory said, placing her hand across her heart. "I skipped breakfast because I heard how great your cookies are."

"I hope I don't let you down," Megan joked, pulling the cookie sheet from the oven and Tim taking it from her. "Welcome to my kitchen."

"I'll place them on the platter for you," he said, nudging her back to the hosts.

Megan stood with them, making chit chat as if they, too, had gathered at a party. This felt a lot like the party at Barry's house. Out of the corner of her eye she saw the cameramen sliding the camera equipment and lights to her corner kitchen.

"Thirty seconds," the director called.

As quickly as it started, Megan found herself handing them the turquoise platter of cookies she had made just forty-five minutes before. Then it was over.

"We're out!"

The cameramen slid the equipment back across the large studio space.

"I wish we could talk to you longer," Tory said, covering her mouth as she chewed. "But before we let you go, we have one question."

Megan looked at both of them and waited.

"Are you really dating Nate Matthews?"

Now Tory and Dan waited for her to respond. Megan didn't know what else to do. All the emotions of the past few months bubbled up and turned to laughter.

"That's a yes if I ever heard one," Tory said, turning to Dan who nodded.

"I'm surprised you didn't ask me on the air?" Megan questioned. "I thought for sure…"

"We were forbidden," Tory said, gritting her teeth. "By Barry, was it? We don't even know who Barry is, but we were told Barry said not to ask you."

On the flight home, Megan relaxed in her seat and thought about Barry. He knew exactly what to do at all times. Except for his romantic relationships, it felt as if every step in Barry's professional career was filled with gold. When she arrived back into Albuquerque, it was dark, just as it had been when she left, she rolled her luggage across the Saltillo tile of the airport floor, clicking behind her and outside down below to the baggage claim area.

Outside, Barry stood next to his car, talking on the phone, waving at the security guy who was about to tell him to move. When Barry saw Megan he waved at her to alert the security guy, who then walked away.

"Hi," Barry said. Megan didn't say a word. She wrapped her arms around his neck and rested her cheek against his light brown blazer. She felt him wrap his arms around her and they stood there together, people getting picked up from their travels all around them.

"Thank you," Megan said, when she had pulled away.

Barry didn't say anything. He squeezed her hands. "You forget sometimes I have a pretty good idea of how to handle just about everything."

"Except maybe Maria," she laughed, wiping her eyes with her hand.

"No," he told her, nodding his head and looking toward the parking garage as if the answer were somewhere inside it, then looking back at Megan. "I think I've got that down now. I hope."

CHAPTER 26

"Releasing a cookbook in the United States isn't enough?" Megan asked, raising her eyebrows as Barry looked at her across the conference room table a few weeks later.

She still had her office, but she wasn't working for Barry's firm anymore. There was a constant juggle of marketing, appearances, and a lot of web work that kept her from her old job. "I'm not sure this is the best place for you to be creative," he had said when she asked if she could keep using it, "but we have that office at the end of the hall where we can put your replacement."

"Yeah!" Julie had whisper-yelled and squeezed Megan's wrist when she heard the news as they passed in the hallway. "We don't want to be here without you."

"We can't just be national," Barry now said, looking at Megan as if she had missed a memo. "The UK, Australia…then one day we'll discuss translation to other languages."

Megan's head started to spin. She was still processing England, but the idea of other languages? She pushed the thought out of her mind and came back to England. "So what does that mean?"

"It means you get to go to England," Maria said, never far from waltzing into the room when Barry had news to share.

"You two are like a Broadway show," Megan said, looking at each of them as Maria placed her hat on the table and slid into the seat next to Barry. "One of those musicals. When there's news, you're ready to break into song and dance."

Barry laughed, he and Maria looked at each other, and then he looked back at Megan, while fiddling with the papers he had in front of them. "You're going to London."

"Why?"

She bit her lip as soon as she said it, surprised it had come out sounding negative. Who wouldn't be excited about going to London? And she had the time without working for Barry.

"To promote your cookbook."

"A stupid question deserves a stupid answer," she admitted, holding out her hands in front of her as if to stop him from saying more.

"London to be on the 'Peter Walker Show.'"

"I've never heard of it.

"Of course not," Barry said. "We don't get it here, but it's popular there and that's all we care about."

"When do I leave? Tomorrow?"

He slid a paper across the table to her. "It's right before Christmas so you have a little time to prepare. You'll be taping for them to air it after Christmas."

"Then why can't I go after Christmas?"

"Why does she ask so many questions?" He turned to Maria who shrugged her shoulders.

"Smart girls ask a lot of questions."

"I should have known better," he muttered.

After Megan left the office an hour later, instead of heading west back to her house, she turned east on Central and drove to the Twilight Sands. It was nicely locked away, not looking like it was closed so much as it was a gated motel. Megan stood in front of the gate, knowing no one was there, and peeked in through the small holes in the metal.

Everything from filming had been cleaned up. She knew they were still waiting to hear if a second season would be picked up or if the Twilight Sands would truly become a motel once again. There were several episodes left and a decision would be made once the season ended.

"It looks good, I think," Nate had said on the phone, Megan not sure if he was hopeful more than he was trying to be hopeful. The reception had been good and she'd read the reviews until someone called it "hoky" at which time she realized mostly these were people writing online reviews with no writing experience, and hokey was spelled without an e. She decided there wasn't more for her to read.

The swimming pool was still full, the water looking cold in the November cool, despite the sunshine on the cloudless day. The motel wasn't full of life like it had been when she had been on the set. Right now it looked sad to Megan, as if it were waiting for people to show up.

"I hope they come soon," she whispered, not thinking her words sounded like a prayer she was throwing out to the universe. Megan took one last look at the neon sign, now dark in the daylight, and walked back to her car.

*****

"Hi Dad," Megan said, surprised her father was calling her. She got up from where she was working on a date cake recipe at the dining room table and walked to the back door where she looked out at Sam, who was smelling the perimeter of the yard. "How are you?"

"So you're going to London?" he asked, obviously having read her last email. She couldn't get him to graduate to text, but email he was happy to do.

"Yes. Pretty cool, huh?"

"I know I haven't been able to tell you, but I'm proud of you," he said.

Megan sensed something was wrong and didn't interrupt him.

"Your mother isn't doing well and I'm…" his voice kept drifting off. She knew he was holding back tears. "Well, you know she has an uncle and some family in Wales."

"Nigel," Megan said, remembering the uncle her mother always talked about. After World War II some of the family had emigrated to the United States– her mother's mother along with her husband– Megan's grandfather– but most of the family had stayed behind, choosing to continue life as it was. Her parents had visited a few times, but not in at least ten years.

"Well, if you're going to London…" He was drifting off again. "Could you go see Nigel?"

"Sure. But why?"

Megan had never met Nigel and wasn't so sure about going to meet a great uncle she had never met.

"Because none of them know how sick your mother is."

Oh, Megan said, her mouth making the words, but nothing come out.

"It would be better if you told them in person rather than my calling or writing them." He paused– Megan figured he had an inkling she wasn't happy about doing it. "Please, you know I don't ask much."

"Okay, okay," Megan said.

CHAPTER 27

Before Megan knew it, she was traveling to Chicago to catch an overnight flight to London, her first overseas adventure. Nate still didn't know if "Twilight Sands" would make it and Megan found herself trying to not think about him. Even though the more she did, the more she found she, well, thought about him. She constantly reminded herself about his house, the house that sat empty because he still hadn't made it back to start the remodel.

She looked around the gate area at O'Hare, filled with people of all sorts of colors and races.

There has to be one of everyone, she thought, studying the various styles of dress and hair.

Megan had stayed in the airline lounge until they called her flight. But now with a slight delay, something about the lavatories needing to be emptied again– she didn't want to know more than that– she found a seat and waited.

"Your first trip overseas and first class no less," Barry had teased her, handing her the flight itinerary.

London. By herself. Not with Simon Le Bon. At least now, she chuckled, she could see where she and Simon might have lived. The one dream in her life, the one that didn't come true. And the one that taught her maybe it wasn't wise to dream, but instead just to live in the present moment.

A kind-looking, male flight attendant led her to her seat. Twinkle Toes, she thought, watching his mannerisms. That's what my dad would call him, not realizing it wasn't kosher to say that anymore.

She looked around at the seat she knew would lie flat and let her sleep the whole way to London– if she desired.

"Well, if it isn't the Overseas Virgin," she heard a familiar voice say.

Definitely not Mr. Twinkle Toes.

Megan looked up to Nate smiling down at her, a carryon bag in one hand, his cell phone with his boarding pass in the other. At first, she looked at him, surprised to see him.

"You weren't expecting me," he laughed as she got up to hug him.

"Sorry to interrupt your reunion," the flight attendant reminded them, "but we have people who would like to take their seats."

Megan moved out of the aisle and Nate followed her. "I'm guessing you're next to me, aren't you?" she asked, looking sarcastic, but secretly she thought her heart was going to burst out of her chest.

"Of course I am."

"Because Maria arranged it."

"With the help of Barry."

He walked to the opposite aisle where his seat was. "We have the middle to ourselves," he whispered, sitting down on the seat, Megan following him. She didn't say anything, just sat and stared, not even sure what to say.

"Are you overwhelmed?"

She nodded, looking at him. He reached his hand across the partition between them and she held hers up to his. He squeezed it. "I promised you it's the beginning of everything, didn't I?"

Megan nodded.

"It is." He looked up. "Now where did our friend go. We need to get rid of this partition."

"Can you do that?" Megan asked, feeling hopeful they could be closer.

"We sure can."

When the flight attendant came back through, carrying a tray of wine glasses as if they were silver slippers, Nate stopped him and asked him how to move the partition. Suddenly, what had been two separate seats looked like one area. Meant for two.

Megan looked around and realized she hardly knew what was going on around her. First class wasn't full, there were two seats that didn't look as if anyone would be using them. The other people were settling in with headphones, wine, pillows, and blankets. Darkness had engulfed Chicago. They would take off at 10:00 pm and arrive in London sometime in the morning.

Megan was set for a night on Hyde Park and then the television filming the following day after which she would board a train to Wales where her great uncle Nigel would pick her up and she'd spend several nights before returning to London for another night. And a party.

"Why am I going to a party in London?" Megan asked. "Can't I just come home then?"

She was ready for a holiday break before she went on a book tour in the spring. Barry was already talking about her next cookbook. And the television show. And the people she would begin to work with after he stepped out.

"Peter Walker is having his annual holiday party and because you'll still be in the UK at the time, his people asked if you'd like to attend."

Maria had told her which dress to pack, what shoes, how to do her hair. And with Nate sitting next to her, arranging his seat for the long trip, she began to wonder what else she didn't know about.

The lights dimmed for the takeoff and Megan sat back and listened to the roar of the engine below her. She thought about this entire aspect that her one dream had never included– the feasibility of traveling over an ocean in a relationship. She had pictured everything between London and Los Angeles. While she knew there were people who did it, she was thankful now that it hadn't happened for her. The distance between Albuquerque and Los Angeles was enough. She looked over at Nate, who was flipping through a magazine. He caught her stare and smiled at her.

"As soon as the seatbelt light goes off, you and I are merging together."

"That's what this is?" she asked. "A merger?"

He laughed and leaned back in his seat. "Yes. We're merging our lives together."

For her though, it still felt as if a gorge existed between them. Not because he wasn't close to her, but because their lives were on such parallel tracks that still hadn't come together. She wondered if– when– that would happen. And she was totally confused why he was taking this trip. And hadn't told her. Her brain felt like words mixed together, but not in any order, as if she couldn't form complete thoughts.

"Why are you going to London?" she finally asked.

He laughed. "I was going to go anyway."

"You were not." Megan whispered, not believing him, yet also trying to let go of why she didn't know. Did she have to know? Wasn't it more important that he was there with her? After all, they hadn't known each other that long. They each had plans the other probably didn't know about. She tried to stop the thoughts and be present with Nate.

He shrugged his shoulders, their faces as close together as possible with the two separate seats. The jet engine hummed below them, making a low noise that Megan could barely hear.

"I'm going to look at property."

"For when you sell Mexico?"

"Yes."

"You want to live there?"

"I don't know. We'll see what the future brings. But I'm also thinking about what's next if 'Twilight Sands' doesn't work out."

Megan didn't ask more questions. She drifted off to sleep, thankful she could, unlike the people sitting up in the back of the plane who were probably miserable.

A driver was supposed to pick her up at Heathrow and Megan saw her name as she walked out of the arrivals hall, Nate next to her.

"I'm hiring a car," he said.

"Trying to sound native with the language?" she asked.

They hugged and kissed and went their separate ways, Megan disappointed he wasn't going with her to the filming.

We still have separate lives, she thought, watching him walk away from her and toward the car rental counters. She then walked to the brown bearded man holding up a sign with her name on it.

London at last, she thought, sitting back in the sleek black car, adjusting to the car on the left side of the road, and watching the scenery go by.

London, a place she always thought she would live even though she knew little about it.

She sat at the window and wondered if this was what it was like to be royalty: to watch the world walk by you outside your window while you stayed inside wishing you could be part of it. People, most of them dressed in shades of black, strolled on the streets, each person looking like he or she had a purpose.

I have a purpose, too, Megan thought, but if it's this lonely, I don't want to do it, feeling as if Nate were a million miles away.

And here she was, the taxi pulling up in front of the large branded hotel, a bellhop opening the door. This wasn't New York or Los Angeles. It was London.

"My suite is huge," she texted both Julie and Stephanie, standing by the window that overlooked Hyde Park. She watched people milling around, as the city was coming alive at 10:00 am.

"As it should be!" Julie sent back. "But you woke me up– it's only 3:00 am here."

Megan gulped and sat down on the couch. She crossed her legs under herself and looked around.

After thinking for a moment, she thought about how tired she was, how she needed a shower. But after that? What would she do?

Megan grabbed her handbag and walked down to the concierge.

"What's the best place to go shopping?" she asked.

"Oh, Oxford Street, of course," the concierge named Colin said, pulling out a paper map and making pen notes for her. "Take the Underground and you'll be there in a jiffy."

The long escalator took Megan to the depths of a city she had no idea existed. "I've spent too much time in New Mexico," she mumbled to herself as several people went flying by her left side. Even traveling to New York and Los Angeles, she was beginning to see the world was much bigger than she imagined. And that was even though all those years ago she imagined she would experience the larger world around her. It just didn't happen until later. Much later.

The platform was filled with people and Megan found herself watching them, catching snippets of the conversations of those who were talking, while watching others who listened to music or read the newspaper.

To her right a young woman stood with a shopping bag in her hand. She had long black hair pulled into a ponytail and dark skin. Megan guessed she was from India. She was a pretty girl and wore a skirt with low-heeled shoes and a long black wool coat.

A man, with brown hair and fair skin, approached her and they began to talk. Old friends? Megan wondered. He was saying he had to go to China Friday and was picking up his visa. They talked about getting together.

The train arrived and both of them stepped on it, Megan not far behind, sitting down opposite them although she had stopped listening. Her mind turned to other thoughts, wondering how people met. Like relationships, she wondered. How did people meet so they formed romantic relationships? Did it happen as easily as on the train platform? Or what about on a plane?

The train came to a stop and Megan stood up to repeat her journey, this time up the escalator and onto Oxford Street where she walked around, the day gray just as she had always pictured London. It was lunch time and people were popping in and out of stores, their hands filled with bags, buying gifts with Christmas just a week away.

"Places to go, people to see, shopping to do," Maria had sung to her a few days ago. "Don't miss the shopping in London."

"You should go to museums," Barry had said, shaking his head.

The map in her purse, Megan thought she would walk along Regent Street and then eventually make her way to some of the sites. With just the afternoon to explore, it only would be the tip of the iceberg.

The windows were filled with signs of the holiday season: glitter, ornaments, shades of green and red. Not just gifts to buy, but outfits for holiday parties. The end of the year celebrations. The little moments people celebrate to keep life exciting and fresh before starting new in January with diets and prepping for spring and summer.

Something caught her eye in front of Louis Vuitton, a store she had never entered in her life. She only knew the ads from the magazines she read or the celebrity gossip that

Stephanie always talked about. "I heard so-and-so wore Louis Vuitton to the Oscars," she would say after reading the latest issue of *People*.

"I have to end that subscription," Barry would always note as he walked by, having heard her comment. "I get it for our clients to read yet you're the only one who does."

"Someone has to keep up with the important news in the world," Stephanie would remind him as she picked up a call.

The holiday décor had been carefully selected for the window, but she looked beyond that and quickly walked into the empty store where an elegant British man with a moustache greeted her, doing a slight bow while rubbing his hands together.

"Good day, madam," he said.

"Hello," Megan said, trying not to sound like a stupid American, but his Britishness leaving her feeling like a country bumpkin. "Do you have that hat box that's in the window?" she asked, pointing toward the display.

"We do," he said, leading her to the far side of the store where the hat box– also available in several other colors– was displayed.

There was the traditional brown and a black, but what had caught Megan's eye was the dark pink. It wasn't the kind of pink that made her feel like she was back in the eighties, but a pink that looked wintry yet sophisticated.

"It's a very unusual color. We haven't ever done a pink like this." He picked it up and gingerly handed it to Megan, as if it might break.

She took the leather into her hands, feeling instantly the quality of the craftsmanship, like nothing she had ever known before. "Have you sold many?"

"They just arrived," he said. "They're special for the holiday season."

It didn't take Megan long. She inspected it. She knew she didn't want to leave the store without it. She liked the Michael Kors bag she carried, but this hat box bag made Michael look boring, as if he had been a stow away in the cargo train. But this hat box? This was the first class car.

"Get yourself something nice," Maria had encouraged her. Maria always encouraged her. Instead, it was Barry's words which influenced the purchase.

"You never get anything," he reminded her. "Just when I tell you. Enjoy yourself. This is only going to grow." There was a twinkle in his eye as he said it.

"How much is it?" she asked, ready to take the blow of the price.

"1,500 pounds," he said, not flinching. Megan didn't either.

She looked up at the salesman in front of her, handed the hat box back to him and said, "I'll take it."

He bowed again and as he walked away, she thought he was smiling. I'm sure he's saying, that was easy, she thought.

Walking out of the store, the hat box wrapped in tissue paper and placed into a large shopping bag, she thought she would head back to the hotel because it was getting late. But as she did, something again caught her eye, this time in the window of a large store called Jack Colin.

A dress.

Not just any dress, but a pale pink-colored short-sleeved dress. Perfect for a party. And she already had the party on the schedule.

That's mine, she thought. It's perfect.

Megan held her head high, searching for the dress in the women's clothing department, but a woman in a blue dress stopped her. "Hello," she said in her British accent, her brown hair tied up in a bun. "Is there anything I can help you with today?"

"Yes," Megan said, pointing. "That pale pink-colored dress in the window outside."

"Oh yes," the woman said, walking ahead of Megan. "That's a beautiful dress for the holiday season."

She stopped at the rack and eyed Megan. "I'm guessing a 38, does that sound right?"

Megan laughed. "Sure."

Inside the fitting room, she slipped it on, making sure not to let Louis– still in the bag– out of her sight. The dress fit. Perfectly.

Megan smoothed it down across her stomach to her hips. It wasn't as shapely as the dresses she usually wore, but she loved the A-line flared skirt and the ¾ sleeves.

She looked in the mirror, her hands lightly on her hips, and smiled. A little bit retro, a little bit modern. It was different than her usual style, not so fitting, but she liked it.

And after all, it was London.

"How are you doing in there?" the woman called from outside the door.

Megan opened it and walked out, knowing a pair of heels would complete the look. And maybe even her hair piled on top of her head. "Marvelous!" the woman said, looking pleased. "You will be the hit of the party in that."

"And I have a party on the schedule," Megan laughed.

"Perfect," the woman said, smiling.

It didn't matter, it was only a fraction of the cost of the hat box at $200 American dollars.

*****

Just as scheduled, Megan's London taxi pulled up in front of the BBC studios at 1:30, an hour before she was due for her scheduled interview. She stood in front of the complex, wearing her dress and heels, looked at the big BBC sign, and then began walking inside where she was greeted at security.

It wasn't much different than filming in New York. Or Albuquerque.

"They just have fun accents," she joked later with Julie and Stephanie.

"You would have married one of those funny accents if you could have," Stephanie reminded her.

"Belinda will lead you out," Peter Walker said, the segment taping over, shaking Megan's hand when they were finished filming the segment. And with that, he disappeared with the plate of cookies she had prepared in that hour before the taping.

"They must be delicious," Belinda whispered, taking Megan by the shoulder and leading her off the set. "He's worse than Gordon Ramsay. I've seen him spit up food."

"What happens to the segment if Peter doesn't like the food?" Megan asked, her eyes opening widely as they walked through large black curtains and into the hallway.

"It never airs," Belinda said sadly, opening a doorway for them both to travel through.

Despite Belinda's overweight frame and the heels that made her look as if she might topple over, Megan found herself working hard to keep up with the assistant.

When they reached the lobby of the complex, Belinda handed Megan a voucher to pay for the cab. "Merry Christmas although I'll see you at the party I hear!"

CHAPTER 28

The next morning Megan watched the English countryside pass her by while she sat on the train, the hat box on the table in front of her. Now onto the part of her trip she dreaded.

A graying man with a beard stood on the train platform and Megan knew instantly it was her Great Uncle Nigel. It was probably all the photos she had seen over the years.

"Hi," she said, walking right to him, a smile on her face, his growing larger as she neared him.

"Well, you look like an Americanized version of your mother," he said, giving her a hug. She could tell it had been a day or two since he showered– her father warning her about that.

"It's all that war stuff," he had said. "They had nothing and to build back from nothing. They think they're saving something by not showering every day."

Megan let it go. Be grateful, she told herself as he finagled her large rolling bag into the back of his tiny car. She wanted to help, but she could see he was making it a mission to show her his strength.

It didn't take long for him to figure out why she was there. He pulled the car out of the train station parking lot. "Your Aunt Matilda will have dinner ready for us. I heard you were filming 'The Peter Walker Show'? It sounds like you have quite the interesting life."

Megan had been worried about what they would talk about. Now she knew that wouldn't be an issue.

"I imagine you're here to tell me something," he finally said, maneuvering the car around a few corners before going straight again. "And if I had to guess, it's about your mother."

"Why would you think that?" Megan asked, unclear about any family politics her father had neglected to share. And then realizing it wasn't because this was good news she had been asked to tell him. Before he could answer she blurted out, "She has Alzheimer's. Dad had to move her into a facility recently and she's …" Megan couldn't decide on the right words. "She's dying fast."

"I had a feeling," he said softly, switching gears, unable to take his eyes off the road because of the turns. "He would have called me with good news. It's been a while since I heard from him."

"I don't talk to her anymore," Megan admitted, feeling as sad as the gray day.

"She doesn't know who you are?"

Megan shook her head. "No. She hasn't in about a year. He told me to stop visiting, too. He said to remember her as she was."

"That's too bad." He slowed the car down for a stop sign. "She was a beautiful woman. I wish I had seen more of her. We all have regrets."

Megan didn't say anything. She wondered why they didn't travel back and forth. She knew they occasionally talked on the phone, switching to email when both had upgraded their lives to computers.

He reached over and patted Megan's shoulder. "But you're here now. So I understand it that your brothers are married, but you are not?"

Oh no, Megan thought, here it comes. "Yes, that's true."

"Why is a beautiful girl like you not married? Too busy building a television career?"

She laughed and he pulled into driveway, even in the winter the grass green from the rain. As she watched him struggle to pull her bag from the back of the car– the boot she would later learn it was called– she waited until they were on their way into the house via the kitchen door. "It just hasn't happened."

"Oh, but my daughter Margaret says you have a suitor," he said, fiddling with his keys. "Matilda went to the store. She wanted to make a cake, but we somehow ran out of sugar. She has always been little light headed," he said, clearly making a joke about her constant forgetfulness.

Megan laughed. "I'm not really sure."

She hadn't talked to Nate since they parted at the airport– he said his phone wouldn't work overseas, holding out his older smartphone that he hadn't had time to upgrade.

"A very famous one I hear. I think I've seen a movie or two of his."

He let Megan inside the house and followed, dragging her bag behind him. The house was small, but filled with light and Megan felt instantly at home.

This is Wales, she thought, but secretly still confused how it was different than the rest of England.

Uncle Nigel dragged her bag upstairs to one of the three bedrooms. "I hope you'll find your accommodations sufficient," he said, leaving the bag on top of a chest and placing his hands on his hips.

Megan sat down on the bed and nodded, feeling sad. But hoping he wouldn't notice. "Yes, they look fine to me."

"Very well then, I'll meet you in the kitchen for tea. Matilda should be home shortly."

The three of them sat in the kitchen at their round table, the dark sky making everything seem later than it was, Nigel showing some signs of his own sadness.

"I knew she wasn't well," he said, looking out into the backyard– the garden, Megan learned they called it– "but now I see we should have made a trip all those years ago."

"Oh, don't beat yourself up over it," Matilda said, pouring more tea into her cup, her short silver curls bouncing as she moved. "We had no idea this would happen."

"You didn't," Megan added, her hands in her lap at the table. "My parents didn't come visit you either. Everyone was wrapped up in their lives."

A light rain began to fall outside the window, making the mood even sadder. Matilda had placed a pan in the oven and now the house was beginning to smell like a hearty dinner. Megan felt her stomach grumble and hoped no one heard it.

"You have a knack for cooking we hear," Nigel said.

Megan laughed. "Let's just say I fell into it."

She didn't want to interrupt the sadness to discuss cookies and yet she realized Nigel probably wanted to talk about something else.

Everything had been moving so quickly in her life and now she sat in the kitchen of her great uncle across the country and the ocean from her life in New Mexico. It felt weird to sit. And not have anywhere to go or anything to work on.

The next morning, the sky looked much the same when Megan pushed back the sheer white curtain. She saw a little boy with a backpack, bundled up in a winter coat as if it were the middle of January in the snow. After a shower, Megan walked downstairs to find Nigel and Matilda in the kitchen. A complete breakfast had been set at the table. While Nigel was reading the newspaper, Matilda looked like she was fiddling in the kitchen.

"Good morning," they both said, echoing each other. Matilda walked to the stove to turn on the gas under the teapot and then motioned Megan to the table.

"This is quite a feast," Megan said, feeling grateful that she wasn't the one cooking.

"I should have asked you if you had any allergies or preferences," Matilda said, a frown on her face.

"So instead she prepared everything," Nigel whispered loudly, leaning over toward Megan.

There was toast, yogurt, fruit, eggs, bacon, cereal in the middle of the table. Megan wasn't sure where to begin; Matilda took care of that for her. "Would you like some tea?"

"She'll have some tea," Nigel said, waving his wife off. "She has the blood in her."

"I didn't want to tell them I never drank tea at home," Megan confided to Julie later. "It seemed insulting."

"Many Americans like to drink coffee," Matilda reminded her husband, then looking at Megan.

"Tea is good," Megan assured her. "I'm adventurous."

Nigel roared with laughter and with that comment, he opened up to her. "I have an idea for today," he said. "I'd like to take you to see Llanddwyn Island."

Megan looked at him having no idea what he was talking about.

"You better go soon," Matilda warned, buttering a piece of toast. "Or check if the tide is in."

"I looked on the internet," he assured his wife. "It looks like it will be low all day."

Matilda looked up at Megan. "He said that once before and we got there and it was so high we'd have to swim to the island."

"We didn't go," Nigel said, looking back at Megan again. "I won't make you swim in the water here."

"I think it's a little cold, isn't it?" Megan asked.

Matilda continued to shake her head; Megan moved between them, watching and listening, buttering her own toast.

"It's never warm enough to swim here," Matilda said. "We go to Spain for that."

"Matilda has a group of women she meets with once a week. A book club sort of thing," Nigel said after they were packed back into the car for the trip to LLanddwyn Island. "I believe it's just an excuse to sit around, eat desserts, and talk about their husbands though."

Once they reached what was a peninsula, Nigel waved Megan toward him as he walked across a wood slanted bridge to an opening that led to the beach. And water.

"We're going over there," he pointed at a peninsula off to the right. A few people were walking across the long stretch of beach to what looked like a windswept area near the end of the peninsula.

As they walked, Nigel– at eighty-some years old– walking better than many thirtysomethings, told her the story of St. Dwynwen and how she was denied the love she wanted.

"He was deemed unsuitable for her," Nigel said, looking up at the peninsula ahead. "She prayed for help and when she was given a magic potion, she then gave it to her suitor. But it turned him to stone!"

Megan looked at him, feeling sad about this tragic love story.

"Then she began to pray that he would get his life back and for her that she would never marry or fall in love again. Instead, she would protect lovers."

"Ooh," Megan said softly.

Nigel looked at her as they walked off the beach and began the climb to the hermitage site, the ruins of a church ahead of them as they came to the top of the hill. There also was a cross for her. They stood in front of it together.

"While it obviously doesn't look the same as when she lived here," he said, looking around, "many lovers have come here asking for her to protect them."

"And has it worked?"

Nigel shrugged his shoulders and looked at Megan with a twinkle in his eye. "Matilda said she came here with her sister the day before we were married and prayed for our love and our marriage." He shrugged his shoulders again. "And here we are sixty years later."

Megan didn't say anything, she simply looked at the cross in front of her. Miracles she thought. You can't be a saint without miracles.

Then Nigel interrupted her thoughts, nodding his head toward the cross. "If I had to guess, you are in love. I don't know what's happened. I only met you in person yesterday. But perhaps your love needs some protecting, if only so you believe in it."

Megan looked at him a moment, opened her mouth to speak, then closed it. As she did, she remembered a trip to the mall in eighth grade, she remembered throwing a penny into the fountain as her mother had taught her when she was younger. "Make a wish," her mother had said, smiling at Megan, bundled up, in her big winter coat.

Ten years later, with her friends, she stood at that same fountain, picking up a penny she found on the floor. "Throw it in the fountain," Sheila had suggested.

Megan did, wishing for Simon Le Bon.

But as she stood, staring at this worn stone cross, she thought about how prayers and wishes are the same. But different. And miracles. But she didn't need a miracle.

"What you need is faith," Nigel said.

How does he know this? Megan wondered. Or does it come with age? You just know so much?

"Let Dwynwen believe for you. That's what she's here for," he said, his hands jammed in the pockets of his large navy blue coat, protecting himself from the wind.

Megan shut her eyes for a moment. She wasn't good at this she knew. She read somewhere that prayer was an art form. It definitely wasn't an art form she had experience with, though, and chuckled inside as she thought about that.

There on that cloudy, windy, cold day, she said a prayer as Nigel stood patiently watching, not judging, not uttering a word.

"Okay," Megan said, opening her eyes and looking at Nigel, who simply smiled at her and placed his hand on her back, leading her back to the worn sandy trail that would take them off the peninsula.

Megan looked up and saw a bit of blue sky trying to work its way out of the clouds.

"Sometimes we see the sun," Nigel said, looking up himself.

"It's the first time I've seen it since I landed here," Megan said, half laughing.

"If you see it at all, you're lucky."

They quietly made their way across the empty beach, the very beach that later that day would be filled with water, making the trek to see St. Dwynwen's peninsula impassable except by swimming or boat, too cold to do either.

Megan took one look back before they finished their walk into the parking lot. "I'm counting on you, St. Dwynwen. Obviously I haven't been good at this myself," she prayed out loud as if St. Dwynwen were standing next to her instead of Nigel.

The scene didn't change: the water continued to rush up on the shore, the wind blew, and the trees moved in the breeze. But there was no answer.

"You'll get your answer," Nigel said, driving the car out of the parking lot and taking the winding roads back to his home with Matilda. "But first you're going to have shepherd's pie with us tonight."

CHAPTER 29

Before Megan knew it, she was back on the train to London for Peter Walker's holiday party.

"What a beautiful dress," Matilda had said when Megan had pulled it out of her suitcase to show her. "You will have a wonderful time."

"You're the American version of Nigella Lawson," Nigel had told her when they dropped her off at the train station.

Megan laughed. "I don't ooze sex appeal."

Nigel shrugged his shoulders. "You're making the family proud and that's all that matters."

As the train pulled away, Megan thought about how lucky she was to have spent a few days with some of her family, watching Nigel and Matilda waving in the distance.

Not everyone gets that opportunity, she thought.

She checked back into the same hotel on Hyde Park and found herself in the bathroom doing her hair and makeup.

Pretending, she thought. I'm pretending to know what I'm doing.

She wouldn't know a soul at the party. She barely knew Peter Walker. Maybe Belinda, the assistant, would be there. But who was going to spend time with her?

And yet Barry and Maria's words echoed in her head.

"You're there to make yourself known," Barry said in a text. "Just mingle, look happy, and know that every little social event helps you."

Sell more cookbooks, Megan thought with a sigh. Keep the bills paid. What next? She wondered.

And then Maria's words. "You'll be the prettiest woman there. Lap it up and enjoy it. And then they'll be doubly impressed when they find out who you are."

With a bobby pin, she pulled the last wisp of hair up into the loose bun she'd created on her head, took one look at herself in the mirror, made sure everything was in place. Then she looked at the clock.

Twenty minutes to spare, she laughed, knowing that if she had started later, she wouldn't have been so lucky. She'd be running late. As it was, she was already going to enter the party thirty minutes late.

"Don't ever be early for this sort of thing," Maria had warned, shaking her finger and her head at the same time. "You want to walk in late enough that you're turning heads because everyone is there already and drinking a glass of wine." She paused and added. "And eating fun appetizers."

The cab dropped her off in front of a large home just off Embassy Row in Kensington. Several taxis and cars were ahead of hers and each one waited as several men with umbrellas, invoking memories of Mary Poppins to Megan, held them up so the people in the cars could walk without getting wet from the drizzle that had begun to come down.

"Someone always loans a house to him for this," Belinda had told her.

Hello," a bald man in a suit greeted Megan as he pulled the taxi door open and held an umbrella out for her.

"Hello," Megan said, feeling as if she were stepping into another time.

Around her, the rain had soaked everything in the dark and it brought on a shiny feel as the lights bounced off the puddles and the wet street. It reminded her of the darkness she felt when it rained in New Mexico and everything turned dark and damp.

Magical, she thought.

She walked carefully across the cobblestones, remembering that just ten months ago Maria had taught her to walk in heels. This was the ultimate test.

"Have a wonderful time tonight," the man said, handing her off to another man holding the umbrella who would walk her up the front steps of the house.

"Good evening," he said. The slight bow, of course.

"Hello," Megan said, pulling her wrap around her, the air chilling as the sky turned completely dark for the night.

And yet another man opened the door for her, leading to a foyer where a woman took her wrap and motioned inside to an even larger foyer with a large chandelier. And a circular staircase that traveled both ways around the chandelier.

"Welcome," a woman with cat-eye glasses and a smile said, several papers in her hand. "May I ask your name, please?"

"Megan Marshall," Megan said.

"Ah, yes, of course," the woman said, looking through the list and nodding her head, as if she knew Megan. "Thank you for joining us tonight. You'll find the drinks off to the left and the food to the right. Please enjoy yourself."

Megan nodded.

Once again, Megan was alone in the world.

"You'll have a wonderful time," she could still hear Uncle Nigel's words echoing in her ears. And then tears in his eyes– the tears that led to tears in her own eyes. "Your mother is so proud of you. Maybe she isn't aware of it. But she is."

Megan took a few moments and walked through the house, smiling at people as she passed them by, many of them smiling back at her.

One woman stopped and asked about her dress. "That's beautiful." And then called another friend over to see it. "The perfect party dress, don't you think?"

"And it's perfect on you," the second woman said, both of them dressed in black.

"Thank you," Megan said.

"Oh! An American!" The first one laughed. "You aren't afraid to wear color like we are."

And the three of them laughed for a moment.

"You must be someone special to be here at Peter's party all the way from America," the first woman said, tossing her black hair over her shoulder.

"I was on his show a few days ago," Megan said, taking a glass of white wine– afraid to get near any red in case she spilled it on her dress as white was easier to hide and disguise as water– from a passing waiter. "Or at least we taped the segment a few days ago. It will air after the new year."

"Oh! We didn't realize he was taping this week. We just knew about the party tonight. Are you a writer? An actor? You must be someone."

"I wrote a cookbook," Megan said. "I've been appearing on television in the states for the last year."

She knew they never would have heard of her, but Maria's words rang in her ears. "It will be a great chance to spread the word. Lots of influential people will be there. Don't miss one chance to tell someone who you are."

"I started making cookies with carob." Their faces looked blank. "It's like chocolate, but actually better for you."

"That's what I need," the second woman laughed. "I can't stop eating it once I start."

"And so you've been making cookies on television?"

Megan laughed. "It's much more than that. It's a brand."

"Sell yourself!" she pictured Barry snapping his fingers as he stood in the background.

"It's a lifestyle. There's a story behind many of the recipes. It's called That Cooking Girl."

"Is there a web site?"

"There is," Megan said. "And in the spring the cookbook will be available here in the UK."

Someone pulled them away– "Excuse us," the first woman said, "but don't go anywhere! We want to know more."

Megan knew it was okay if they didn't know more. She had given them the information so she moved on, continuing through the maze of the house and really wanting to see what the kitchen looked like. She stayed in the dining room, looking over all the food before deciding what she would have.

Get a plate of food, she told herself, and then go find a place to sit. She resisted the urge to pull out her phone and text Julie and Stephanie, who were still at work.

"Don't text us from the party!" Julie had warned. "Text us after the party!"

"Text us the next day," Stephanie had winked.

"Oh geez," Megan said putting her head in her hands.

But here she was at the party looking for a corner to sit.

"It's nice to see you again," Peter said, coming up behind her and putting a hand on her shoulder.

Megan turned and smiled. "Hi," she said, feeling so American, forgetting she should say something more regal like hello. "Thank you for inviting me. I'm surprised you remember me with all these people here."

"Of course I do!" he said, smiling at several people who walked by. "You're That Cooking Girl! We want you to enjoy your time here and go back to America and tell everyone how great we treated you."

'That won't be a problem," Megan said with a wave of her hand.

Someone pulled Peter away– "We'll be in touch," he said as he strolled toward where he was called. And Megan walked to the end of the table to find a plate. As she picked one up, a voice came from behind her.

"Are you sure you don't want some gummy bears?"

She turned around to see Nate standing behind her with a small red paper bag in his hand.

"Are you sure that Maria hasn't planted you everywhere that I go?" Megan laughed, looking for a place to put the plate as Nate handed her the bag.

"She might have had something to do with me knowing where you are," Nate admitted.

Megan looked inside the paper bag. Gummy bears. She burst out laughing.

"I was worried you might have run out," Nate said.

"So you tracked me down here?"

He leaned up next to her. "Do you know how hard it was for me to get into this party? It's not like I was on the guest list, you know."

"And I'm sure they minded having you added."

"I had to have my people prove to them who I was."

Megan shook her head, opening the bag that held the gummy bears. "Do you want one?"

"I think they have quite a spread here," Nate said, tilting his head toward the table. "Maybe you could save those for later."

She didn't respond. "How did you find me here? Did Maria get me an invitation to the party just so you could find me?"

He laughed and held up his arms as if to surrender. "I don't know that part. I was just trying to find you and I finally tracked down your Uncle Nigel only to find out you'd already left. I just now had to sneak in here after running for trains this afternoon to get back to London to get you before you left back home."

"And when are you going back?"

"Tomorrow– with you."

"Conveniently planned," Megan said.

He took her elbow and started to lead her toward the front of the house. Suddenly, it felt as if everyone was in the way, Megan thought. The path wasn't clear; there were people, appetizer-filled dishes, and full glasses of red wine keeping them from getting out of the house.

But she let Nate lead her, no one seeming to notice who they were or the fact that they were leaving.

Once they retrieved her wrap, the helpful men held up their umbrellas again, a drizzle still falling in the night air.

"I feel like I'm in 'Mary Poppins,'" Megan giggled.

"Then you should have an umbrella to pull out of your carpet bag," Nate teased, looking at the small clutch she carried.

"Oooh," Megan said. "I bought something."

"What does that mean?" She didn't notice that Nate had waved off the cabs and somehow he was now carrying an umbrella, and they were walking along Embassy Row, Hyde Park on their right. Cars and cabs drove by, stirring up the water on the street.

She giggled. "For the first time in my life, I bought something at Louis Vuitton."

He raised his eyebrows and stopped for a moment. Megan looked up and saw a streetlight behind them. "Are you sure you didn't plan this? It seems like something Nate Matthews the actor might have dreamed up in a script?" she asked.

Nate laughed. "It doesn't matter what I say because you'll never believe me."

"That's right. You're an actor. You act. No one knows what you really think."

"Even if I get politically involved."

"Then everyone will think you're political and be more suspicious."

They started walking again, turning right at the corner toward Megan's hotel.

"I know I love you," he said. "Do you believe that?"

She laughed and held tighter onto the crook of his arm. "That I do. And I love you."

Nate stopped again. "And you're happy with where we are today?"

Megan looked at him. She didn't say anything at first and then she nodded. "I am."

He looked to the road ahead and then back to her. "I think it's time we started to take our lives and merge them. Would you be okay with that?"

She raised her eyebrows. "Do you have an ending for this script? I need to have some idea of what I'm supposed to do."

He laughed and started to walk again. "Well, I have some idea of how I'd like it to end."

"Might you tell me how?" Megan asked, trying to be nonchalant, like it didn't matter.

"In time, I think you'll find out. But for now, I think we've got stuff to do."

"Like what?"

They reached the front of the hotel and once under the covering, he closed the umbrella. "We need to fly home for one."

"I hope you booked yourself a first class ticket because I'm not going back to coach after that flight over here."

"Right next to you."

"Maria?"

He nodded. "How else?"

Just then, a couple– both wearing jeans– walked up to them. "Excuse me," the woman said, holding out her hand as if she wanted to keep them from going anywhere. "Aren't you Nate Matthews?" Then she looked at Megan. "And you're– That Cooking Girl?"

"Her name is Megan," the man said, wiping the rain off his glasses. "Megan Marshall."

"How do you know that?" The woman asked him.

"The same way you know who Nate Matthews is."

The woman looked stumped.

"The paper bag pizza. Have you already forgotten?"

Nate and Megan turned to leave, the woman asking her husband questions to refresh her memory.

"It's already begun to change," Nate said, taking Megan's hand and together they walked up the steps into the lobby of the hotel.

"Yes, it has," she said.

www.ingramcontent.com/pod-product-compliance
Lightning Source LLC
Chambersburg PA
CBHW070732280626
47159CB00023B/3118